Praise for *Alligator*:

"Lisa Moore is a highly inventive wordsmith. . . . [Her] rhythmic sentences and powers of description create a strange reality for her readers as she writes of a place and time that is at once modern and mythic, and wholly her own." —*Books in Canada*

"An utterly gorgeous gathering of images." —*See Magazine*

"A writer who is at the top of her game and a novel of distinct merit." —*Atlantic Books Today*

"Lisa Moore brings to her pages what we are always seeking in fiction and only find in the best of it: a magnetizing gift for revealing how the earth feels, looks, tastes, smells, and an unswerving instinct for what's important in life. . . . Ms. Moore can flat-out write." —Richard Ford

"Appeals to the senses, and to the soul." —*Newfoundland Herald*

Praise for *Open*:

"Dazzling . . . daring . . . [Moore] has a genius for nailing the physical world on the page. One image after another is a feat of seeing, of waking up the senses." —*The Globe and Mail*

"The stories are full of nerve and verve. They brim with an irresistible mix of adrenaline, compassion and insight. They laugh and cry and rage. . . . *Open* is like this from start to finish: perceptive and wonderful." —*National Post*

"Nuance and cunning, and every time, of all the possible words, exactly the right word. The making of a wondrous fiction demands both compassion and hard choices and Lisa Moore seems born to it." —Bonnie Burnard, author of *A Good House*

"An accomplished, polished collection. . . . Over and over Moore expands the universe, then shrinks it back to a beat of individual consciousness. . . . She has mastered the short story."

—*Quill & Quire* (starred review)

"Moore is one of those rare writers who can change the way you see the world, who can make your own life feel infinitely more fragile, more real."

—Michael Crummey, author of *The Wreckage*

Praise for *Degrees of Nakedness:*

"A stunning debut collection. Shot through with riffs of startling and vivid imagery, Moore's stories are urbane, offbeat and sophisticated. Moore makes a metaphor of art and turns art into life—the characters literally glow on the page and peak of love."

—Douglas Glover, author of *Elle*

"Lisa Moore captures not only the landscape of contemporary Newfoundland, but the particular strains of family life in the late twentieth century, in supple, sensuous prose."

—*The Globe and Mail*

ALLIGATOR

Also by Lisa Moore

Degrees of Nakedness
Open

ALLIGATOR

LISA MOORE

A NOVEL

BLACK CAT
New York
a paperback original imprint of Grove/Atlantic, Inc.

First published in 2005 by House of Anansi Press Inc.,
Toronto, Ontario, Canada

Printed in the United States of America

FIRST AMERICAN EDITION

Library of Congress Cataloging-in-Publication Data

Moore, Lisa Lynne, 1964–
Alligator : a novel / Lisa Moore.
p. cm.
ISBN-10: 0-8021-7025-0
ISBN-13: 978-0-8021-7025-5
1. St. John's (N.L.)—Fiction. 2. Teenage girls—Fiction. 3. Domestic fiction.
I. Title.
PR9199.3.M647A78 2006
813'.54—dc22 2006040133

Text design and typesetting by Brian Panhuyzen

Black Cat
a paperback original imprint of Grove/Atlantic, Inc.
841 Broadway
New York, NY 10003

Distributed by Publishers Group West

www.groveatlantic.com

06 07 08 09 10 10 9 8 7 6 5 4 3 2 1

For Nan Love

COLLEEN

IT STARTS OFF there's an alligator with its jaws open on a dirt road. The man's back is bare and gleaming with sweat, and those trees they have, hanging with moss. The whole thing is overexposed. The sun is relentless. A crowd has gathered around the man and the alligator. There are kids in the front, a little girl with blond hair and a silver helium balloon tied to her wrist.

The balloon looks hot. For some reason the camera lingers on the balloon. Perhaps the cameraman has forgotten what he's supposed to be doing. The balloon looks like a hole burned through the sky. There's no wind, but the balloon jerks when the little girl shifts her weight. It jerks to the side and bobs and then settles, becomes still. There isn't a cloud. The little girl's blond hair is spread over her shoulders and bits of sunlight come through it and some of her hair is full of static and it stands up and the sun makes it buzz with light. The alligator footage was part of a training video about safety in nuclear power plants.

Some plant in Ontario.

My Aunt Madeleine made a lot of industrial training videos in the 1970s and 1980s. For a while safety videos were her bread and butter. She had a niche. I was watching Aunt Madeleine's archival footage and came across a man who puts his head in an alligator's mouth.

There's something low-budget about the event. The man is strutting around, trying to rouse the crowd. He has a sheen and there are beads of sweat all over his back and he is trying to create anticipation. But he looks exhausted by the heat.

The alligator doesn't move. It looks like a tree trunk in the middle of the road.

But it also looks untrustworthy. The way it stays still makes it look sly, though it may just be asleep. It's probably asleep is what's going on.

A shimmering curtain of heat rises from the dirt road and the man walks through it. This shimmer makes everything behind it look saturated with colour and blurred. The child with the balloon has a red dress that seems to lift and float over the person beside her, an elderly woman in a straw hat sitting in a lawn chair. Two walking canes rest against the woman's knees. The aluminum frame of the chair looks like it would burn your skin.

Several people in the crowd are fanning themselves with pieces of paper that must be some sort of program.

The veil of heat is a warning, like what you might see in a crystal ball, of something bad.

Then there's a cut.

I've also been downloading the beheadings off the Net. They are available. The wet concrete wall behind and a man in a black hood kneeling on a concrete floor next to what appears to be a drain, and a few people amble past the camera behind him, then out comes the machete. It's slow and gritty and takes a while to download, or it downloads instantly. I never watch further than out comes the machete but I watch as a kind of duty because I don't want that man to be alone. It looks like the courtyard of a compound. You can see the leaves of palm trees over the top of the cinderblock wall. It looks hot there too.

For a while I watched one of the beheadings every night, the man with the hood, two men behind him with rifles, a glint when the sun strikes the bayonet. After the second glint on the bayonet the hooded man stops walking and the hood turns toward the camera. He's small-boned, this man, and his hands are tied behind his back. Just briefly, his head turns toward the camera, though he probably doesn't know what he's turning toward. One of the soldiers behind him, they look like soldiers, gives him a nudge. I watch because how lonely to die so far from home with nobody in attendance.

I'm attending.

I stop watching before they commit the act, not because I'm afraid to, but out of respect. This is in a bedroom painted pink and a pink canopy over the bed in a house in the suburbs of St. John's, up behind the Village Mall. I have a high-speed connection to help with homework. I go into the kitchen for supper and there's Mom.

Mom says, Why the face? You've always got a face on you.

I often sleep over at Aunt Madeleine's and watch her old footage. She's saved all the takes from pretty much everything she's ever shot. It's a nuclear power plant and there's a scientist talking. I'm watching the footage and I'm reading *Cosmo*. Reading is not the word, flipping, leafing. I like the crinkle of the pages and the weird dresses and the raunchiness you come across. Big jewels and bulimia, perfume bottles and lots of glossy mouths ready to whisper something dirty.

A nuclear power plant on the mainland, the guy is talking.

He says, A distinction must be made between the safe operation of the nuclear power plant and protection against sabotage. He cocks an eyebrow, like, is he ever smart.

Cut.

The best part of the footage is always Madeleine, off-camera, yelling cut.

Sometimes I see Madeleine in the footage. The camera swerves and she's pacing with her arms folded, looking at the floor. She's younger, much younger, and she's crouched with her back against a wall next to a stainless-steel cylinder, which is the kind of ashtray they had in public places back then.

She's always smoking, eyes squinted, patting her back pockets for a notebook, silver hoops tangled in her black hair. A pencil tucked behind her ear.

The scientist is trying to talk about sabotage and this is pretty much before sabotage.

This is before the twin towers and web sites that show a mounted rifle aimed at a corral of exotic animals and for a fee you shoot from your armchair. You press *Enter* and an emu goes down.

Emus and orangutans lope through the crosshairs of a mounted rifle somewhere in Montana and you watch on your screen and kapow, they send it to you in the mail. An emu on ice chips, via PayPal.

Or the bum-fight videos you can find on the Net. A Jeep pulls up and five guys jump out and they attack a pile of cardboard and filthy blankets in a back alley and two bums crawl out from beneath the frost-coated debris they're sleeping under. The bums are bearded and lost and the five men from the Jeep beat them on the head with billy clubs, these poor half-retarded alcoholics with their arms thrown up to protect their ears; they beat them until the bums agree to fight each other so they can make a video that they'll post. Like something on the Animal Planet channel, only winos.

I saw a bum fight on a plasma screen at a party in Mount Pearl but eventually the police were called because the parents were in Florida, because of the noise. Everybody cleared out, but I saw through the front window as I was heading down the street, the four cops standing in front of the plasma screen, their brawny shoulders slumped, like they couldn't believe what they were watching.

The scientist is talking nuclear accidents and I go into the kitchen to make a peanut butter and honey sandwich. He's talking risk assessment and creating default systems that activate when other default systems fail. Water coolants and bugs in the programming.

Someone put a finger in the peanut butter.

There's a gouge the width of a finger. The honey has crystallized. It's gone whitish and hard and it's a squeeze bottle. It makes farting noises. I love Madeleine because she has honey and multigrain bread, and the smell of her cashmere sweaters and her big silver jewellery. She's always rushing and she has grocery bags or video equipment or luggage because she's just off some red-eye from Paris or Madagascar. Once, I saw a black shawl get away from her and go flying over the pavement, tripping all over itself, until it caught on a hedge.

There's an article in *Cosmo* about winding a scrunchy around your lover's balls to maximize his orgasm. Guaranteed to double his pleasure, it says.

There's a diagram. You just wind that sucker around the scrotum, and this wows him so much he never leaves you because he's not going anywhere because you've done this incredible thing with the scrunchy and he's immensely grateful. I'm just sitting on the couch, leafing through.

Then there's the actual nuclear power plant and it's all chrome and steam. It's all shiny surfaces and echoes and ominous footfalls, which people forget the importance of the sound effects in a safety video.

The guy's voice is still going about safety. Safety this and safety that.

There are pistons dropping into cylinders, pipes sighing, gusts of steam lit by cherry-coloured *Exit* signs or orange lights and beeps and dings and shrill whistles like kettles that sound not very state-of-the-art.

Make sure the scrunchy isn't too tight, then just tickle his balls a little and see what happens. I know soon they will have a shot of a mushroom cloud because any excuse for a mushroom cloud, wait for it, wait.

There's a Dr. Newman who says about the flow of blood and engorgement and tumescence and the scrunchy will tighten during the normal course of and if you put your mouth.

And there it is, billowing, smoky, and lurid gold underneath, against an aqua blue sky, spreading over the desert. What we don't want to happen. What they have the capability of in China now. What they have the capability of in who knows where else. A dime a dozen, these mushroom-cloud shots.

There can be no strangeness while watching the footage because it's random. Everything is strange. Strange boils over into strange. But then something strange happens. We are out of the nuclear power plant, suddenly, and there is the man and the alligator. But there's also narration.

The man gets down on his knees before the alligator.

He has a handkerchief and he's sweating. The scientist is narrating about how you must always follow the exact same procedure in any sort of dangerous work in order to achieve safety, whether we're talking nuclear power plants or circus work.

He says, This man *always* wipes the sweat from his face before he puts his head in the alligator's jaws, because if anything, even a drop of sweat, touches the alligator's tongue it will cause an instinctive trigger and the jaws will snap shut.

But, as you will see, on this day of extreme temperatures in Louisiana, this performer forgot to wipe one side of his face.

Watch closely.

The man does wipe one side of his face, but he forgets the other side.

And, unfortunately, a drop of sweat falls onto the alligator's tongue and triggers an instinctive response.

The crowd rushes backwards, stumbling, falling, getting up, spreading out. People trip over the abandoned lawn chair and the walking canes.

The man's body is flicked back and forth. His fists are on the alligator's snout for a moment. He's flopped over and flopped back. His legs are kicking. Then, on his bare back, stripes of blood because of the claws, or being dragged in the dirt. The alligator shakes his head as if he's having a disagreement. He really disagrees. He disagrees vehemently. The alligator is trying hard to tear the man's head from his shoulders. Everything about the way the animal moves is repulsive and quick. Its tail stamps and lashes the man into the dirt.

The camera keeps rolling because maybe the man, should he survive, will want to view the accident later.

Or maybe he will want it viewed by others.

There must be a school where they teach, don't turn off the camera. Because the cameraman forgets to turn the camera off, though for long stretches the only thing in the frame is dirt.

For long stretches, it's dirt and the toe of the cameraman's boot. Veils of dirt float across the frame and a black boot scuffs in and out and there's a jerk and the alligator and the man are back in the centre of things.

He is not dead, his legs are moving.

How long will it take?

And then there is a corridor. An empty corridor of white walls and tile and the colour bars.

Peanut butter stuck to the roof of my mouth. I rewind and watch and rewind and watch. I look for some reason to believe the man is still alive. If you watch for long enough you will see everything.

I watch until Madeleine comes home. She leans against the door frame with her arms folded under her chest. She tugs at her amber pendant, back and forth, on the chain. It's the beginning of August and we've had weather in the high twenties for three weeks. Madeleine has a dewy look from the heat; she's tanned and blousy and she's getting ready to shoot the second half of a big feature film she's working on.

He's still alive, she says. He runs an alligator farm in Louisiana, an ecological reserve.

Loyola, she says.

She pushes herself off the door frame with one shoulder and goes into the kitchen and then I hear the frying pan. I hear cupboard doors and oil sizzling, glasses clinking. Madeleine will cook at midnight if she's hungry.

She comes back out and stands and watches the footage with me.

Loyola somebody, she says. It'll come to me. Nice guy.

She has a glass of vodka with ice and tonic and she works one toe behind the strap of her sandal and kicks it off. She hobbles over, still wearing one high heel, and drops into the leather couch and kicks off the other sandal too, and removes her rings. Big silver rings, with amber and turquoise, and they clink on the glass coffee table as she puts them down.

He lived through that, she says. Loyola Rosewood.

Madeleine's entirely consumed with her new film. She acts like someone in a dream.

I rewind to the beginning. The man is strutting around the perimeter of the crowd again and his stomach is washboard ridges and his fists are by his hips and he has serious muscles. He has a proud, worn-out look. There is the silver balloon burning a hole in the sky, the kinetic halo of sunlight in the girl's hair.

I had a thing with that guy, Madeleine says. An ice cube in her glass busts open.

The alligator guy?

We had a little thing.

FRANK

Frank's got the windows open and the warm night breeze jostles the handful of forget-me-nots sitting in a Mason jar of yellowish water on the windowsill. A few petals move on the surface of the water like tiny boats on a still lake. The glass jar and the submerged flower stems are coated with silvery beads of air. There's a housefly near the jar, bluish and iridescent, cocooned in a spider's web and dust. The fly has been there, lying on the crackled paint of the windowsill, since Frank moved in a few months before Christmas, two days after his nineteenth birthday. The breeze draws his door shut with a loud slam.

Frank has been selling hot dogs on George Street since April, but he knows this will be his best month. He has four weeks of steady sales until September, even longer, if the weather holds. He'll work every night until the cruise ships have left for the season and the university crowd heads back to school.

He hears a band warming up on George Street. He lives a few streets up from downtown in a bed-sit, the cheapest housing he could find. There's a retired Avon Lady on the floor beneath Frank and two Russian drug dealers on the floor above. Carol, the ex–Avon Lady, says they're drug dealers.

There used to be an Inuit guy on the third floor, but he hanged himself on Boxing Day. They'd never got his name and it was something Carol felt bad about. She had been the one to call the police, when she noticed the Inuit guy wasn't coming and going.

Frank dropped a bag of laundry on his bed and, opening the zipper, took out his pressed, folded shirts in a neat stack. There were eight. The woman at the laundromat on Gower Street put sheets of crisp white tissue paper inside Frank's shirts when he had them pressed and he liked the soft crumpling sound when he was getting ready for the evening. He paid extra to get his shirts done and it was his only extravagance. He liked to wear a white shirt when he was selling hot dogs. He liked to look clean, and whatever kind of detergent the lady used — she had spiky black hair, wore tank tops and leopard-print leggings — his shirts always smelled as if they'd been hanging on a line. He wore a baseball cap to keep his hair out of the way of the hot dogs. He'd never had a complaint about hygiene.

He and Carol had known the Inuit guy was in trouble, but they'd tried to mind their own business. They'd listened to him shouting and crying in the middle of the night; they'd seen him with his cases of beer. Then there had been no sign of him. The cops had arrived seven minutes after Carol called them, ducking under the icicles that had hung from the door frame. They'd brushed against each other trying to wipe their feet on the welcome mat Carol had bought at her own expense and put out to cover the hole in the linoleum. They'd shut the door and the draft made the light bulb swing and their shadows dipped and stretched. The cops looked windburnt and content, as if they had worked most of the day outdoors and were ready to get home.

Have you got any reason to worry? one officer had asked, directing his questions to Carol, who seemed self-important and frail in their company.

Frank turns on the shower and takes the can of shaving cream out of the cabinet over the sink. He pulls the chain overhead and the light from the bare hanging bulb swings a soft gold arc on the beige wall. Steam roils above the shower curtain, which is transparent except for a print of big red roses. Frank takes off his T-shirt and leans over the sink to look at the stubble on his chin. He stretches his neck, checking both sides of his jaw. The mirror clouds with steam and he wipes a streak with a face cloth and begins to shave.

There was nothing in the bed-sit when he moved in except a hotplate and fridge and the bathroom with a toilet and shower stall. There was a mantelpiece above a bricked-in fireplace and he'd taken the urn with his mother's ashes out of his suitcase first thing and put it in the centre of the mantelpiece.

A rectangle of autumn light had come through the window and he set the brass urn down so the light struck it and the urn looked like it might become warm to the touch if it sat in the sun long enough. He didn't know if it was right to display the urn but he decided he felt more comfortable with it in view.

He'd sold all of his mother's furniture in an open house he'd advertised in the *Telegram*. He stood in the centre of the bed-sit, on that first day, and he could see his breath. He stood there thinking about his mother. There were two windows and they gave an unobstructed view of the harbour. Frank had sat on the floor with his back against the opposite wall and looked at the harbour for a long time. He'd had a pencil and a notepad and he was jotting down the items he wanted to list in the *Buy & Sell* under Freebies. There were things belonging to his mother he couldn't bring himself to sell or keep: a vinyl recording of the Pope's address to the people of Newfoundland when he visited in 1984, still in its Cellophane cover, a set of rosary beads carved from narwhal tusk, and a hooked mat his mother had done herself, a portrait of the Pope, his hand raised in benediction.

While he sat there he decided he would buy a waterbed. He had always imagined owning a waterbed when he was successful, but now it struck him that getting the bed might invoke the man he wanted to become. You bought a waterbed and so became the sort of man who owned a waterbed.

Frank had waited until his mother was dead to give her landlord notice. He kept up the belief that she might get well as long as she was alive out of a sort of respect and faithfulness, though he had given up hope of getting the money together to send her to the Mayo Clinic. He talked every day, during his hospital visits, about the airfares he was checking into and the medical advancements the clinic offered that were superior to anything she could hope for in Newfoundland. But his mother's cancer had progressed so far by the time it was diagnosed that there had been no hope, even if he'd had the money for the Mayo Clinic.

The police knocked on the Inuit guy's door several times. Then one of them came back down to Carol's to borrow a butter knife and they used it to jimmy the door. Frank stepped out onto the landing and listened with Carol. They both stood, Frank staring at Carol's fluffy pink slippers and her peach toenail polish, and they heard an utterance. It was not a shout but not muffled either, it was a human noise that expressed surprise and awfulness at the same time and it came from the cop's gut. Frank heard him say, He's after hanging himself in here, Greg.

Frank dragged his eyes up from the floor and Carol had covered her mouth with her hand, and her eyes looked watery behind her glasses and her fingernails were painted the same colour as her toes. They hadn't decided to stand on the landing but they found themselves there. The Inuit boy was twenty-one, two years older than Frank, and he had arrived three months before Frank and drank continuously and kept to himself, except one morning when he and Frank had shovelled the walk together.

Frank heard a thump and this must have been the body being lowered from whatever kind of noose. The police were speaking quietly to each other. They sounded respectful and upset. Frank and Carol stood, almost unable to move, because they'd both felt a dread building in them all through the week before Christmas without ever talking about it.

On Christmas Eve, Frank had knocked on Carol's door and given her a box of chocolates and she said she had something for him. He told her not to bother but she said, Come in, come in. He saw her place was bigger but he stayed just inside the door while she opened and slammed drawers in her bedroom and took a long time, and he heard tape.

He stood waiting and finally she came out and handed him the present, blowing the hair out of her eyes as if she were winded. He opened the present and it was a bottle of Avon cologne for men. The bottle was in the shape of a stallion, one hoof pawing the air. Half the cologne had already been used.

Carol asked him did he want to come in and have a glass of Scotch with her if he were old enough to drink and then the bagpipes started from the Kirk across the street and Frank had said that maybe they should call the police about the guy on the third floor. He was holding the glass horse in his hand and the balled-up wrapping paper.

Carol was shorter than Frank and she wore bifocals. The lower half of her lenses magnified the soft pouches under her eyes, which were pale white and delicately veined; her eyelashes were almost transparent. She gripped the edge of the door frame and looked up at him and her eyes snapped several times while she decided what they should do.

Neither of them wanted to go up and knock.

They'd seen him stumbling out of taxis and they'd heard him singing to himself at all hours. Then there had been nothing for two days, not a sound.

The very afternoon Frank had moved into the bed-sit he'd gone outside to the bus stop and caught the number two to the Village Mall and went to Sears and lay down on five or six beds. He lay there and spread his arms and was careful to keep his boots off the mattresses. A man came by and asked if he needed help and he said he wanted a waterbed and he'd want it delivered.

The man said that a waterbed was the most expensive bed you could buy. Frank was still lying on his back. The ceiling was a long way up.

I have lots of money, Frank said.

The police came out of the apartment and passed Frank and Carol on the landing and Frank became aware of himself, just standing in the way, and went back into his room and shut the door. Then he opened the door and stood watching in case someone needed help moving the body.

An ambulance arrived and two attendants got the body on a stretcher and with the help of one of the cops carried it down the stairs. They were giving instructions to each other, wincing under the weight. One of the attendants caught his knuckles on the banister on the second-floor landing. He had to stop and rest the stretcher on his hip and shake his hand because of the pain. He'd grazed the skin on each of his knuckles on the left hand and blood got all over the front of his white shirt. Frank got him some paper towel and he wound it around his hand and dropped the roll and it went bouncing down the stairs and rolled all the way to the front door.

Frank and the Inuit guy had shovelled the walk together one morning after a snowstorm when the sun had come out and the street was an achy ultra-white and the ploughed banks were way above their heads. All down the street cars were buried.

Children had come out in their snowsuits and their voices rang out in the clear air and the chink of shovels. People were shovelling and veils of snow trailed after each shovelful and hung in the air sparkling. The pavement, where it showed through, was as shiny and black as patent leather. The traffic could hardly move.

Frank and the Inuit guy nodded to each other and they shovelled for more than an hour. They didn't introduce themselves. The moment for doing that came and lasted and passed without either of them speaking up.

The Inuit guy had sunglasses on and a yellow anorak and his hair was blue black and he shovelled effortlessly and took regular breaks to lean on his shovel for a moment and still made more progress than Frank.

The young nurse who lives across the street, a new single mother, was backing out of her driveway over a ploughed hill and she made the engine rev until it was squealing. They went over to push and Frank gave her directions on which way to turn her wheels and saw her eyes in the rear-view and they were brown and he would give anything to kiss her and make love to her because he had been watching her since she moved in, and she'd call out hi and wave and sometimes that was all anybody said to him in the run of a day.

He and the Inuit guy leaned into the fender of her car with all their might. The Inuit guy had pushed his sunglasses up into his hair and he was grinning at Frank and he knew, had seen Frank looking at the girl in the rear-view, and they were laughing and rocking this big mother of a car and finally it gave and the girl covered them from the waist down with slush, and she then pulled over a little farther down the road and ran back to them and brushed at both of them with the end of her scarf, almost down on her knees flicking the slush off, saying, I'm sorry, I'm sorry, and he and the Inuit guy grinned at each other.

Frank got out of the shower wrapped in the only towel he had. He lifted a shirt off the pile of shirts and, holding it by the shoulders, gave it a little shake and the tissue paper wafted to the floor. He had dried his back but he was damp with a fine perspiration because of the heat and he put the shirt on and rolled his shoulders to get it to hang nicely. He took a float from the envelope of money he kept under his bedside table and buttoned it into his shirt pocket. He turned off the lights and gave the door a good slam behind him.

Out on the sidewalk a flock of pigeons lifted as he came down the stairs. They cooed and settled again to peck at the bread crumbs left for them. Inside Frank's empty bed-sit, water drops travelled in hesitant, zigzagging paths down the plastic shower curtain, and in the window several air bubbles on the stems of the flowers in the Mason jar floated to the surface and broke soundlessly. The breeze nudged the flowers into one another and the stems tippytoed across the bottom of the jar.

COLLEEN

THE ELEVATOR DOORS fling themselves open and Colleen sees a judge heading toward her from the end of a long hallway. He's in full stride, forehead first, the arms of his black robes billowing. The reflection from a tube of fluorescent ceiling light runs over his oily bald head like a charging train.

She assumes he's a judge; he towers above her. Colleen is seventeen and slight, with pale white skin, a light spray of freckles over the bridge of her nose. Her hair is kinky, almost black, like bitter chocolate, and gathered loosely with a rainbow-coloured shoelace at the nape of her neck. Her expression is forthright and blatantly innocent. But she has recently been caught trying to destroy several thousand dollars' worth of privately owned forestry equipment. Colleen Clark had poured sugar into the fuel tanks of some bulldozers belonging to Mr. Gerry Duffy; the youth diversion meeting had been set for early August and she had waited, feeling sure of herself and unsure by turns, all through July. She had wanted more than anything for the day to be over. She had fervently imagined the rest of her summer with the youth diversion meeting behind her. But she had not imagined being in an elevator about to come face to face with Mr. Duffy. She had not imagined this judge or the light sweat she could feel at her hairline on her forehead. She had not imagined the pitch and tone of her fright.

Mr. Duffy is waiting in an office several floors above to talk about the damage and how she might pay for her vandalism with community service.

Colleen looks at the judge's reflection in the brass panels of the elevator. His eyebrows hang down into his watery eyes. His face is warped in the polished metal.

A haze of smarting cologne hits her; she can taste it at the back of her throat. When she was six years old she gave a gift package of four bottles of Aqua Velva to her father for Christmas. David was her stepfather, really, though she has never thought of him that way. She thought of him only as her father and she was obsessed that Christmas with buying him a present. She had received an allowance that year and saved most of it in a pink plastic bank shaped like a pig with a rubber stopper in its belly. She'd had to fish the bills out with a fork.

Two days before Christmas, at the door of Wal-Mart in the Avalon Mall, with a flurry of snow and wind at their backs, Colleen and her mother, Beverly, were greeted by a woman in a white plastic apron with eggplant-dark lipstick and big teeth who brought a hand-held whirring set of blades in close proximity to a carrot and sent film-thin coins flying into the air.

Imagine all the time you'd save, Beverly had said, giving her hands a quick clap. Beverly had short, curly hair that she dyed a dramatic, solid black as soon as streaks of silver appeared at her temples. Her eyes were large, strikingly luminous — the white visible below the pupil. The wrinkles at the corners of her eyes gave her an etched intensity. She could look rapt and full of judgement, but when she smiled her face was entirely altered. When Beverly smiled she looked girlish and wantonly generous.

Her expressions were too honest and full of bare emotion for anyone to think her pretty. But she was strongly attractive.

The woman with the vegetable dicer attacked an onion and, most disturbingly, a chunk of purplish meat. Everything the blade buzzed near held its shape for the briefest instant and then fell into a thousand limp slices.

It had been snowing since dawn on that day. The parking lot was covered in snow; the cars looked crammed together and restful under sloppy white caps. Men and women in orange vests waved glowing wands to direct traffic. The buses were sweeping their headlights into the grey dusk of the afternoon.

The Aqua Velva was the first gift Colleen had ever picked out by herself. A tower of boxes ingeniously piled one on top of the other, each with a corner slightly off-kilter so the stack rose like a spiral staircase. There were giant Christmas bulbs hanging from the rafters, carols bubbling wordlessly through the overhead speakers, shoppers in bright coats rushing forward and away like the bits of coloured glass in a kaleidoscope.

Inside the department store Colleen's tight red wool coat with the black velvet trim and matching buttons smelled of the cold. The coat had been purchased at an expensive children's clothing boutique on Duckworth Street, the first of its kind in St. John's, which had closed after only one season. Beverly had eyed the coat for four months, watching the price go down, and bought it in the spring close-out sale for the following winter. As a result the sleeves were too short, but Colleen had to wear it anyway.

Beverly had lifted Colleen into a shopping cart and she was hanging on tightly while her mother charged forward into the crowd, unwilling to slow down for the customers who wandered into her path, until the front of the cart hit a motorized wheelchair and snagged on a protruding bar.

The woman in the wheelchair was obese. Her body was composed of three distinct rolls of fat that settled on top of each other and made Colleen think of soft-serve ice cream pouring out of the nozzle at Moo Moos. The woman's shiny red rubber boots didn't quite reach the footrests and the appliqué Christmas tree on her sweater had green lights that blinked on and off.

Colleen was well into Grade 1 and had been taught to look adults in the eye, to shake hands when introduced, never to mumble. But the woman in the wheelchair frightened her. Colleen looked down from the cart, now jerking back and forth on only two wheels, to the top of the woman's head. Greasy white hair lay flat over her skull. The grooves made by her comb were still visible and the pink of her scalp showed through.

It was all her mother's fault — the bravado she brought to every gesture that most often paid off and sometimes went very badly.

BEVERLY

BEVERLY WAS WAITING in the food court on the ground floor of Atlantic Place, having watched Colleen get into the elevator near the bank. Before the doors closed Beverly had called out, There's nothing shameful about being wrong.

They were not speaking very much these days. Beverly had taken the vandalism as a personal affront. Colleen was trying to protect the Newfoundland pine marten, an endangered species.

A whole species wiped off the face of the earth, she had screamed at her mother.

Pine martens, Beverly had said. She could not fathom what Colleen might mean by trying to save them.

They're rodents, her mother said.

They're dying out forever, Mother, Colleen said. Somehow Beverly had raised a daughter whose voice could be as shrill as a fire alarm. Was that genetic? Does it skip generations? Beverly had never even seen a picture of a pine marten. There was a whole subgroup of animals — squirrels, badgers, beavers, rats, mostly grey-haired or brown, flicking through peripheral vision if seen at all — in whom Beverly had no interest. Why not albino tigers?

I'm sure we can manage without them, she'd answered. She wondered what David would have thought.

Beverly had met David, Colleen's stepfather, at a prenatal class. David was with a downtown barmaid whose husband had left her during the pregnancy. The barmaid had asked him to accompany her to the classes — be her birth coach — because she was afraid to do it alone.

She'd served David a martini with a twist during happy hour at the bar he'd been drinking in since he'd turned nineteen. Then she put her fingers over her mouth as if to hold the words back. They'd known each other since high school.

What's wrong? he'd asked. She told him about the pregnancy, working her wedding ring off her finger as she spoke. She came out from behind the bar and went into the bathroom and he heard the toilet flush and she was out again without the ring. When she asked him to attend the birth he'd blushed deeply.

We're friends, right? she'd asked. He said he would be honoured.

Beverly was attending the prenatal class alone, having broken up with her lover the weekend before discovering she was pregnant. She could not consider abortion; she had been overtaken, swiftly, with a passion for the idea of a baby. The pregnancy heightened her senses, gave her extra glow, softened her. She became more graceful and deliberate.

She'd told the father, a tepid Catholic lawyer who lived with his mother, over lunch, downtown.

He'd scrunched his napkin into a tight ball and raised his fist and released the napkin. They both watched it unscrunch on the table. The napkin opened like a flower blooming in a time-lapse film.

How could you let this happen? he'd hissed. What she'd imagined to be gentleness — his quiet, unassuming demeanour — had been complacency. Tepid, and given to petulance, she decided. She waited for what she knew was coming. She watched the thought light up his face with rude, desperate hope.

Are you sure it's mine? he'd said. His voice was weak. Hardly a whisper.

She had thought to include him out of a sense of obligation. She was astonished and relieved to discover he was terrified about what she would demand.

David had made jokes throughout the prenatal classes, brought the barmaid tea during the break, waited while she took the first sip, consulted, and then trotted back to the cafeteria to get her more milk or sugar. He misted up while watching the videos of births, and rubbed the barmaid's belly with vigour when the lights snapped back on, as if he couldn't wait to get started.

Many of the men kept their eyes riveted to the floor, Beverly said, but David was watching intently, along with all the women. She found herself in the lineup behind him at the Tim Hortons counter one evening. They spoke about the rain and traffic and then Beverly's eyes flew open from a kick in her belly — a look of undiluted awe spread over her face — and David fell in love for the first time in his life.

Your mother was so damn beautiful, he'd often said to Colleen. Colleen loved him with a loyalty that kept her from asking too many questions about her real father. They had met several times and he seemed elderly and foreign. She thought of it this way: David had chosen her.

COLLEEN

THERE HAD BEEN a stomach virus going around Grade 1 just before Christmas when Colleen was six. While sitting in the shopping cart that was hooked into the wheelchair Colleen felt a mild altering taking place inside her. She could not have said what she was afraid of; the woman's red rubber boots were too bright and childish.

Colleen's stepfather died suddenly of an aneurysm when she was thirteen. At the funeral home she'd heard a man say, He went down like a ton of bricks. The death, when it came, was obdurate and biting; it just was.

The fear she felt in the mall on that day was magnified by the noise and a nascent fever. The Christmas bulbs were swaying, moved by a mysterious internal breeze near the rafters. When she remembers it, she feels the dangerous, oozing seepage, the disintegration of the membrane between adulthood and childhood.

She would soon know things she was too young to know. The woman in the wheelchair twisted her head around and shouted, For the loving honour of Christ. The green lights of her sweater cast a reflection of jiggling dots on her neck.

The engine of the trapped chair roared and there was a faint tinge of burning metal in the air. Colleen's mother rattled her cart savagely, trying to knock the wheelchair free. Colleen was slammed to one side of the cart, her cheek pressed against the wire mesh, and she nearly fell out.

The crowd gathering around the wheelchair began to shout advice. A man in a tweed coat finally stepped forward and lifted Colleen free. Then with an easy move he disengaged the shopping cart.

The woman in the wheelchair shouted at Beverly, You are a piece of shit. She glared with a depthless hatred that, Colleen saw, had instantly diminished her mother.

Then the woman turned the wheelchair in a series of deft jolts and zoomed off down the aisle, swerving around customers and hitting the display of Aqua Velva, the uppermost boxes of which slid one after another to the floor with dull slow-motion plops until the entire tower seemed to bend in half and fall apart all over the aisle. The man in the tweed coat removed his glove and offered to shake Beverly's hand.

You're an absolute angel, Beverly said.

She closed her eyes and put her trembling hands over her ears and smoothed down her hair. She stood like that, eyes closed, hands on her head, while the ramifications of the woman's rage beat against her.

And during the festive season, she whispered. Then her eyes opened and she was restored. She could make effortless recoveries. She could be dazzlingly bright after near collapse.

People have to watch where they're going, she said.

I'm just trying to buy a microwave, the man blurted. I told my wife, whatever you want. But there's not a single microwave to be found in the whole goddamn mall.

Of course everybody's so fraught, Beverly said. She raised both her hands, asking the man to take in all the wreckage of Christmas. The man looked up and down the aisle. The scene made him draw back his lips from his teeth in a kind of parody of extreme merriment.

If I had my way there'd be no Christmas, the man said.

That's exactly how I feel, why not some quiet, private celebration of life, Beverly said. This comment mystified the man.

I'm thinking about a dishwasher, he said shyly. That's what I've got in my mind right now, but my wife said a microwave.

A dishwasher and a microwave amount to the same thing, Beverly announced.

A nice dishwasher, the man said.

Is she a stay-at-home mom? Beverly felt a mild disdain for women who gave up careers with the excuse of raising children when most normal people could do both, but she felt guilty about the opinion, and often claimed to be envious.

Never worked a day in her life, the man said proudly.

I'm telling you, a dishwasher.

She'd like a dishwasher, he said.

Imagine her face on Christmas morning.

Colleen wandered over to the Aqua Velva. She picked up a box, which was red with a print of holly leaves and had a clear plastic window on the front to show off the bottles inside. Each bottle of cologne was a different colour — turquoise, dark green, navy blue, and rust. Inside each bottle an oblong air bubble wobbled toward the lid. When she gave the box a shake the bubbles jiggled madly and burst into a thousand tiny bubbles and rushed toward the neck like foam and then slowly fizzled out to reform the single bubble. She tried to get the bubbles in each bottle to hang exactly in the centre of the glass. It was the perfect gift for David. One thing was for certain — he didn't have it already. As far as she knew, he had never used cologne of any sort in his life.

Colleen had been promised the shopping trip for three weekends in a row, but something had come up on each occasion — her mother talked on the phone or studied a cookbook — and by the time her intense absorption with these tasks had worn off it would be too late to do anything. Colleen would try to catch her mother's attention with a winning look. Sometimes she would whisper, *Mom*, reprimanding and pleading at once. But that only provoked; Beverly would hold up one finger and then turn her back on Colleen.

When she hung up the phone or snapped the book shut she would be awash with whatever world she had been dipping into, whatever had taken place there, and would seem to have no recollection of their plans. It was a delicate mood to negotiate — even a sigh might cost Colleen everything. She would have to take off her red coat and go back to colouring.

She went to bed each Sunday night, for three weekends in a row, overwhelmed with anxiety about getting David's present before Christmas morning. Once, her mother slapped her calculator against the dining-room table and shouted, Didn't I say I'll get you there before Christmas? What did I say?

You said you'll get me there.

And have I ever let you down? It was a question that stumped them both for a few moments.

Later, after putting Colleen to bed, her mother hesitated, standing at the door in the bar of light from the hall. She idly turned the doorknob a few times and the tongue made a clicking noise. It was an old house in downtown St. John's. It had previously been a boarding house and when Colleen's parents moved in all the bedroom doors had padlocks on the outside. A few had been kicked in and the splintery holes were badly repaired with plaster. David had found enough antique doors, over the years, to replace the cheap modern ones. Doors that needed to be stripped and planed and fitted with heavy glass knobs that looked like jewels.

I'll get you there, now stop sulking, her mother said. If there's one thing I can't stand it's a baby. Then she closed the bedroom door and left Colleen in the chilly darkness. Colleen listened to her mother's heels on the hardwood floor and then in the kitchen until she was overtaken by sleep.

The words *piece of shit* uttered by the woman in the wheelchair had brought Colleen's nausea to the surface. She felt as if she had been sliced into a thousand limp pieces and was about to fall apart. Colleen had never heard adults speak to each other quite so honestly, had never seen her mother treated with anything less than strict attention or the sort of incidental admiration glamour inspires.

Now she saw there was something spoiled about her mother. With this one profoundly dirty phrase — piece of shit — everything had been laid bare. She threw up all over the front of her coat and her new boots and the glaring tiles of Wal-Mart. Her mother was down on her knee at once, unbuttoning the soiled coat and folding it into a tight knot with the shiny black lining on the outside. She took a tissue from her purse and wiped Colleen's mouth and then her boots and then she stood.

Okay baby, let's get the hell out of here, she said.

I'm getting Daddy a present, you promised.

Honey, you're sick. We'll have to come back later.

It was abominable. Her mother had nearly knocked a woman out of a wheelchair, and now they were leaving without a single purchase.

Look at the lineups, her mother said.

Colleen had a Christmas list crunched up in her pocket — it had taken hours to write in different crayons. David had helped her, his bristly silver hair tickling her cheek, the softness of his flannel shirt. How abruptly his giant hand spilled the crayons over the table and spread them. He was short and his eyes were wolf blue and he could take her onto his lap and cover her hand with his and they wrote the list together like that, his chin resting on the top of her head. She loved David with an intensity that had nothing in common with what she felt for her mother, which was a duller, more enduring, inevitable love.

A glaze of tears came to her eyes. When she cried it generally sent her mother into a short-lived fury that resulted in Colleen getting what she wanted. She hardly ever cried, and never on purpose. She hated it as much as her mother, but she was suddenly exhausted. Then, strangely, she was swept with a fury of her own. It felt new and disorienting.

You're nothing but a piece of shit, she said evenly.

Colleen thought, Goddamn her. Nothing hurt more than her mother's cold shoulder, mostly because it was involuntary. It was a dry-ice, burning kind of cold that required massive amounts of energy to ignore. Colleen was terrified and compelled by her mother's anger. She was drawn, against her will, to be in the same room with her. Everything was amplified when her mother was in this mood; the squeak of the cupboard hinge was ultra-meaningful. The low rumble of the kettle starting to boil, building without hesitation to a sonic weltering until lifted off the heat, somehow expressed everything between them. It was best to stay out of the room but Colleen could not stay out of the room. She wanted the full blast of rage, but Beverly either guarded it vigilantly or was oblivious to it.

The elevator lifted and Colleen thought of the runny egg she'd had for breakfast, a spot of blood on the yolk, nastily red and glossy. The judge took one of the files from under his arm and, licking his finger, flicked through the pages until he found something. Then turned to her and stared.

You the bulldozers? he asked.

I'm the bulldozers, she said. The wattle that hung under his chin shook after he spoke.

If you were mine I'd have the snot beat out of you, the judge said. They rose to the fifth floor. The doors started to open and then half-closed and then opened and the judge started down the corridor and then turned on his heel.

I knew your father, young lady, he said. And let me tell you, he's turning over in his grave.

On Christmas morning David had taken a long time with the present, shaking it next to his ear, pausing to register bewilderment, careful with the wrapping paper. Even at six years old, she could see that he was genuinely moved. He unscrewed each lid, sniffed, and then screwed it back on tightly and fitted each bottle back into the squeaky Styrofoam box.

This one smells like a walk in the woods, he said.

The cologne eventually made its way up to the cupboard under the sink in the guest bathroom, behind the pipes, containers of Comet, cleaning rags. It remained there, even after David died, the plastic window of the box covered in a fur of dust.

BEVERLY

BEVERLY WATCHES THE numbers over the elevator doors flick up and then down. The doors open again and close and her daughter is gone. Colleen will be scolded and made to feel small. She wills her daughter a spiny fortitude, even if she was incomprehensibly wrong. Let her stand up to the lawyers and social workers and Mr. Duffy of the tampered-with bulldozers. It had turned out — thank God — sugar doesn't do much harm to an engine, but Mr. Duffy had worked up the sort of self-satisfying rage that requires a refined feminine cunning to mollify.

Beverly thinks suddenly of the rooster eggcup that had once belonged to her grandmother. As a toddler, Colleen had hurled the eggcup at the fridge and cracked off the rooster's head. Beverly had been inconsolable. An instant, jagged disappointment entirely out of proportion had ripped through her as she watched the china head dance over the kitchen tiles. The broken eggcup had brought her to an understanding: being a mother was an entrapment.

She had felt from the moment Colleen became visible in the mirror of the birthing room (she had screamed at the nurse,

Tilt the goddamn thing, I can't see) a profound rapture the magnitude of which dwarfed any sort of emotion she would ever feel again. It was a flooding hormonal love that never balanced itself out, never gained an even footing.

But her life was also irrevocably changed after the birth. She had been robbed of a store of vital, combative energy. Breastfeeding was an enchantment that caused her to drift into afternoon naps full of erotic dreams from which she woke blissful and useless.

Beverly had loved her grandmother — a fisherman's wife with a loose, shiny grey bun and a network of delicate blood vessels over her cheeks. Her grandmother had bequeathed the beloved eggcup just before her death.

This morning Beverly had put the eggcup in front of Colleen without a word. It was an inscrutable reproach. Then she'd turned and stood at the kitchen window.

Colleen tapped the shell and the undercooked yolk streamed a hazard-tape yellow over the rooster's wing and onto the saucer beneath. It made her gag, quietly, but she ate every quivering spoonful.

There were crystal prisms hanging in the windows all over the house. When it was sunny in the kitchen the crystals cast trembling rainbows over the white walls and chrome appliances. Beverly had collected 183 of these crystal prisms, not because she believed they had mystical power, but because they were pretty. But there were no rainbows that morning. The prisms were spitefully ordinary-looking.

MADELEINE

TREVOR BARKER'S APARTMENT was in the same condo as Madeleine's on Military Road and was all coarse fibres and bran-coloured. It makes her worry about what he will cook. Why hadn't they gone out to eat? She'd seen the fennel bulbs in his grocery bag and this was what decided her.

His skin was warm-toned and Mediterranean and he made her think of Paris when she was twenty-one. Her honeymoon with Marty, and it was Marty she was thinking about, really, and she didn't want to be thinking about him. Marty had remarried and had a child on the way and he called her every night when his wife conked out with exhaustion.

A weekend she'd spent in Paris on the way to Germany after a month in North Africa and the city was streaky and saturated with colour. She's been to Paris since, but it's the honeymoon she thinks of when she thinks of the city. A grocer putting out his buckets of tulips, she'd posed jauntily with a baguette, and later there was a pool by the Seine. Before the children, when she and Marty had no money and spent every cent they could get their hands on.

She'd watched Trevor carry a bike on his shoulder and work

it into the elevator. There were days last winter when she was torn apart by her work on the film, distracted, elated.

First she'd had to secure the funding. To bring an idea like this off the ground required a serious budget. She could be convincing. She could drink, she wore red and black and big silver jewellery. She carried a lucky rabbit's paw and she was hilarious and sexy, the way she dragged both her hands through her hair and looked up under her brow.

She didn't do coy because she hated coy. But she could do savvy and raunchy and acerbic. She could do spiritually enlightened if she had to. Coy she would not do. Girlish she would not do. Tenacious she could do.

Madeleine was entranced by her film and she stayed that way all through the winter shoot. She'd wanted Isobel to play the lead. She had written the lead with Isobel in mind. Snowstorms and ploughs and in the night they towed her car and there was all the talk of her heart being weak, angina, clogged arteries — they'd wanted to take a blood vessel out of her leg but she wouldn't have it. She could barely pay attention to the boy she'd chosen for a doctor, his pen tapping a diagram of the heart, because she was besotted by her film.

She had a fist in her chest and sometimes it squeezed with all its might. Her daughter, Melissa, phoned from Europe to check up on her.

Mom, go back to the doctor, she shouted.

Madeleine felt the pain in her arm and her neck and her jaw but she didn't give it any attention. She'd given up drinking and red meat, she'd started to exercise. She felt like a born-again Christian after laps in the pool. She'd embraced fad diets, vitamins. She'd tried, fleetingly, to meditate; her son, Andrew, the surgeon, had said about stress; but the tremendous pressure around her heart increased. The winter shoot was over and now they were gearing up for the summer shoot. Thirty days in the snow and sleet, mostly exterior shots. Madeleine had wanted landscape. Isobel had come from Toronto; she had a disturbing fragility, an odd, eerie edge Madeleine had not seen before. Or maybe it had always been there; maybe all the great actresses are fragile. But Isobel had been professional and strong and she'd carried the winter shoot. The rushes were everything Madeleine had hoped for. The landscape was stark and glittering white. She had been dead right about the cinematographer. She could hardly believe they'd got this far, she and the cinematographer, sidestepping ruin at every turn.

They did this on the Southern Shore back in the 1830s: two young men stole a priest's collar and went up the Southern Shore hearing confessions.

It didn't matter if they really did it; they couldn't have really done it, but what a film. A claustrophobic community bandaged in snow squalls. And a girl is possessed by the devil.

There's always a young virgin, and this one has streaming red hair and a white, white nightdress. A girl on a cliff in her nightdress, sleepwalking or fairy-led, the church bells rippling through the icy darkness.

And there is Archbishop Fleming! He comes from St. John's to exorcise the old church bell and finds the girl, all windblown curls and shawl snapping in the gale. Isobel plays the girl's mother; how Isobel commanded a scene, even without lines, everyone off set huddled around the monitors gripped by the simple arrogance of a woman in control of her craft. How Isobel makes the archbishop falter.

Madeleine has been haunted by the ghost of Archbishop Fleming ever since she read his letters in the Roman Catholic Archives — the rolling sentences, each clause stepping over the back of the last, blistering with vindictive ambition and scalding faith. They'd given her white gloves at the archives, and let her hold the actual letters in her hands. The paper was brittle. There was the old-man smell. Her heart would constrict in the middle of the night and she'd wake slathered in sweat, thinking, This is it, this is it. And she'd find Archbishop Fleming in the corner of her bedroom baring his yellow teeth like a dog. Once she dreamt he'd crossed the room, moonlight on the gold embroidery of his loose cream-coloured sleeve, and he put his pale, liver-spotted hand on her bare breast, and the pain receded. The pain left entirely and she woke rested and fresh. Sometimes it was just indigestion.

She had chosen a man for a doctor because despite her feminism — back in the late 1960s she had been on a floor of the Women's Centre with twelve other women convulsed with laughter all trying to work a speculum and a hand mirror — she had chosen a man because the awful truth was she trusted a man more and now she gave him a look full of doubt and loathing. She was just her film and how much energy it would take to make it happen and she didn't have time to argue with a doctor two decades younger than her. She needed to pass a physical in order to begin the summer shoot. Nobody would insure the film if the director had not passed the physical. The broadcasters wouldn't release a cent.

My heart will hold up, she told him. She could unsettle and stir even a very young man by raising an eyebrow.

Stress is a determining factor, he said. He was rubbing his stethoscope against the inside of his thigh as if to get rid of some kind of static. His chair was on wheels and he pulled himself this way and that with his hand on the desk. He couldn't seem to hold still.

You're not a young woman, he'd said. He pulled himself a little closer to her with his heels on the tiles. He leaned forward, elbows on his knees, hands clasped before him, head bowed, as though lost in thought. Then he lifted his head and a lock of hair flopped into his eye. He ignored it.

You're pushing your luck, he said. The casual gravity of his tone frightened her.

I know my own heart, she said, drawing herself up. He swivelled the chair suddenly and the castors battered over the tiles like a drum roll and he was at his desk ruffling the papers. He signed each form. She had wanted him to sign, but now that she heard him scribbling, it felt like a betrayal. He was casting her adrift. She was responsible for herself. He swivelled in his chair again and handed her the forms.

Must be some movie, he'd said. He turned his back on her and gathered up his papers and a plastic container of tongue depressors. He rose and slipped his pen into his shirt pocket and she saw he was wearing Birkenstocks. Grey wool socks and leather sandals. What had she done?

The film was all about the desolate, violent landscape and human triumph over nature, but it was also, in a much quieter, private way, about evil. A community in the grip of some religious fervour that had sprung out of the tyranny of mild, constant hunger and a giving over. The girl's mother was a scapegoat the town would mercilessly devour. What a part! It demanded an actress of Isobel's stature — an ageing beauty, a haggard temptress. Isobel's cheekbones, her wide, full-lipped mouth — the strength in her face — an absorbing iconic face, the dark, heavy eyebrows, sooty lashes, almost masculine, except for a vulnerability you couldn't put your finger on.

The cinematographer spent a long time getting the shadows right, her face becoming remote as marble and mesmerizing. The light struck her brow and cheekbones while she stood in a window, and it was a naked face. The church bell rang out in the middle of the night when there wasn't a breath of wind. The priest dashing buckets of water over the bell, shouting incantations to rid it of whatever spirit had crawled inside. And there was Isobel, in candlelight, looking lost and alert.

It had taken Madeleine a lifetime to build the kind of career one had to have in order to pull off a feature. Investors saw at once that she could be trusted. These were the credentials she put forth when she argued in her head: I have never failed. I have never given up. I don't take no for an answer. I'm a hard ticket.

The snow came and when Trevor Barker from the condo upstairs got in the elevator he smelled of snow and nighttime and childhood and lost love and she could smell the cold dripping wet titanium bicycle. They'd made small talk about the bike and keeping in shape. A titanium racing bike she'd seen him ride through snowdrifts going uphill. She had hardly noticed him all winter. But then he'd said about cooking for her. He was a man who enjoyed cooking. There were things he was willing to try. There were things he could do with sesame oil he was pretty certain she'd never tasted before. He had a way with fish, he'd said.

And here she was, their first date. She'd knocked on his apartment door and she heard something drop into a frying pan, something hissing and spitting and she could smell ginger. For a brief instant she thought of turning around. She thought of standing him up. But the door flew open and he was holding a champagne flute and there was bossa nova and the living room was blond and pine but not too much pine. The living room was inviting and she could see the definition in his arms.

The blondest thing in the room was his guitar.

It leaned against the bran sofa and it cried out to be played and she hoped he would not play it. It would be awful to watch him be overtaken with a special absorption, to watch his face go stiff with concentration. She did not want to be reminded that he was younger.

She was certain he had a secret and she didn't want to know it. The last thing she wanted was to be implicated in some sticky moral rupture. She felt certain he was in a situation, he was just the right age for a situation, perhaps twenty years younger than her, and she hoped she had not been asked up here to listen.

She would indulge. She would pamper. She would cry out in ecstasy later on if things went that way, but she would not placate or console or absolve.

What she wanted was sweaty naked slippery fast slow deep hurtful tender altering sex with some Wagner in the background.

Wagner or the new Loretta Lynn.

She wanted to be drawn out, rapt, spanked. She wanted feathery touches and massage oil, handcuffs. She wanted to eat naked and she wanted him to feed her from his fork.

She hoped they would maybe smoke a joint. He drove the bike with such presence of mind. He was always on it and his body was without flaw. He was long-limbed and his shoulders were woody-looking and his clothes were new.

She had been paying attention to when he came and went throughout the winter, in a vague, distracted way — the way you watch a neighbour come and go. She heard him walk across the floor in the evening.

She could hear water running through his pipes and when his phone rang and his philosophical, turgid guitar. She had heard "Bridge Over Troubled Water" again and again.

She had seen him in the dark and at dawn. What she knew about him she'd read in the *Express*. He'd run a branding consultancy firm in New York. The sort of work one retires from early, he'd said. He was, according to the article, an enthusiastic supporter of the arts. He'd donated a ton of money to a local art project. Juvenile delinquents would paint murals all over the city. They didn't say delinquents; what did they say? What was the word these days? Gloria Garland was co-ordinating. Gloria who was known for her clubbed seal pup paintings on silk, mostly grey paintings with splats of red, gushing blood, and her affair with a bank manager.

There was a head of radicchio on the counter and she'd seen a package of mascarpone. She had a craving for whatever Trevor Barker would cook and to have sex and for it to get dark and he could light the fat candles on the mantle and she could just take the elevator back to her own condo when they were done.

She wanted to be done. She didn't know what she wanted. How irritating to be ruffled. She had been jubilant moments ago — a date with a younger man — pushing the tiny leather strap of her shoe through the tiny buckle just below her ankle, the swish of her gauzy skirt, atoms of sprayed perfume still hanging in the air. How instantly her granite confidence evaporated. There, not there.

But here was the wine in an ice bucket and she bet it was very cold. She didn't want a relationship with Trevor Barker; she didn't want a relationship. What she wanted, actually, was an idle conversation on the phone with her ex-husband, Marty.

She wanted to hear Marty puffing his cigar. She wanted to hear the ice in his glass. She wanted to hear the scratchy static of a baseball game, broadcast from some southern state, on the transistor radio he keeps on his desk, turned down low. There is no such thing as a one-night stand; she has never seen one.

Three thirteen-year-old girls had jump-started cars and driven them all over town last winter. The police tailed one girl and she tried to outrun them. She'd gone through the red light on Topsail Road by Brookfield Road and through the light after that and it took seven police cars to box her in by the Village Mall. She would be painting the murals Trevor had financed all summer. They were doing waves because waves are about change and empowerment, Madeleine had read in the *Express*. The girl boxed in by seven police cars was at present in charge of waves rolling toward a sandy beach. She was a girl who had never held a paintbrush before.

Please, no *what do you do* or *who are your parents* or *what kind of books*. Nothing of the ex-wives and children and seashore reveries, no life-altering moments and minor illuminations.

What if she said about his bike, and how she had heard him practise "Bridge Over Troubled Water" and whatever was that delicious smell, sautéed ginger and what?

She could forgive "Bridge Over Troubled Water." She could be magnanimous when she had to be. She glanced into the bedroom. There was a futon on the floor. This made her reassess.

There was a spiritual aspect to a futon, some mystical benevolence that she wanted to steer clear of. She did not want to make love on a futon. Her futon days were over.

Will we sit? Trevor Barker asked. He was pouring the wine into glasses he had taken from the freezer. They were foggy with frost.

We could sit, yes, let's just sit.

Then sit, sit wherever you like. She undid the tiny buckles on her sandals and slipped them off and stretched her legs. The sofa demanded this sort of casual sprawl. It was dark out now and the city was lit up and Mount Pearl was lit up and it spread much farther than five years ago. There was a yielding hardness about the sofa and she realized it was a beanbag couch. The couch threatened to slowly, gradually, swallow her whole, and she thought she might just let herself be swallowed. Why not give in? If there was a mess later on, let there be a mess. Strings of orange lights and a few pink and thousands of white and the headlights of cars moved through the whole city like quick, quick drips of liquid. Trevor dropped onto the couch beside her and there was the scrunching noise of beans rubbing against each other while they settled into place. It was the sort of view that took root inside you and blossomed later, when you were working or scrubbing the bathtub. It was a view that had nearly bankrupted her, and she loved it all the more because she couldn't afford it. She had got away with it. Two glass walls. Trevor had the same view, only slightly higher. Would he be sleeping with Gloria Garland of the bloodied pups? she wondered.

So Trevor, she said. What do you do? He clinked his glass against her glass.

BEVERLY

SHE HAD WATCHED Colleen, just last week, from the guest-room window that overlooks a long, gentle hill and the playground beyond. The park was sunlit and pulsing green and after a moment Colleen lay down on the grass and rolled down the hill.

She turned over and over very quickly and then lay on her back with her arm thrown over her eyes.

She looked both joyful and shipwrecked.

Beverly felt a thud of relief: she's still a child. When she turned away from the emerald-bright window to finish her ironing, the room dimmed and she was satisfied as when a good movie ends.

The vandalism Colleen had inflicted on the bulldozers was a rogue act — Beverly had this thought watching a documentary about a demolition team on television with the sound muted — a rogue act so charged with alien zeal that she imagined Colleen had been brainwashed.

Eco-terrorists had kidnapped her daughter and turned her from her mother and everything she'd ever been taught, such as being polite at all costs, using cloth napkins, wiping the sink if there's toothpaste crusted on it, achieving excellent marks at school, avoiding sexual intercourse, and oral sex in the back of school buses, which is the rage, recycling, and eating what's on your plate — all of this had been erased.

On the television screen a quick succession of shots showed a leaden ball hitting a New York tenement in slow motion, and then a hotel in Bombay and then a skyscraper in Paris and the buildings bowed down like supplicants greeting a Japanese emperor.

What pissed off Beverly the most was the brutish lack of imagination.

Self-indulgence she could have forgiven; self-righteousness pissed her off.

It was a calculated and dull-witted act; Colleen had got caught.

Beverly had been drinking blueberry wine by herself at the dining-room table when the pale red and blue washes of light swept across the glass doors of the cherry-wood cabinet. A police cruiser had pulled into her driveway. It was late afternoon and the officer who got out from the driver's side wore sunglasses and a gun. The other cop was a short woman with plump hips and a heart-shaped face.

Beverly had watched them coming up the driveway and there was an elastic moment when it seemed they might have lost their way. Colleen had been staying at a friend's for the weekend. Jennifer Galway had asked her to sleep over. Jennifer's mother played bridge with Beverly.

She saw the police officers and imagined Colleen asleep on the mauve-and-blue shag carpet of Jennifer Galway's rec room in Mount Pearl. A wooden bowl of chips nearby, crunched cans of soft drink; what else did they eat? And the other girls too, Sherry Ryan and Cathy Lawrence, all asleep in the gloomy renovated basement smelling of old sneakers, cigarette smoke, and dampness. Beverly tried with all her might to imagine Colleen's dark hair shushing over the nylon sleeping bag when she turned her head in the murky morning light from the basement's grimy, half-sunken window and knew at once that her daughter was not there. She had not slept at Jennifer Galway's last night. She had not, had not, had not slept at Jennifer Galway's. Colleen hadn't mentioned Jennifer Galway in months, except to say that's where she would be sleeping. Beverly had been delighted.

The male officer drew a small pad of paper from his breast pocket and flipped a few pages and then studied the front of her house. Beverly immediately assumed Colleen was dead, but also believed she could not be dead.

If Colleen was not dead, why were two police officers coming up the walk? Colleen could not be dead because Beverly couldn't live without her.

She had come to think of life not as a progression of days full of minor dramas, some tragedy, small joys, and carefully won accomplishments, as she figures most people think of life — but rather a stillness that would occasionally be interrupted with blasts of chaos.

The wine was the last of the batch David had bottled just before he died. David was — had been — a short, pudgy man with fine silver hair and a lot of cufflinks. Beverly keeps a brown velvet box with a stiff hinge under her pillow. She gives it a shake, listening to the cufflinks rattle around, before she drifts off to sleep.

He'd had a thing for cufflinks. He'd believed in finishing touches, nice soaps, napkin rings that had some heft to them. He'd smoothed eye gel under his eyes every morning because it felt cool and helped him wake up. He'd clipped his toenails with his foot resting on the toilet seat. The wine was surprisingly right for homemade wine. The trick was real fruit juice. He'd squashed the blueberries himself, with his knuckles. What she missed most were his eccentricities. The weird constellation of qualities she would never find in anyone else. She didn't want anyone else.

The wine was potent, full of the four lost summers and suspended sediment. She had been saving the bottle for a special occasion. But the day had been unbearably forlorn, the weather windy and sunny, all the trees finally in bud. Daffodils whipped back and forth. David had never cleaned the sink after he shaved. The porcelain peppered with bristles is something she misses, though it had always mildly shocked her when she came upon it before he died. She had never expected it; now she misses it like a stab with a sewing needle right through her heart. How white and cold a sink can look when you live without a man. How sterile. She misses the smell of sex, is what she misses, a shadowy smell, full of lapsing time and cut grass and seaweed.

The alcohol slammed like a door, perhaps because she was dieting. She had decided David's death would not destroy her entirely. Here was her prescription: behave as if you are unaffected and never stop behaving that way.

There had been a lot of cottage cheese, iceberg lettuce.

In yoga class she lay on her mat, allowing the smell of socks to be a form of comfort, and let tears stream from the corners of her eyes over her temples and into her ears. She was fifty-eight and kept her house very clean and always set a formal table, even when she was eating alone.

A badge or decorative square of metal on the policeman's cap flared with light. They were standing near her tulips. The man looked up and Beverly could see he was young and she saw her bungalow in his mirror sunglasses. She had bought the bungalow two weeks after David was buried. It had been cowardice that had made her sell their house. She sold their house because she was brave beyond measure. She drove past it almost every evening trying to peer through the curtains. She had once seen the silhouette of a woman with oven mitts carrying a giant pot aloft and there were people around a table and candlelight. It had provided her with stores of comfort. Whoever they were they were young and celebrating. She wanted it to go on until dawn.

The officer touched the row of buttons on his shirt before starting forward.

Beverly wrote her sister, Madeleine, occasional e-mails, though they spoke on the phone once or twice a day. Madeleine had a headset she wore while driving.

I like to get my emotional work done on the move, Madeleine said. Beverly could hear squeals from the tires, as though Madeleine were taking the bends recklessly.

Is it work? Beverly had asked. Madeleine, the eldest by six years, had always been vigilant and uncompromising about Beverly's well-being. Often there were car horns in the background; Madeleine running red lights or pulling U-turns, absent-mindedly enraging other drivers.

But her e-mails were hard-nosed and terse. No matter what new fear arose, Madeleine's e-mail advice was the same and consisted of a single phrase: Drive on.

Beverly frequently wrote: I'm losing it. Just that.

The officers started up the concrete walk to the front door. The buzzer rang twice. Beverly had begun to believe in the inevitable. David's aneurysm had been inevitable. More disaster was inevitable. She would have liked to have written

Madeleine at just that moment: I've surrendered. Tell them not to shoot.

For four years there had been a physical ache that started in her solar plexus and pulsed through her whole body just as if she had been shot.

People think sadness is ephemeral and romantic, she wrote to Madeleine. On another occasion: People must think I'm an ice queen, carrying on as I do with ordinary life.

She didn't know what people thought. She had thought nothing herself about sadness until she was penetrated with it.

Every sensual act since David's death fell flat. More than once she'd noticed orange peels next to her lawn chair and realized she had already eaten the orange.

She found herself saying things to people she had already said. Two or three times she said the same thing.

People hesitated.

They tried to behave as if it were fresh, what she was saying, but it subdued them. They had a look. A certain numb look that made her feel like her slip was showing.

Beverly had told one of the secretaries at work about leather couches, she'd received a flyer. She had stopped by the coffee machine and the secretary was putting in the creamers. They were almost half-price, because the secretary had said about wanting a new couch, and this was a real opportunity, these couches, they were a find.

She went into her office, closing the door with her foot, and stood there surprised by how dark it had become. She heard the rest of the department faxing and printing and phoning each other from their cubicles — all the burgeoning, insipid vitality of the tourism sector where she had worked for the last twenty years — but behind her office door, alone, she was dazzlingly lost. The room was very dark in the middle of the afternoon. Every object grainy in the shadows, her fountain pen, the snow globe from Banff, her winter boots drying on a rubber mat, bent over each other, each object, indistinct, hardly there at all.

It was later than she thought.

It must be much later.

She usually left the overhead lights off, but in the time it had taken her to get a coffee, it had become dark and quiet. She felt disoriented; she hardly knew what year it was or how old she was.

She might have been twenty, flying down a hill on her bike, the wind making her squint. She remembered a skirt she had when she was twenty and brown knee socks and the wind billowing the skirt; she was going to see a boyfriend. She arrived at his house, Darren Jones, and he'd had a hose. She opened the latch on the garden gate, and a spray of water full of rainbow shimmer and spears of late-afternoon sunlight and a man she hardly knew — he was just a boy, she realizes in the darkened office — and she thought she was in love with him.

That wasn't love, she said out loud.

She snapped on the overhead light and everything became hurtfully present and stark. She had been fifty-five then and already a widow. She went back out to tell her secretary about some leather couches that were on sale.

The wine tasted like what it was: homemade wine, too sweet, too strong. She had expected a visitation. The wine slammed into her.

The wind took the aluminum door from her and it crashed against the wrought-iron rail and it rang like a gong. The male officer asked if she was the mother of Colleen Clark. Beverly slumped against the door frame and her eyes rolled back in her head. The male officer caught her elbow before she hit the floor.

I have relinquished my hold, she imagined writing to Madeleine, once the officers had put her head between her knees at the dining-room table. The female officer unrolled the yoga mat that had been pushed against the wall and had Beverly lie on it. Then she took Beverly's legs and lifted them into the air, resting the woman's cold bare feet against her chest.

I think I'm very discouraged, Beverly said.

You may just have to cheer up, said the officer.

She came to after only a minute but she felt chilly and had broken a sweat. She heard vandalism and bulldozers. Apparently Colleen had not been hurt. There had been a car accident, she'd got a good crack across the nose, but that was it. Her nose wasn't even broken. She deserved a broken nose at least, Beverly thought. Thank God her beautiful little nose was okay.

The male officer was in the kitchen checking the cupboards for a glass. He came back out with a beer stein full of ice cubes and orange juice.

Electrolytes, the officer said, and Beverly closed her eyes and saw fireworks on her eyelids. She imagined killing her daughter. She imagined putting her hands around her throat and squeezing tight. She imagined the cartilage of Colleen's windpipe snapping under her thumbs. How dare Colleen frighten her like that?

Colleen had been saying eco-terrorism, but Beverly had not been listening. Colleen had been saying change the world, the plight of animals, the environment, radioactive waste, the World Trade Organization. She had said Seattle, she had said Quebec City. She had been going on, but Beverly had not listened.

Are you listening? Colleen kept asking.

Beverly had said about new shoes.

We should get you a nice pair of shoes, Beverly had said.

Of course she's a minor so the complainant has no way to recoup costs of the damage, the male officer said. The sun came out at that instant and hit the prisms in front of Beverly's window and a rainbow fell on the officer's cheek and another on the front of his blue shirt. The glass of orange juice flared with sunlight as if it were a fire in his hand.

I have a daughter, the female cop said. They're nothing but trouble.

Colleen was wilful and lovely. She had become beautiful overnight, large blue eyes and full lips, long, shiny hair. Her trembling, towering empathy, her insistence that the world play fair. She would not allow injustice; she would not stand for it. Beverly had seen the colour rush to her cheeks and tears brighten her eyes over nothing, over some insult visited randomly on one classmate or another — a girl disfigured by acne who had been teased, someone left out, someone who was poor, the kids who had no lunch. And then came the animals. She could never stand the immense unfairness to animals, the chicken factories, cows led to slaughter, even fish. As a four-year-old she had worked herself into an inconsolable rage when Beverly flushed a dead goldfish. She could not bear the indignity of the funeral, her little fists white at her sides, the stamp of her small foot on the bathroom tiles.

How did you catch her? Beverly asked. The worst was how thoroughly she had been betrayed, how befuddled and old she felt. She felt dangerously foolish.

We had a call from a gentleman who picked her up hitchhiking, the male officer said. The officer had been distracted by the crystals. He gave one of the spears of glass a little flick with his finger.

She dropped her knapsack at the scene of the crime, he said. We found the address in there. A rainbow jittered over the wall like a new butterfly.

She'll have to come down to court, he said. Your daughter will have to admit she's sorry for what she's done and then she can avail of the youth diversion program.

You're thinking of diverting her, Beverly said. She thought of rivers in the developing world that were diverted for hydro-electric power, how plains were flooded and birds had to abandon their nests and whole villages were made to move with their belongings on their backs. She had seen this on the documentary channel.

We have a very good program, the kids do community work, said the female cop.

COLLEEN

Beverly had made crustless sandwiches for the funeral home three days in a row when David died. Colleen remembers her leaning over the bathroom sink applying mascara, her eyeball very near the mirror, her mouth stretched open between each stroke. She had pulled the matted hair from her brush and wiggled her fingers so the hair fell into the toilet. These were the ordinary gestures of getting ready. There would be no hysterics; for whatever reason, Beverly had decided she would appear completely intact.

I'm still intact, she'd said.

David was dead but she would apply mascara.

At the funeral home she gripped the hands of visitors and held them. Colleen watched her squeeze each hand for emphasis when she was recounting some memory. Madeleine stood beside Beverly throughout, directing friends toward the casket, bringing cups of tea, sometimes holding her arm above the elbow as if to keep her on her feet.

Late, on the last afternoon of the wake, Colleen had followed her mother into the bathroom of the funeral home and saw her leaning on the sink, her arms straight, her knuckles white, her head hanging down. The water was running in the sink and she might have just thrown up. Finally, she tossed her hair back and they stood like that, mother and daughter, looking at each other in the mirror.

They were absolutely still and they didn't look away from each other, nor did they touch each other or speak. Colleen became aware of the ticking of her mother's watch over the running water, and the thrum of a heater and the murmuring of guests in the rooms over their heads.

There were five separate rooms in the funeral home for separate wakes and each room had a slotted board near the door with the dead person's name in movable white letters that slid into the slots. What sounded like voices might have been steam in the pipes running under the floor.

The lights pulsed slightly, a surge of electricity that caused them to buzz, and still Colleen and her mother stood there not moving until her mother closed her eyes and drew a deep breath through her nose and exhaled with a shudder.

She rubbed one of her eyes hard with a knuckle and there was the wet sound of the knuckle and eyelid and eyeball, a watery, interior, extremely private noise. Colleen's mother yawned deeply and Colleen yawned too. She saw herself yawning in the mirror and she could not stop yawning. They might have fallen asleep on their feet; they might have been generating the same dream.

David's body in his charcoal suit with his wedding ring and white rose, his hands, and the creamy ruffled lining in the casket and all the old women and men who had come to visit might have been something from a deep, deep sleep. The way part of a particularly exhausting dream floats back throughout the following day, overtaking the dreamer, portentous and absorbing.

Then her mother shattered the gathering quiet.

I think a trip to Florida after the funeral, Beverly had said. She closed her purse, which was beside her on the sink, with a hard little snap. She turned off the water.

In the evening, after the funeral, they drove home without talking and when they pulled into the driveway Beverly turned off the car and they just sat there. All the lights were off in the house.

Let's go in, Beverly said. But neither of them moved.

Finally, Colleen's feet were so cold she got out of the car and her boots broke through the thin glossy crust on the banks of snow. Each step she took toward the house made a loud crunching noise.

When she got inside she went to the bathroom and when she lifted the toilet lid she saw the thin nest of her mother's hair, pulled from the hairbrush earlier that morning, floating on the top of the water in the toilet.

The hair in the toilet was floating in an idle circle and there was, in that subtle movement, something sinister.

It struck Colleen her mother had aged with David's death.

She became instantly ancient. She had always been older than all the other mothers who wore jeans and got on the toboggans with their kids and knew, instinctively, the right kinds of junk to put in loot bags. But now she was ancient.

Colleen stared at the hair and thought that her mother had been hurtled into a remote solitude, far away from Colleen or anyone else, sealed away forever. She had been robbed of sex and the intricate privacy and rituals of a couple who have been in love for a long time — the aspects of her mother's life that had been invisible to Colleen before David's death. But, yes, they must have had sex, they must have loved, they were each other's best friends, they'd spoken together in murmurs while they cooked; she saw the staggering, bald truth of it, the bottomless loss. Her mother's vast, new solitude was a stigma, banishing her from fun or lightheartedness, banishing her unequivocally; it was a solitude that seemed to Colleen infectious.

The dark hair, floating in the toilet bowl, embodied the simplicity and horror of her mother's grief and it terrified Colleen. She wanted to be as far away from the voyeuristic intimacy of that floating nest of tangles as she could get.

She woke up on her bed, the light still on; she was wearing her winter coat. The snow on her boots had melted all over the bedspread. She woke as though she hadn't slept at all but it was 4 a.m. and she went to the living-room window and saw her mother had fallen asleep in the car, her forehead resting on the steering wheel, the windshield frosted over.

BEVERLY

COLLEEN FINISHED THE undercooked, mucuslike egg Beverly had prepared. Beverly believed in a proper breakfast. She believed that even a daughter who disappoints irrevocably deserves breakfast.

She put the cracked eggcup on the placemat in front of Colleen.

Just eat it, she said. She stood at the window with her back to her daughter. She was watching a cat stalking a robin in the backyard. She looked vindicated and dreamy.

What can possibly happen to me next? she whispered. The cat pounced and held the bird under its paws for a long, considered instant, then tore off its head.

You look lovely, she said. They had fought over the piercing in her tongue for three months and, as a concession, Colleen had removed the stud.

Off to youth diversion then, said Beverly.

FRANK

HE HAD BOUGHT the first hot-dog cart with his paper route money. He put every cent of it away for four years and during the winter he went door to door asking if people wanted shovelling and he asked if there were beer bottles they wanted to get rid of.

There was a restaurant downtown that let him wash dishes in the summer when it was busy.

His friend Kevin got him a part-time job at a photocopy place; he helped cut posters and business cards, he fiddled with the machines when they wouldn't work. He put every cent away and paid for his own school supplies in September.

One day in June he and his mother got the bus to the Village Mall and took a taxi the rest of the way out Topsail Road. They told the taxi driver the address he'd found in the *Express* and when they arrived it was a used-car lot with a string of faded plastic flags sagging from one street light to another.

They'd arrived at dusk and it was cold and had been raining for eight days and the lot was muddy and someone had laid down two-by-fours on the walk up to the house. The cars had their prices marked in white shoe polish on the windshields and some were missing a tire or two and the rusted axles sank into the ground. There was a small bungalow at the end of a dirt driveway. It had pale blue vinyl siding and two narrow windows. The front door was six feet above the ground with no front steps. They went around the side and found the back door and rang the bell. A row of faded men's jeans hung on a clothesline. There was a German shepherd on a short chain tied to a doghouse. Someone had written *Shep* on the doghouse in red, dripping paint that looked like horror-movie blood. The dog rose when they approached and it sniffed the air and turned three circles and lay down again on a patch of concrete. They had heard the doorbell chiming through the house but no one came to the door so they knocked.

The man who finally opened the door wore jeans and a white undershirt and he asked them in and they had to take off their shoes in the tiny porch and step through a pile of children's boots and toys. In the kitchen the heat was on bust and a kettle started to whistle and the man waved at the kitchen table for them to sit down. He took out three cups and he got a tin of Carnation milk from the fridge.

There was a TV on in the living room. He had a belly that was hard and round and grey hair sprouted out from under his arms and above the neck of the white undershirt and he got out a package of Jam Jams, slit the plastic with his thumbnail, and put them on the table.

Frank saw the man's hands had a kind of tremble; they hovered over the cookies as if he were deciding how best to offer them. The trembling made Frank think the man was in financial need and would demand a good price for the hot-dog stand.

His mother reached across the table with a sigh and poured the Carnation milk from a bit of a height and gave the tin a jovial little dip and twist when she had enough milk and she stirred the tea very quickly and knocked the spoon on the edge of the cup three times.

He saw that his mother was prepared to engage with the owner of the hot-dog stand as if he mattered greatly to her. She would warm him the way she warmed everyone who came into her path, and this might be enough. His mother's natural, enduring warmth might carry the day.

The kitchen was clean, there were dishes drying in the rack, and a cuckoo clock sent out a bird nine times and they had to wait for it to stop before Frank felt comfortable talking about the hot-dog stand. He felt a reckless anticipation.

The truth was he wanted the hot-dog stand and he had only $1,000 and the man was asking $1,300 and it was possible, Frank felt, that if he went home without the hot-dog stand it would break his will.

COLLEEN

SHE HAD HITCHHIKED on a Friday evening for six hours and then began her walk up the timberline. She walked for three hours with just the moon and a flashlight beam to show up the stumps sticking out of the earth. She felt a blister form on the back of one heel and felt it break and rub against her leather sneaker. The breeze was chilly and when it rushed through the trees, making them jostle together, she became aware of how audacious the vandalism would appear. She felt adrenalin rush through her and she was exhilarated and weary. Nothing could compel her to turn back.

There had been a short-lived group at the university who had come together to protest the clear-cut that was endangering the pine marten. They'd argued whether it was true about the Newfoundland pine marten being a separate species and how it could be saved and how they could raise funds and how urgent it all was. There was a definite sense of urgency. There was talk about a bake sale and a letter to the premier. They were dressed mostly in Polarfleece, and hiking boots; they were studying biology or literature or geography. Colleen had gone because of an ad she'd seen on a paper placemat at a café downtown.

She'd downloaded material about international groups and people who had handcuffed themselves around the trunks of trees and people who had gone without food or set themselves on fire. She had photographs of Julia Butterfly Hill, who had climbed a tree and refused to come down for two years. But she couldn't bring herself to speak up. They were all older and seemed to know each other. She sat in a desk at the back and listened and her cheeks burned red and her blood thumped in her temples and finally she drew her material from her knapsack and flicked at the edge of the folder with her thumb, but she couldn't bring herself to open it. She'd gone to a meeting in April and only two other people had shown up. At the final meeting in May, when university was winding down, no one had shown up but her. She'd sat with her back against the locked door of the seminar room and waited for a half-hour. She felt oddly humiliated. She decided to act by herself.

The shadows of the underbrush stretched out and swivelled away from her as the beam of the flashlight travelled over the brush and the stars were very bright. She had to be in and out before the morning shift showed up. Twenty-five men were employed to raze the forest. They would come bouncing up over the timberline on ATVs at dawn.

By the time Colleen reached the clear-cut it had begun to grow light. A gleam appeared along the edge of the river at the base of a very long hillside that had been scraped of vegetation. A dawn light showed the tips of the trees against the sky. There was a streak of bluish green at the horizon and the indigo darkness was turning a softer blue. The bulldozers, in silhouette, looked like prehistoric animals, majestic and slouching.

She had already climbed up into the first bulldozer, had opened her knapsack and taken out the bread and cheese she had packed, when the door of the plywood shed at the edge of the clear-cut smacked against the wall.

A man in a plaid shirt and jeans stood in the doorway of the hut and began to piss. When he was finished she could hear him moving around inside, pouring water, and there was a clatter of dishes. She stayed crouched inside the bulldozer for a long time.

Finally she took a zip-lock bag of sugar from her knapsack and found her way to the top of the machine where the lid to the diesel tank was. She unscrewed the lid, keeping her eye on the shed.

She thought about what she was doing. She closed her eyes and imagined the sugar falling into the guts of the machine, working its way through all the pipes and gaskets. She thought of the surprise and consternation all the men would feel when the five machines cut out almost in unison.

She could hear a radio. There was no way to know when it was safe to move without being seen. Not getting caught required a telepathic vision of the future and an ability to somehow manipulate it, the power of positive thinking, or dumb luck.

She heard a sudden slap and it was the man tossing a bucket of water on the rocks beside the shed. She waited and then she moved to the next bulldozer.

The noise of the pouring sugar, a loud, erotic gushing, caused the hairs to stand up on her arms.

She moved under the window of the shed and tripped over an enamel cup and it clattered against a rock and she ran for all she was worth. The man yelled at her. But she was running and she heard him running behind her. She got over a hump in the path and she ducked into the woods and he ran past her. She stayed where she was and once he was out of sight she dug her way back through the woods so that she was sure she could not be seen. Her neck and wrists were bitten by blackflies and they were burning. She felt a bite between her toes and she tried to rub it against the weave of her cotton sock and couldn't wait to scratch it until it bled. But she stayed perfectly still. The man came back over the road and passed her again. She waited for an hour and then crept out of the bushes and ran as fast as she could.

What she'd felt when she reached the highway was elation. There were fifty pine martens left in this forest. She had not saved the pine martens of course. The clear-cut would continue. But it would take a few days to replace the machines. There would be men who would be paid to sit around and do nothing.

VALENTIN

VALENTIN AND ANTON sat in opposite chairs, each with a row of seven shot glasses in front of him. They were methodical about drinking, taking very little pleasure in it. They were not talking to each other. Once, Valentin, the older man at forty-five, put his fist against his chest because the alcohol burned on the way down. Anton stood and shrugged himself into his leather jacket and headed for the bar.

Valentin was a steady drinker who never slurred or swaggered, but when he drank his face became softer. He was a brutal man and drinking made him decisive and composed. Even the scraggly, bleached-out, delicate women who always gravitate toward nasty men were shy of him when he was sober. Drinking made him resolute in a dangerously attractive way.

Often, he had the bartender send a drink to a woman who interested him. He'd watch while she scanned the room and when she found him he'd tip his glass in her direction.

There was nothing for her to do but nod back.

He knew that tipping his glass, as he did, appeared disdainful; he knew there was some slight adjustment required; some subtle aspect of the North American culture he needed to grasp before his attentions could be appreciated. But he had never mastered an easy charm. He attracted women, instead, with a wily sense of purpose that was itself intoxicating.

The door to the bar was open and it was raining hard. He could smell the rain and heavy cigarette smoke and some dank, despairing smell — the mouldy carpet, briny harbour, and pigeon-shit reek the rain released.

He was waiting for a young woman who had a supply of prescription drugs he was willing to sell for her. She was fifteen minutes late.

The woman was on a month-long OxyContin binge and he imagined she would probably be dead by the end of the summer. It had impressed him how long she had hung on already. She might have been beautiful, but the binge had left her jaundiced, bony, and drawn. He might have made love to her, but she was fitful and distracted. He found that when he made love he liked to have a girl's attention. It was a mandatory courtesy he hadn't cared about or noticed when he was young.

Valentin had a heavy brow and broad cheekbones. His eyes were large and almost rusty brown and his mouth was crooked and sensuous. He assessed himself every morning when he shaved, gave himself a cold look, but he found himself handsome.

In Russia, as a teenager, Valentin had been a chess champion. If the girl didn't show he would play a game of chess. He had an Old World cunning that amounted to a talent for being flexible.

He knew he was the picture of European sophistication when he sat behind a chessboard with his arms resting on the table. He affected a brooding look. He could win without much effort. He liked the feel of onlookers. He liked the way they didn't speak, and would wander away and come back to see how the game progressed. He liked the good-natured losers who shook his hand or clapped him on the shoulder.

Flexibility meant a prismatic comprehension of all aspects of experience. A burst of intuition that stripped a situation of its complexity and made plain what was most advantageous. What he believed in most was being thorough.

He had travelled through countries where the worth of a loaf of bread had soared and dropped in the time it took him to eat it. He'd seen a Jeep fly into the air; he'd seen legs torn from bodies.

He'd seen his father dragged from his bed and made to kneel on the ground and then shot in the back of the head. It was a night that came back to him frequently in dreams. He had not seen it; he had heard it through an open window. Or it had been recounted to him. His sister had whispered the story to him while he was falling asleep; he had heard the neighbours speak of it. Here or there, a spoken phrase so vivid he couldn't remember what he'd seen for himself and what he'd been told.

His father kneeling in the mud is a memory he feels he must have seen with his own eyes, first one knee then the other, the concentrated spot of a flashlight jiggling on his father's bare white neck and then becoming diffuse, flying off into the trees. But he cannot remember a gunshot.

Valentin and his sister were hiding under a bed, he remembers, and the smell of mothballs still brings the night back distinctly, though he was only three, though he might have been sound asleep throughout. *Mothball* is not a word he has ever read; he doesn't even know what they are made of. Perhaps mothballs are natural, occur in nature.

He had been tortured once for six days in a cinderblock cell and believed himself to be abandoned in this cell, buried alive, and lived with this belief for two and a half days and three cracked ribs and an eye swollen shut — they had dislodged the retina in his left eye and now it caught the light in a strange way, like the irregularities in a piece of amber — and had then been released for no reason he could figure out, though he'd examined every detail of his experience in confinement for logic or pattern. When he got out into the light of day it was supernaturally bright and he recognized that he had been altered so radically that he could no longer be certain of who he was.

It was an uncertainty that lasted for almost a month. During that month his hearing became unbearably sensitive. Words failed him. What do you call the utensil you eat soup with? The struggle for the word caused an acute anxiety. He would think he was speaking Russian and realize it was English. He would tell a French waitress he wanted a thing to eat his spoon but he would be speaking English. He would say he meant soup but he had switched to Russian.

He'd made love to the widow of a dentist in Bosnia and had taken her husband's dental instruments in a satchel and claimed he was a professional for so long that a weak paper trail identified him as such and he had crossed some European borders he would not have crossed if they'd known he was a common thug. By the end of it he could remove a rotten tooth with the appropriate tool causing minimal pain.

Thug was an English word with which he identified. He liked its truncated sound, its gangster-movie anonymity, its gritty truthfulness.

He'd read a book called *The Successful Executive* published in the 1930s and found everything he had already assumed to be correct. Ask questions later. Don't ask. There was a stream of philosophy that recommended reflection but those guys were all dead. He could persuade, or coerce, he had both these abilities. He had an intermittent genius that came and went like a bad cellphone connection. Plans came to him this way: fully formed and without flaw.

For example, he had decided he would douse the house on Morris Avenue with gasoline. He would take the pickup to every gas station in St. John's over the period of two weeks and fill up three five-gallon plastic tanks in each gas station.

The idea of torching the house came to him when Isobel Turner was opening her mail. She had a letter from her insurance company and as she stood reading it she opened the breadbox and then became still, transfixed by the statement.

She put the statement on the counter and took out the loaf of bread. She said insurance rates had doubled since she bought the house. She said this to the toaster. She picked up the statement again and the toaster began to smoke. At first she did nothing.

The fire alarm began to bleat and it was a new design with a female voice between each peal of shrilling rings that said, This is an automated message. This *is* a fire alarm. This *is* a fire alarm.

Isobel flapped at it with the dishtowel, dragged a chair over, and pulled the batteries out. The toaster made a grinding squeal and she got a fork from the drawer and poked at the bread that was blackened and tossed it, smoking, into the garbage bucket under the sink.

She'd bought the house fifteen years before, filled it with her grandmother's furniture. The contents of her grandmother's house in Old Perlican had been left to her in a will. She'd rented out the house to a family until she came home from Toronto. The husband had worked for the telephone company and his wife had kept the house immaculate, as if it were her own.

Valentin had sent her flowers in December, after they had spent their first night together. He had been gentle with her and he found a way to respect her during the evening. She was a woman who enjoyed sex, who could summon a kind of exaltation. There was no trace of selfishness in the way she made love. When she came, Valentin thought of it as a kind of giving over; the soft clutching of her orgasms sent tremors through him. He decided, too, that Isobel Turner had been smart once, but something had got away from her. She wasn't smart any more.

She was working on a film shoot that winter and after they made love she would put in a fire and go over her lines. He watched her lips move while she silently memorized the script. She hardly knew he was there.

He could see a gaping weakness in her, a profound vulnerability that he knew he could take advantage of. He'd known nervous people; he'd seen people fall apart. People who had struggled doggedly against far worse odds than Isobel Turner would ever know; people who had suddenly given up, without warning or obvious cause. He had seen it in prison, during his brief stint in the Soviet Army, in the crews of the ships he sailed with.

His own mother had left Valentin and his sister without a word and no way to support themselves when he was ten years old. They had gone without food for a day before his sister left the house to ask the neighbours for something to eat. Those kinds of collapses came in incremental stages; his mother had worried about natural disasters, earthquakes, floods. Some days she wouldn't get out of bed and kept the curtains closed; they'd had very little money after his father died. He remembered waking up on the morning she had left, knowing something was wrong. He'd walked down the hall from his bedroom to hers, his fingers on the wall beside him. He stood for a long time in front of her bedroom door, unable to turn the knob, afraid of disturbing her. He felt someone watching his back and he turned and there was his sister in her nightgown and she was standing still, waiting. He turned the knob and gave the heavy door a push and there was his mother's bed. She had made it and the sunlight from her bedroom window lay over the bed in a bright rectangle and the pillow squarely in the centre of bed beneath the headboard. A bird was singing outside. No object had been tipped over or smashed in the kitchen; his mother hadn't taken anything but the clothes on her back. The house had boomed with her absence.

He had started to drop by Isobel's regularly for tea when he was certain she was alone. He liked it when she offered him food. Her cupboards were full of pharmaceuticals and tinctures. Bunches of dried herbs were bound with thread and hung from the window frames. She didn't eat much, and there were expensive cheeses and withered vegetables in the crispers. She was cool and firm with him, but she was also vulnerable. Sometimes when he arrived there were three or four loaves of hot homemade bread covered with checkered tea towels sitting on her kitchen table. She was compliant and self-absorbed, and she intrigued him. He began to realize she was taking lots of pills, and maybe her languid sexiness was nothing more than a doped funk. They'd seen each other throughout the winter and spring, mostly when he felt like it. She was starting to prepare for another shoot for the same film. She had become more focused over the last week, contained and distant.

Outside her kitchen the garden was brilliant green, sun filtering through the overgrown trees. The leaves had been eaten by the elm spanworms so the branches were naked. From the window he could see the spanworms hanging. It was the third consecutive summer of infestation and the trees would not last, they said. If it were his house he would have sprayed. He would have blasted the worms straight back to hell, where he imagined they had come from.

She was wearing a sheer, lime-coloured nightdress while she read the insurance statement. She had taken her foot out of one slipper and scratched the heel of her other foot with her bright red toenails. She put the slipper back on and turned the statement over, continuing to read. The sun from the window showed the lines around her eyes and he liked that she was much older than him. He'd guessed she was older but she would not say by how much. He knew she would never spray the worms.

I have my tomatoes to think of, she'd said when he told her to spray. She stood reading the statement from the insurance company and the toast smoked and he decided. He would burn down the house.

Last week they'd both gone out into the backyard after making love and they had stood beneath her mature maples and listened to the worms. It was a sultry evening, and Isobel stood with a shawl over her bare shoulders, staring up into the trees. It was a clicking noise, like the inner workings of a combination lock, all the wheels and dials and tumblers falling into place. Tiny jaws munching persistently, killing everything. She was an actress, she'd told him, which, as a skill, amounted to looking into the camera as though it were another person.

That's not a skill, he'd said.

Sentient beings, she'd whispered, staring up into the branches of her trees.

He would burn the house down, Isobel Turner's house, and when she collected the insurance money he would take most of it from her.

Valentin asked how much money she would collect and she said $82,000. She answered him without realizing she had spoken, so absorbed was she in the mail.

This $82,000 was definitely the right amount. He would not stay in St. John's for another winter. He had been in Newfoundland for more than a year and he hated the place as he had never hated any place in his life.

He told Isobel Turner what he was going to do and he said she would get a cut and he threatened to kill her.

You must have someone you can visit around the bay for the weekend, he'd said.

He had gone to her several times during the week and said these things over and over, sometimes cajoling, sometimes threatening, and one night she turned her back on him and took a bottle of pills from the cupboard and tapped them into her palm while the water ran and he saw she was taking too many and he slapped her hand so they bounced all over the floor and she crumpled slightly.

He took her in his arms and she was absolutely still, except a gentle heaving of her shoulders, and he could feel the front of his shirt getting wet. He could hardly believe how moved he was by her crying. He almost cried himself.

Instead, he reached his arm along the wall toward the light switch and snapped it off. He began kissing her and she kissed him back and they had sex on the kitchen floor and she came several times and was slippery with sweat and she felt very strong in his arms.

When he got off the floor, there was some kind of grit, perhaps dried breadcrumbs, imbedded in his knees and elbows, which he brushed away, and his legs were watery and he was full of a spiritual freshness. He reached down and helped her up. She gathered up her clothes, held them against her breasts, and left the room and he could hear her bare feet on the stairs and he counted her footsteps.

He felt he had attained, through the lovemaking, clarity of thought. He decided Isobel Turner would benefit from the fire too. As a gesture of goodwill, because she was such a profound lover, he would drag her out of the entropic dreaminess she was mired in and get her started on some venture. She could sell luxury items of one kind or another. He was certain she could convince older women to pay great amounts of money for things they didn't need. That was a skill.

He realized, then, that the water was still running in the sink. She had turned the water on so she could swallow the pills he had knocked from her hand. She had put a finger under the tap and flicked at the stream of water waiting for it to get cold and she had tapped all the pills into her palm. A whole handful of whatever they were.

He turned off the tap and thought about the extreme heat of her body, she was like a furnace, and the fresh slick of sweat that had glistened on her chest in the street light from her kitchen window and how she gripped him so tightly with her thighs and how she had shuddered after each orgasm, and how the whites of her eyes had shown in a thin silvery line through her lashes — he understood all of this had to do with the fact that she was close to eating those pills. She had reached around with one hand and held his ass, her nails digging into him, and the palm of her other hand squeaked on the cold kitchen tiles.

When Valentin turned off the water, it became silent in the kitchen and he couldn't hear her walking around upstairs, but knew she was awake. He knew she was lying in her bed in the dark with her eyes open and she was probably very afraid. Afraid was good, he thought. Change requires fear, he knew this too. He wanted her to change for her own sake. Part of him had fallen in love.

He put his clothes back on and left the house quietly. He left the house thinking he had saved her life. He strolled downtown whistling and lighthearted.

He drank the last shot and ordered five more and decided the OxyContin addict wasn't going to show. He'd lost Anton to a shadowy corner of the bar. Anton was small-boned and bald and was now leaning over a young woman, his hand spread on the wall near her head. Valentin watched as he leaned forward to kiss the woman and a blue spotlight that had been blocked by Anton's shoulder struck the pints of beer sitting on the bar: one, two, three.

Valentin believed that groupings of three precipitated a streak of luck. He had a habit of counting stairs and neighbourhood blocks, or cars of a certain make, and believed in a system of recrimination that was visited upon anyone who didn't pay attention to these signs. It was important to be fluent in the language of signs and never to stand still when the signs advised action. He was convinced that the way to escape a dark fate was never to stand still. Traces of superstition, of one sort or another, infected every decision he made.

Earlier today he'd ordered soup at Tim Hortons and watched the girl dip the ladle three times and when he stepped outside he'd found a five-dollar bill in the gutter. He has a recurring dream of his mother stirring soup that fills him with exploding ambition. Always the same, simple moment, steam rising from the pot, wisps of her hair falling away from a long dark ponytail, she turns and smiles at him, she touches the top of his head, and then she bends and folds him in her arms; he wakes full of abstract terror. He wants to get ahead. Getting ahead is the way he thinks of it; racing toward a different end than his mother's, whatever it was. She had gone into St. Petersburg to find work, they'd heard later from the neighbours, and they had lost track of her altogether. They never heard from her again.

There was a girl at the pool table, Valentin saw, who was wearing white leather spike-heeled boots that were laced up to her thighs. He watched the girl from the corner of his eye. He put the chess pieces down on the board, setting up a new game. They were pieces carved from marble, they looked like Inuit hunters and the rooks were walruses and the pawns were seals. Valentin held the queen in his fist and moved his thumb over her carved cloak.

Sometimes when the girl at the pool table bent over to line up her shot, one of her boots lifted off the ground. There were seven balls left on the green felt. Valentin gestured to the bartender and the man poured a pint and brought it to the girl just before she took her shot and she looked around the bar.

When she finally glanced at Valentin he tipped his shot glass. The girl turned back to the table and she struck the ball sharply with a hard jut of the cue and everything on the felt rolled and smacked against each other. She sank three balls.

He would set fire to Isabel Turner's house and he would collect the insurance. He would start her on some business venture and he would get out of Newfoundland. He would never return, nor think of it again. He had come to a cold and ugly island that hardly existed, could not be found on many maps. He was nowhere. He could imagine the house on Morris Avenue collapsing in the heart of a roaring fire.

COLLEEN

BEVERLY AND COLLEEN were in the food court of Atlantic Place and Beverly had chosen a table as far from the one with the four police officers as possible. The courtrooms and Colleen's meeting with the youth diversion officer were upstairs. Her daughter would soon go up and meet Mr. Duffy and he would have his say and Colleen would spend the rest of her summer, the long, hot month of August, doing community work, begrudging all of life, Beverly's existence and her own. And Beverly would have to be supportive and motherly throughout. It was her job; what was expected. She was tired of her daughter and the heat and her own loneliness. She wanted to drive to the ocean and get in. She wanted to feel that kind of cold, end up with hypothermia, be washed ashore and discovered by someone willing to take over. But, instead, she was in the food court of Atlantic Place, jittery from bad coffee and a suffocating, unconditional love for her daughter with the bruised nose.

They were one table away from Mr. John Harvey, a downtown vagrant who had settled into his seat and had bent over and unzipped the rubber boots he wore, exposing ankles so pale and veined and bluish white they looked opalescent.

Mr. John Harvey wore an army-surplus parka done up to his chin. Beverly could only imagine how hot he was. Looking out at the harbour, she found she suddenly felt like talking.

This time you've gone too far, young lady, she said.

And then a moment later, One day I suppose you'll be able to say you're sorry for all this.

A cruise ship crept into the window frame. There were thousands of black portals and the ship was fiercely white, even through the tinted glass. It was a monstrous vessel casting a cool shadow over the families walking along the harbourfront.

Mr. John Harvey thumped his chest several times with his fist and eventually, raucously, coughed up something he folded into a paper napkin and put in his pocket.

Colleen suddenly wanted her mother to accompany her to the youth diversion meeting. She would give anything to have her mother there. This was what mothers were for: to swoop in and rescue.

Tough love, her mother said.

The cops on the other side of the room burst into laughter. One of them removed his cap and hit the female cop on the shoulder with it. She pretended to topple off her chair. They were just people, these cops.

Beverly asked, Have you ever given me a thought?

I wanted to change things, Colleen said. When she said this phrase she saw the planet earth from a great distance. It was so far away it appeared to be dislodged from the present, a part of some distant future. They had all lived past this moment: the police, Mr. John Harvey, her mother. The world was still the world but they weren't in it any more. They had long since died and been replaced with new, better people.

Once, her mother said, I left you in a basket on the kitchen table and went upstairs to get something. And when I came back downstairs fifteen minutes later the kitchen was full of smoke. I'd put potatoes on to boil and burned the bottom out of the pot. I'd almost asphyxiated you. Why am I feeling so sentimental?

I'm sorry this happened, Colleen blurted. She wanted to be rewarded with her mother's forgiveness, and then the sun would fire all the prisms in their empty kitchen, the cruise ship would pass, and the arms of the sun would reach beyond its massive, gliding bulk.

Colleen was willing to accept the consequences of her actions — in imagining them she had seen a beer-bellied developer stomping his foot with impotent rage — but she hadn't imagined getting caught.

David had always said, Goodness prevails. He was like a mason laying bricks. There was a right and honest way; things must stack up.

So few things are worth doing, he'd once said. It was after the construction business failed and he'd spent a week in bed. He said he had contracted some virus, more than likely contagious. He'd come out of the bedroom only to smoke in front of *Canada AM*, wearing pyjamas — the buttons done up wrong — and a terry-cloth housecoat of maroon and grey stripes with the belt dragging on the carpet behind him.

David had once organized a benefit to raise money for teenage rugby players. He'd spent weeks selling tickets for a gala dinner and dance so that children from lower income families could go to Sweden with the St. John's rugby team. Colleen had heard him on the radio — he'd spoken with emotion in his voice, seemingly overcome with conviction — Every kid on this team gets to play ball.

How different is that from pouring sugar into bulldozers? David had e-mailed photographs of himself and the team. In one picture David stood in front of a butcher's window with several goats' heads hanging upside down behind him, white against the blackness of the shop's interior; there was a reflection in the window of an oncoming bus; it seemed to be tearing through David's back.

When Colleen thought of the consequences of her actions she had allowed herself a secret, forbidden, helium-filled self-regard — powerful enough to make her cry. Tears were spilling over her cheeks. If she was given the chance, she would do it again. She thought of Joan of Arc. The black-and-white version, the actress dewy-eyed, bathed in celestial light. The planet, animals, trees — these were the things that needed to be saved.

Mr. John Harvey rose from his seat and came toward their table. They caught a whiff of the velvet-thick, rancid stench with maybe traces of shit that rose from the neck of his zippered coat.

Colleen remembered seeing him last winter in a sleet storm. He'd sat on a park bench across from City Hall, and a tree, completely encased in ice, was snapping over him in the wind.

The whole city had been shutting down because of the storm. Telephone poles had cracked in half. Slanting ropes of sleet cut through the soft, concentric aureoles of pink and white haze around the street lights. Colleen had wanted to bring him home, give him her bed, anything to get him out of the cold.

Mr. John Harvey stopped at their table and offered Colleen a tissue. The fingernails on his outstretched hand were brown and bitten.

It breaks my heart to see a young girl crying, he said. One of the police officers stood. Then the other three stood with him. They were alert and ready.

I'm having déjà vu, Mr. John Harvey said. Sometimes these fluorescent lights affect me. He waved a hand at the ceiling. I have moments of clairvoyance since Vietnam, but they don't amount to much. What they did to us there. Mr. John Harvey shakes his head.

Beverly also stood, and her purse fell over and her lipstick and a bunch of coins spilled out. Some of them ran on their rims off the table and onto the floor where they rolled to the four corners of the food court. Mr. John Harvey was transfixed by Beverly.

You must be the mother, he said. The policeman shook out one leg of his uniform. Then he sauntered over toward them.

I was just explaining how lost a mother feels, Beverly said to the officer.

Of course you do, said Mr. John Harvey.

I'm all alone these days, Beverly said.

We're always alone when you boil it down, he said.

Officer, shouldn't this man have a pair of socks? Beverly asked.

They choke my feet, ma'am. The policeman touched Mr. John Harvey on the arm.

You've had your coffee, haven't you, Mr. Harvey?

Yes, I've had my coffee, said Mr. John Harvey. He patted his coat. I've had my coffee, he said again. He turned and searched the policeman's face.

You've had your coffee, the policeman said.

Officer, something has upset this young lady, Mr. John Harvey said. He put a hand on Colleen's shoulder as he spoke.

This young lady has an appointment upstairs, said Beverly lightly.

It's okay, Mom, Colleen said.

There's a man, Mr. John Harvey whispered to Beverly. He took his hand off Colleen's shoulder just as if he had been burned.

Okay, Mr. Harvey, calm down there, said the officer. Beverly gathered a handful of coins from the table and she took Mr. John Harvey's wrist and, turning his hand palm up, poured the money into it.

What sort of man? she asked. He reached into his pocket and took out a salt shaker and put it on the table between them with a little clicking noise.

You see that salt shaker? Mr. John Harvey asked. They all looked at the salt shaker. It was ordinary, with a stainless-steel screw-on perforated lid and a fluted glass bottom. The salt looked very white.

Do you see the salt shaker? Mr. John Harvey asked again. In Vietnam the CIA gave us that much heroin every day just to keep quiet about what we'd seen.

What did you see? asked Beverly.

I've seen the beast, Mr. John Harvey said. The cop shifted uncomfortably and he picked up the shaker and sprinkled a little into the palm of his hand and touched it gingerly with his tongue.

Don't encourage him, the cop said, putting the salt shaker back on the table. He's had his coffee and now he has to have a nice stroll in the sunshine.

Let me walk you to the door, Mr. Harvey, the policeman said. There's a cruise ship in the harbour.

FRANK

FRANK HAD BEEN saving to send his mother to the Mayo Clinic, but she died before he'd got the money together. He had read in the *Telegram* about a local millionaire who had been taken by helicopter to the Mayo Clinic and had recovered. Frank wanted his mother to go in a helicopter. Sometimes he sat by her bed with his head resting on the metal bar and waited until an overwhelming impatience built in him that forced him out of the room.

No part of him wanted her to die faster, even though allowing that much suffering to continue was indefensible.

He was afraid to be without her. He wasn't ready. But he wanted to be free of dread. Dread dogged his every move. His mother had resigned herself to her death. Sometimes she was agitated, but this had more to do with wanting it over than wanting to recover.

Once, after a dose of morphine, she had gripped his hand with remarkable strength. She hadn't spoken for three days and he wanted her to say something. He longed for advice or for her to share a memory, or even an unvivid comment about a nurse. He watched her eyelids quiver and finally open. Her eyes were foggy but she made the effort to focus and he saw her battle whatever hallucinations were threatening to cloud the room. She recognized him; he saw it at once. Her voice was hoarse. She said, E.T. phone home.

As soon as she had spoken her eyes rolled up in her head and then closed. He saw her settle into the pillow. The grip on his hand loosened. But he saw her smile and realized it was a joke. Ba-da-boom.

Frank left the hospital and walked down LeMarchant Road marvelling at his mother's joke. They had watched the video together when he was a kid. Her eyelids must weigh as much as transport trucks.

The way you see the elm spanworms is you are almost on top of them and what you see is a blur that registers in some primitive part of the brain as danger, you focus involuntarily on the worm before your face. It comes into focus, the way it inches up the clear thread, and the other worms hanging beside it become visible. They look like twigs. You can mistake them for inanimate objects, except they move. They waver slightly as if they are uncertain of what to touch next. They look like they think. They inch forward. They are sticky and have a feathery touch.

Simultaneously, the street and cars and houses behind the worm become out of focus. There was a screech of tires followed by an anti-climactic crunch because Frank had stepped off the sidewalk into the lane of traffic to avoid the worm that hung an inch from his right eye.

A minivan swerved into a station wagon. After a moment the drivers got out and looked at their bumpers in silence. Then the older man extended his hand and the two drivers began to speak. One bent to touch the other's fender. Frank ducked into the Shoppers Drug Mart and went through the air-conditioned store out the back door into the heat. There was a worm on his forearm and he swore softly at it.

Frank made sure there were fresh flowers in his mother's room every week. He kept the curtain around her bed drawn so the other patients wouldn't disturb her.

The day before she died Frank's mother opened her eyes again and said, Frank, I want you to get a university degree.

She started to choke. She had Frank by the arm so he couldn't reach the buzzer to call the nurse. He could see the buzzer on her side table but he could not reach it.

His mother's grip was very strong, the tendons inside her wrist stood out from her thin arm. He didn't want her to choke to death. He needed it to be a graceful death. He would not withstand it otherwise.

He did not want to be present. He could not see her off. Her body was rigid and her face was dark red. She kept choking, the colour of her skin went a deeper red, and deeper, the shades changing, her eyes watering. This was it. His mother would choke to death holding his arm, as if to drag him with her. If she died like this he would go with her.

He couldn't reach the buzzer but the woman in the bed near the window had already buzzed for the nurse. The woman, who had come to Newfoundland from Britain long ago, and who was bald and had no visitors, raised her fist in the air and called, Steady on, young man.

Then the coughing subsided. His mother let go of his arm and her fingers had left white marks. He felt a line of sweat trickle down his temple.

Frank picked up the glass of water on the meal tray and bent the straw with the accordion pleats toward her mouth and she drew the water halfway up the straw, but didn't have the strength to get the water to her mouth. She had hurt his arm, actually hurt his arm. But now she could not drink from a straw. The choking had ravaged her.

She tried again and still couldn't get the water all the way up the straw. Frank saw himself looking on, saw his frantic attention to the straw, how earnestly he watched the rise and fall of liquid in the straw, never quite reaching his mother's pursing and slackening lips.

Frank giggled. It started as a quiver and spread a chill over his skin as he tried to suppress it, but he was giggling. Then he erupted with laughter. His mother was startled, but it was as though she had the same vision he did, how intent they were on the straw and some sort of palsy took over her face, the muscles stretching weirdly, her shoulders heaving, and then, because of a familiar look around her eyes he knew she was laughing.

He felt tremendous relief and shock. His nearly dead mother was laughing with him.

They were both soundlessly racked with laughter.

He could not breathe, nor could she, they were laughing so hard. He watched tears come to her eyes and move quickly down her cheeks and this made him cry too. His stomach was clenched. She waved her hand, the weakest kind of move, begging him to stop, but he wouldn't, and this struck them both as even more funny. He couldn't get enough breath and she put her finger to her lips to tell him to be quiet.

He leaned forward and whispered in her ear, Steady on. It made them laugh even more.

Just as abruptly she stopped laughing and he gave her the straw again and this time they were focused. She got the water to her mouth, three fast strawfuls of water. He got a face cloth and ran the water in the bathroom until it was as cold as it got and wet the cloth and folded it.

He thought about their apartment and how he would get rid of it, but not before she died.

They both knew he couldn't afford it, but they had never discussed it. He put the cloth on her forehead and told her to rest. She closed her eyes, and she said, That's nice. What a nice boy.

She was silent for a half-hour. He was watching the clock because he wanted to get out into the sunshine now. He wanted a sandwich before he went to work. He took the face cloth off her forehead slowly so as not to wake her.

Then she said, No one in my family has ever had a degree, and I want you to have one, Frank. I want you to go to university.

MADELEINE

WHAT SHE REALLY wants right now is to spend an afternoon with Marty. Some hotel restaurant somewhere with a threadbare Persian rug and waiters in pressed jackets and the tea comes in a stainless-steel pot with a leaky spout and they have all the time in the world to discuss her film, that's what she wants.

Lately, she's been thinking about hitting him up for a loan. There have been unforeseen expenses. She misses him fiercely. She finds herself arguing with him in her head. He's in the room and he's cantankerous. She asks him what he thinks about this or that shot: the girl in bed, her red hair spread over the white nightdress, how pale and possessed she looks, and the surf smashing against the cliffs and the four white horses galloping over the road at night.

Archbishop Fleming's cape, the scarlet lining in the moonlight, the cracking whip. Newfoundland has never looked so beautiful and dangerous, she wants to tell him.

They'd just got married and had figured out the cities in Europe that were nine hours apart so they could sleep on the train and save on hotels. A honeymoon in Europe, this is 1961 and she is what?

Twenty-one?

Chairs, four to a cabin, unfolded into cots and the train rocked them. They slept in their jean jackets and made love with their clothes half on and hoped no one would interrupt.

Sometimes they shared the cabin, once with a girl from Switzerland with fat red cheeks and thick blond braids whom Martin mistakenly called Heidi, though her name, she said, was Giselle.

Madeleine socked her bum into his hips, his cock pressing against his fly and the seam in the bum of her jeans and that was as close as they could get under the circumstances. Good night, Heidi, Martin said over his shoulder.

They were both twenty-one and couldn't make love enough. There was never enough sex. They hung on to each other in their sleep, his arm under her shirt between her breasts, her chin resting on his fist. He always slept in longer than she did.

In the early mornings she made her way down the rattling train for coffee and she would see the fields, luminous green with blue shadows under the clouds, and the Alps, smoky and cold.

Cows that watched the train with profound interest and started a quick walk with their heads hanging low between their shoulders having decided to keep the train company and in midstep forgot what they were trotting after and stood as still as stone.

She saw villages, forests, and windmills sweep past and returned to the cabin and he was still sleeping.

She read *The Magic Mountain* and went for another coffee, but he did not wake until the very last minute when the train jolted and screeched and emptied out. They had to take their knapsacks down. She pulled on the collar of his jacket and his eyes flew open as if he had been administered electric shock.

He stretched his face and had a little shake and sat blinking, his fists dug into the cot, staring at the floor. He had no idea where he was.

Come on, she said. She was taking down the knapsacks by herself, grunting under their weight, Come on, come on. By then she had lived a full life, felt vast gushes of euphoria and boiling impatience. The day was half over by the time he opened his eyes.

They brushed their teeth in filthy bathrooms with warped mirrors and naked light bulbs in mountain villages. The porcelain sinks had flares of rust and the drains went down into the earth and bubbled up close by. She thought about the phrase, *My husband*. She said it to herself, This is my *husband*, Martin. Or, *This* is my husband, Martin. She hated the word *wife*. It was not a word she could bring herself to say.

Husband, too, was questionable. It sounded stout, bifocaled, and involving of a cardigan.

There were things she would not do: she would not iron his shirts, she would not mow lawns or ever, ever, ever fake an orgasm or put her children in tennis or sailing or allow Martin to buy a motorcycle because she was afraid his head would get smashed in, though he wanted a motorcycle more than anything in the world, nor would she ever get fat or sleep on the couch or let the sun set on a fight or have an abortion or make meatloaf, although a recipe with orange rind and brown sugar had caught her eye.

She would not outright deny the motorcycle — how could she — but she would connive against it.

She would never freeze seven meals because she was going on a trip and didn't want him to have to cook.

It frightened her, what she had got into. In her mother's deep freeze there was a crown of rosebuds that she had worn and a wedge of wedding cake wrapped in tinfoil. Her dress had been cream-coloured, full of understated flounce, and belonged to her godmother. She'd stood on a stool at a dressmaker's with her arms out from her sides and had the zipper moved so the dress would fit in such a way that she could draw breath.

She had fully expected, at the dinner in which they announced their wedding plans to his parents, to be told they were too young, that they had their lives ahead of them, that they'd known each other for only six months and if they were not pregnant what was the rush? She already knew she wanted to make films and she knew the marriage would make it hard to make films but she did not know how or why and so she didn't think about it.

She'd worn a black turtleneck, a rust-coloured skirt, and square shoes and she can still see the way his parents looked up from their plates, how startled they were. How their eyes met and how they decided in unison what they thought of the news. They both took another forkful of food before they spoke.

She had called his parents' house once, looking for him, and they hadn't hung up the phone properly and she heard their conversation about the groceries they were putting away. She heard them say about the price of peas going up and then heard a can of peas, she assumed, slide across the cupboard shelf. She heard his mother say about her back, his father say about his card game. She was riveted to the phone. They chuckled at some remark about a turn of fate; Father Hearn had been dealt the ace just when all was lost in a game of bridge. They both chuckled, a comfortable, private chuckle, and the phone disconnected, but it had been a glimpse into an intimacy so rich it left her light-headed.

Their forks and knives, which had stopped over their plates, began to move again and she saw they were happy with the decision and she could not believe it.

The toilets were clogged and the floors were sometimes packed earth and straw, sometimes covered in a sluice of shit and chickens ran in and out, and they could not believe their luck. They were in Europe.

They hitchhiked to Madrid and fell asleep in a transport truck and the driver pulled over on a hill and got out to smoke under the stars and came back with a flowering branch of an almond tree cold with dew. She woke because the rain from the almond branch dropped on her cheek. She was disoriented and the flowers filled the cab with a green, sugary tang and the smell of cigarettes reminded her of her father, dead for years then.

Groggy with sleep, the flowers and cold night wind made her potently frightened. She was way too much in love.

Smell the flower, the Spaniard said.

I am too much in love, she said.

Smell the flower, he demanded. And he shook the twig near her nose and raindrops fell on her face. She wanted to know what was in the back of the transport truck. What they were carrying.

The landscape had been slipping past them for weeks and it felt like having a tablecloth pulled from beneath an elaborately laid feast.

For the rest of her life she would judge every trip against this trip and every love again this love and none would measure up.

No love would ever measure up.

The truck driver said they had come through the mountains and it had snowed. She saw a rim of slush outside the arc of the wipers and was surprised because two days before they had been swimming in the ocean near Marseille. Marty had pulled a pink starfish out of the waves, handed it to her, and the arms curled around her wrist.

BEVERLY

DAVID HAD MADE a substantial profit in downtown development in the early '90s. He'd had a hand in the construction of many downtown buildings whose main architectural characteristic was an arrogant disregard of the skyline they butchered. This sort of construction — fast and ugly — had inspired months of bitter letters to the *Telegram*, and left a handful of Newfoundland men as wealthy as any men in the world. David had come very close to attaining that sort of wealth.

Or who can say, Beverly thought, what is close. For years, thinking about how close they'd come to extravagant wealth was a metaphysical exercise that gave Beverly pre-migraine symptoms. A blurry spot hung over her newspaper all morning. The altered vision was accompanied by a hypersensitivity to smells.

She vaguely associated the condition with the supernatural. When she felt a migraine coming she almost always bought a lottery ticket.

The two and a half years of wealth had been the best years of her life. She started to work part-time and had time for watercolour lessons and played tennis three times a week. She sunbathed on the veranda that ran around their house, even in May, when the snow was sliding off the tree branches and the icicles on the eaves were dripping. She never wanted to have to work full-time again.

David had taken the family on three trips to the Caribbean during those wealthy years.

Colleen would remember for the rest of her life a sugar plantation in Barbados she had visited when she was seven; a plantation mistress had poisoned a series of husbands with voodoo.

Colleen had fed wild monkeys from her hand, and later heard they'd torn a Rottweiler limb from limb. She remembered crouching indefinitely on a floor of dried palm leaves, the ground full of flashing spears of light and shadow, waiting with the banana held before her. The monkeys blinked quickly and rushed forward and held still and fled to a safe distance. With each brave, wily scramble toward the banana the numbers of monkeys grew until there were perhaps thirty.

They screamed to each other and bared their teeth and a small monkey snatched the whole banana from Colleen's hand. Then the gardener came out waving a machete and telling her to back away slowly.

As quickly as David had got rich, he'd lost everything. He returned to his job at a computer imaging company, specializing in hospital software; three-dimensional graphics that allowed surgeons to watch a laser operation three provinces away, then pick up the phone and tell the guys who were gouging away at someone's tumour that they'd missed a spot.

He had handed in his resignation two years before with some flourish.

I'm getting a fat ass from all the airplane food, he'd said. He was an engineer and liked the clank of one steel girder lowered by crane onto another steel girder; he liked the smell of outdoor work. He hated the rinky-dink hospitals he'd had to visit and their earnest staffs. He wanted to work with men who had tattoos on their forearms, who could swing a sledgehammer without throwing out their backs.

Although David had not exactly told them to stuff their job, as Colleen had heard him rehearse in the bathroom mirror, his chin raised to the ceiling while he dragged viciously on the knot of his tie, speaking through gritted teeth and looking as though he might strangle himself, he had returned to the position bitter and flinty.

The company rehired him for almost double what he had been paid two years before. He had to travel for work and was gone once a month.

Beverly got calls from Provo, Utah, where David said the women were athletic and blond and dazed.

Impossible to get a drink, he said. He was doing pushups as he spoke, grunting after each sentence. He called from Texas to say they were having a windstorm. He had opened the patio windows because it was exhilarating.

Long white curtains are billowing into the room, he said. She heard a smash.

My God, he said. Now there's porridge all over the floor.

He called from Ireland and when she hung up she heard a racket in the living room and her heart beat jaggedly; a bird had flown in through the chimney, an unmistakable omen of death.

The next time she spoke to David he was in Berlin and he said that he'd stood at the edge of a cliff in Ireland, in a small village full of ancient Druid dwellings of stone, and the wind through the crevices had sounded like voices and he'd suffered from vertigo and nearly given in.

Given in? she asked.

I could have jumped, he said.

Something had been compelling in Ireland, that's what she remembered. Something had almost drawn him away. She could hear techno music bleating in the background like cash registers or air conditioners or hundreds of women panting toward orgasm.

I'm in an underground bar, he said.

What do you mean underground? she asked. She was imagining catacombs and rats.

Illegal, he said. It moves location, it doesn't exist.

Do you still feel like giving in? she said.

That was Ireland, he said. Berlin is all broken glass and BMWs.

She was feeling around on the nightstand for her glasses. She hadn't said anything about the bird. She'd had to ask eighty-six-year-old Mrs. Fowler from next door, who had taught botany at the university, to come over and catch it. Mrs. Fowler had Parkinson's and stumbled in, gripping her walker from which there was hanging a clear plastic bag of urine. She positioned herself in the centre of the living room. She wore a lilac cardigan with a large stain that looked like pea soup and her glasses were hanging on a red satin ribbon.

The bird dive-bombed them twice, then settled on the curtain rod, and cocked its head, blinking inquisitively. Mrs. Fowler slowly put a quivering hand into the pocket of her black polyester pants and removed a plastic whistle.

The whistle shook violently in her hand and she dropped it twice and Beverly retrieved it and wiped it clean. When Mrs. Fowler finally had the whistle clenched in her teeth she blew with all her might and it was piercingly shrill and had an otherworldly warble. The bird flung itself at the opposite window and fell with a thud to the floor.

You've killed it, Beverly whispered. Mrs. Fowler shut her eyes in the effort to speak.

I am so often uncertain these days, she said. Beverly picked up the bird carefully and the fragile neck tipped over her finger but she could feel its heart, faster than anything, under her thumb.

I don't know who you are, my dear, Mrs. Fowler said. Wasn't there a nurse or someone to accompany the poor woman? How had she managed to find her way through the hedge? Mrs. Fowler had held annual garden parties for the neighbourhood several years ago. She served punch in a crystal bowl with floating slices of lemon and orange. People had smoked dope in the back of the garden. Mrs. Fowler had worn jeans and had participated in the New York marathon a decade before. What had happened?

The bird's heart terrified Beverly, so speeded up and frantic. The heart said the bird mattered. And David, who must have been staring into an abyss, the seductive roil of the Atlantic, convinced it might be pleasant to simply give up; David mattered.

But when she got to the front door, the bird was fighting against her cupped hands and she opened them and it flew straight into the sky.

It flew with such unexpected purpose — it made Beverly wonder if they might have been spared whatever ill luck was about to befall them.

Everybody here is naked, David shouted. Beverly heard a woman speaking German very near the phone.

Your speech is slurred, she said.

They've got on leather hoods, he said. I wish you were here.

Where are you? she said.

There are girls in cages with nothing on but go-go boots.

Are you with friends? she asked, tilting the bedside clock so she could see the time. She would be awake now until dawn.

David called from Toronto the next day to say his flight was delayed and he wanted more than anything to be home.

You would not believe my head, he said. He said he would give anything to be in her arms. He thanked her for their marriage which he said was the best thing that had ever happened to him. He felt like weeping because he was so hungover, he said, and jetlagged and because she was his wife and he loved her and he was unbelievably lucky to have her. He told her these things couldn't be said often enough and no amount of talking could ever express how he really felt.

I've come to an understanding, he said, about how lucky I am to have you. He said that he'd taken some kind of pill, something a woman had dropped in his drink.

I feel all hollowed out, he said.

A woman put something in your drink? she asked.

I think she was a woman, he said. Beverly had hired a teenage boy from down the street to mow the lawn. It would be the last mowing of the season. Already the trees were bare and the dogberries were violent orange all over the sidewalks. The air had stiffened. The boy was wearing a red eiderdown jacket. She watched him flick the extension cord and bend into the lawn mower.

It was a matter of putting your weight behind something, all of your weight. Giving yourself over to a chore, believing it was worthwhile. She would raise her daughter the same way that boy mowed. She would love her husband that way, no matter what infidelity or loss of faith had occurred. She had wanted the lawn done before the snow arrived.

She was practically naked, Beverly, and very muscular, David said. She had dropped the pill into his beer and he guzzled it down.

Too muscular, if you know what I mean, he said. Beverly could hear, in the background, the wheels of luggage rumbling over tiles, airport announcements. The blade of the mower hit a rock, a bright dangerous clank. She had no idea what he meant.

Too muscular for a woman, David said after a long pause.

You gave me a start, Beverly said. She closed her eyes and saw him falling off the cliff in Ireland.

It's already winter in Toronto, David said.

Maybe you need a good meal, Beverly said.

Everything is white.

Get yourself some juice, she said.

I'm just looking out a big window, he said.

It makes me wonder, David.

They have those guys on the runway. I love those guys. All suited up. They're so alone out there, waving those beacons. They are the unsung heroes.

I'm left wondering.

I have to get something to drink, I'm parched, he said. Whatever it was in his drink had changed him and he couldn't wait to get back and hold her, because he saw now that his life was nothing without her.

She was stirring linguine noodles and the steam covered the window, obscuring the garden, and the boy pushed the mower past a flare of condensation on the glass and walked out the other side, his red jacket seeming even brighter than before. She told David she loved him too. She remembers saying that. Or she has the impression she said it. She left him with the general impression.

Whatever had happened, she'd given the impression she was willing to push through it. She'd made that clear she's pretty sure.

There was no call from Halifax. The aneurysm had struck — if that is what aneurysms do, for some reason the word brought to mind a clock tower swathed in fog, a clutch of pigeons rising in the air, desolation, and the final hour — around four in the afternoon. The storm had hit St. John's around the same time, everything shut down in a few hours, her lawn mower almost buried. David had been coming through the revolving door of a shopping mall. He had a drugstore bag in his hand that contained dental floss and medicated bandages for planter warts. In the pocket of his suit she'd found a restaurant bill. He'd had two draft beer and a cheeseburger at The Keg, bought a *New Yorker*, which was open to a story by Arthur Miller.

VALENTIN

VALENTIN WALKED DOWN the road to the Robin Hood Bay dump until he came to the fence. Beside the fence was a small shack with a single window and the door was locked. Valentin eased the frame of the door gently with a file he'd brought in his backpack and the nails squeaked but he was able to lift the frame without splintering the wood and he jiggled the door handle until the lock gave.

There was a scarred wooden desk with a brown plastic tray on which there was a teacup on a saucer and a squeezed teabag sitting beside the cup. A kettle, a glass dish of sugar packets, and coffee whitener were sitting on a miniature fridge in the corner. The electrical panel that controlled the fence was over the fridge, and Valentin threw the switch and heard the noise of the fence die away. Then he heard the gulls in the distance. A ring of keys was hanging by the electrical panel, and he assumed one of the keys would open the padlock on the gate.

When he touched the fence his peripheral vision turned black and closed in like the shutter on a camera closing, almost instantly, until there was only a point of light and that was also extinguished and he found himself on the ground and the back of his head had hit a rock.

He lay on his back for several minutes tingling all over and aching deeply in his bones. On the side of the road were several flatbeds with stacks of flattened cars, rusty crinkled sheets of metal hanging out between the brightly coloured, smashed hoods like lettuce in a sandwich.

The blue of the sky was so blue it hurt his eyes and the gulls were very white and far away. There was a field of concrete culverts, but Valentin couldn't remember the word *culvert* in English and he doubted he had ever known it. He remembered, or thought he remembered, a train ride where he had been jostled from a dream and saw, out the window, thousands of culverts in an industrial yard, stacked high, like a honeycomb. There were cranes gently lifting them into place and men in hard hats standing around in pairs or alone. The sun was going down and bands of golden light streamed through the cylinders and he couldn't remember what country it had been. He felt jangled all through his body. He felt weepy and childlike and he was afraid of the dump.

The earth he was lying on was packed down hard and threaded with pieces of metal and bits of fabric and plastic bags that had been churned with the gravel and ploughed under and then packed down by bulldozers and the tracks were still visible and he stood up and felt dizzy. He went back into the shack and sat down on a swivel chair, the seat of which was worn and a tuft of foam hung out, and Valentin started to cry.

He was afraid of rats. He had been in prison and he knew how to inflict pain effectively and how to endure it. The way you endure pain: you make up your mind you will endure it. He had given up smoking cigarettes in prison and he had taken part in the organization of a sex racket that he profited from, and that eventually got him out of prison altogether. He had been through all this, but he was still mortally afraid of rats. The ship he had arrived on was overrun with rats, though he had not seen them.

The Russian vessel had been seized by the Canadian government in Harbour Grace with a crew of forty-three sailors on board. The shipping company responsible for the vessel and crew had folded without a trace and the men's wages were frozen or there were no wages and they had run out of supplies and had used up all their fuel after only a week in port.

The Catholic Church in the parish of Harbour Grace held a bingo game when it realized the predicament the sailors were in and raised $600 and the men came ashore for the evening and stood around the parish hall, looking ashamed and hungry. They cleaned out the bowls of chips and pretzels that were put out on the card tables where people were playing bridge. There were bowls of Bridge Mixture and the Ladies Auxiliary had made sandwiches and the Russians ate those too.

The cash from the bingo night was handed over to one of the Russians the next morning and Mrs. Furlong, who was the parish priest's housekeeper, and who was a member of the town council, took the cook from the vessel to the supermarket and drove him down to the dock with the supplies.

Everyone expected the Canadian government to intervene quickly on behalf of the sailors, but by the following weekend the crew was out of food again and had no electricity and there was another bingo game and enough money was raised to provide groceries for another week.

An emergency meeting was called by the town council and Mrs. Furlong said she had heard from the gentleman who bought the groceries that the ship was overrun with rats. She said they had purchased several tins of baked beans at the supermarket, but the Russians were eating them cold, directly out of the tins.

Someone pointed out that the money from the bingo games had been previously allotted to the town library for the purchase of computers.

The minutes of the council meeting reflected all of these comments and were distributed the following morning to the council members, the media, several other members of government, and a copy was delivered to the vessel and Valentin read about the rats, which he hadn't known about, and became terrified and knew he had to get off the ship.

He rowed into town from the ship the next day and went to the Family Restaurant at twelve and sat beside a terrarium built into the wall enclosing eight budgies, blue and yellow and lime green. The back of the cage was lined with a poster of a half-dozen kittens. The budgies mostly stayed still, their eyes closed, their heads cocked to the side. They might have been stuffed except the glass was encrusted with bird shit and there was a small cardboard sign in the corner, written in ballpoint pen, which said, Please don't tap glass.

The restaurant was noisy and the waitresses sprayed the plastic tablecloths with Windex as soon as they cleared the dishes and wiped them down vigorously but the blue ammonia scent hung over Valentin's table along with the smell of gravy and french fries and trapped restaurant heat.

Valentin ordered a hot turkey sandwich. It came with dressing, peas and carrots, and cranberry jelly, which still held the ribbed indentation of the can it had slid out of. He ate all of it quickly and wiped his plate with the dinner roll that came with the meal and pushed the plate away with his thumb. He had tucked his paper napkin into the collar of his shirt, but he looked around now and saw no one else had done so and he took it off.

The waitress came to clear his plate and she asked if he wanted his bill and he said he'd like to pay tomorrow. He took his watch off and laid it by his plate. He saw right away it was the wrong thing to do. The offer of the watch had depressed the waitress.

She stood with a bottle of vinegar and a bottle of ketchup in one hand and his cleaned-off plate in the other and she put the bottles down and wiped her forehead with her free hand. It was as though his removing the watch had made her extra tired, and her shoulders slumped. She had a warm, damp look because of the heat and the place was crowded but she didn't look hurried.

The waitress, Valentin saw, was beautiful and calm and disappointed. She stood with the back of her hand pressed to her warm forehead and his plate in her other hand, staring out the window. The water in the harbour was electric with sunlight, a spank of blinding white light, and his vessel was almost in silhouette. He could see someone walking around on the deck, pausing to lean on the rail. The waitress seemed arrested by the sight of the ship. Then, as though she could feel him looking, her fingers fluttered down from her forehead to the neck of her blouse and she touched a wedding ring that was hanging there on a chain.

You can put your watch back on, she said. She picked up the bottles and walked away and only turned around to put her bum against the kitchen door and push through it and he saw in her face she had already forgotten him.

Outside, on the front step of the restaurant, Valentin found a man having a smoke. He offered to drive Valentin into the Robin Hood Bay dump outside St. John's, but he said the dump was closed on Monday afternoons and there was no use going there and you weren't allowed to scavenge anyway and you couldn't go in without a vehicle and he wasn't taking his truck in because every time he did he got a flat, besides they had an electric fence.

Do you understand the concept *electric fence*? the man asked. He was squinting up at Valentin, his hand over his eyes.

The man tossed the butt of his cigarette and said, I'll take you to the dump and you can see for yourself since you got your mind set on it. It's no skin off my arse if you crowd decide to electrocute yourselves.

Valentin flicked another switch in the electrical panel and turned off the electric fence and touched it again and nothing happened so he opened the padlock. He walked past the weigh station and the fields were ploughed hard on both sides of the road. In the distance he could see the gulls sliding sideways across the sky.

They moved the sky sideways in long white sweeps and then there were sweeps of white sky sliding in the other direction. The gulls filled up the sky, gave it volume and motion. He came upon a small mountain of green garbage bags covered in gulls and there was a TV and a toy castle of durable plastic in primary colours big enough for a child to climb around and play inside.

Valentin thought for a moment he heard a baby crying and it chilled him, but it was only one of the gulls. They screamed in different voices and some of them sounded human and some of them sounded like evil spirits. He didn't see any rats. He was sure the rats would appear all at once and he would realize they had always been there. The garbage bags were too real and the gulls in the distance were not real enough. He shook his head because the landfill was vast and there was no one else there and he had a hard time drawing his thoughts together because of the bolt of electricity that had jangled every atom of him and seemed to dismantle his sense of purpose.

Valentin had a son in St. Petersburg who was three, a boy with pale blond curls and brown eyes. He loved the child with a quick, hard, religious depth. If it wasn't for the child, Valentin would have killed himself in prison, or allowed himself to be killed, but instead, he managed to get out and found himself a berth on the ship because he wanted to buy the child things like the plastic castle and, later, an education.

He had an idea that his son would never ever find himself standing in a vast sea of filth, confronting helplessness. He would make certain of it. Near the garbage bags there was a pink velveteen armchair, it looked brand new, without a scratch or stain, and there was a gull perched on the back. He thought of his son and picked up a piece of pipe and raised it over his head and yelled at the top of his lungs. He flung the pipe at the gull on the back of the chair and the bird lifted itself a foot or two out of the path of the tumbling welter of metal and settled down again.

Sometimes the boy fell asleep on Valentin's chest while they watched television and Valentin was greatly moved by the rhythm of the child's breathing, which was deep and committed and gentle and trusting. He would never let the boy see what his father was really like, Valentin had decided. As the child grew older Valentin would show up at the apartment less and less, gradually establishing a distance between himself and the boy. But he would provide for the boy and watch from afar and send money and pay for his education.

Valentin loved to run his fingers through the boy's hair or hold one of his feet in the palm of his hand. He loved to feel the spring of his curls in his fingers. He loved the smell of him.

The gulls were very big and they tore at the plastic bags, puncturing them and pulling out the contents. He saw a gull dragging the carcass of a chicken from one of the bags. The gull's wings flapped hard but it was moored to the bag and then the bag gave and the carcass came out and the gull squawked and tossed the chicken, and grabbed at it with angry pecks and abandoned it.

The stink came in dense clouds and went away and came back. He saw a stove with a red-and-white-checked dishcloth still folded over the chrome bar of the oven door. Valentin came upon six scattered paper plates that still had gravy on them and green peas and tiny cubed carrots, the same frozen peas and carrots that were served with his lunch. The bright orange of the carrots on the white plates had a menacing buzz and he had to look away.

He left the road, walked for perhaps ten minutes over the hills of ploughed garbage, and the gulls became thicker and he could feel the breeze from their wings near his head; he was not afraid of gulls. He saw, on the distant hills, narrow pathways beaten into the grass and knew they were rat paths, probably several years old and when it started to get dark the rats would pour down the paths like oil.

In less than three hours he had filled two sacks with copper pipes and brass fittings. Then he hitchhiked to St. John's and found White's Salvage, where he sold the piping for $187.

He found the Salvation Army twenty minutes before closing time and he bought a suit jacket and a pair of jeans and a white shirt that fit him well, though under the arms the shirt was slightly yellowed. Valentin went into the bathroom in the back of the Salvation Army warehouse and he found a small bar of soap wrapped in paper on the sink and he unwrapped it and stripped naked and washed every part of himself, even his feet.

He dried himself with paper towels and put on the new clothes and tore the tags off.

The woman who had sold him the suit banged on the bathroom door and told him to come out because they were closing and he'd been in there long enough.

She waited outside the door and he stood still on the other side and for reasons he could not understand, the noise of her fist on the door made him break into a cold sweat and he jammed his own clothes into the garbage bin and flung the door open and it frightened her and he saw all the lights were turned off and they were in the building alone.

Valentin went to a downtown bar and ordered five shots of vodka and sat in front of a chessboard. By eleven o'clock in the evening he had played fourteen games in four different bars and won each of them and had $325 in his pocket.

He slept in his new clothes on a bench in Bannerman Park that night.

In the morning he went to a house on Gower Street he'd heard about and purchased seven cartons of stolen cigarettes; he was back on the ship by suppertime and sold the cigarettes to the rest of the sailors by the package or singly and had $500 by the end of the evening. That night he went back into St. John's and rented a room and slept on the floor. Before leaving Harbour Grace he stopped at the restaurant and paid the bill. He asked for the waitress who served him but she wasn't there. He left a garishly large tip for her. That was sixteen months ago.

MR. DUFFY

THIS SEVENTEEN-YEAR-OLD girl had walked into the forest, Duffy was thinking, came upon his bulldozers, and she nearly destroyed them. Sugar doesn't do much damage when you get down to it, but she had certainly tried to destroy them. She must have walked all night. The nights might still have been pretty cold in early July; she must have gone without sleep. The mother had called ahead to ask if she could be present at the meeting.

The mother is not welcome, Duffy shouted to the social worker. This is no time for the mother. The mother should have been around when her kid was dumping sugar into my heavy equipment. Where was the mother then?

He was sitting in a shed of plywood with one window and there were chainsaws and falling trees in the background and insects taking pieces out of him. He slapped bug repellent on his arms and they had an angry sheen. Sweat crept from under his hard hat, tingling in his hairline. The hard plastic band inside the hat was wet and it dug into his forehead. He could take the hard hat off talking on the phone but you forget to put it back on. Leave the hard hat on, he's always saying. His shirt was stuck to his back.

He'd had to hire a truck and a crane and four mechanics. There was a guy came to him with his finger hanging by a flap of skin and blood made Duffy weak. These were some of the things he'd dealt with that morning. He had to shout to be heard, but the social worker was meek and keen and he took advantage of it.

The purpose of the meeting, the social worker said, is to give the incident a human face.

I have no interest in the mother, he shouted. Bring on the youngster. She wants a human face, I'll show her a human face.

But the mother had ambushed him in the underground parking lot of Atlantic Place. Duffy saw she was an attractive woman; the fawn-coloured suit she wore fit snugly, a filmy scarf at her throat, pointy shoes with high heels, as he had seen all the women wearing this season in Montreal. Even without the heels she was a good three inches taller than him. Duffy liked tall women. He liked the way they commanded attention on a convention floor or in a ballroom. He liked a woman who could dress with formality in a heat wave.

I'm Beverly Clark, she said. I was a Holden. I think my mother knew your family. We were the Holdens from the East End. My father's family had the Meat Market.

Even in the underground parking lot, where Duffy thought it might have been cool, the air felt close and smelled of warm tar and exhaust.

Now that Beverly Clark was right there in front of him he felt deflated. He looked for the daughter.

I forgot my purse, Beverly said, putting her hand on his arm. Colleen is upstairs already.

She was intent on making him feel bad, the hand on his arm, and he was irritated by it. He wanted to turn the full bulk and range of his considerable might against the daughter when he met her. She had not committed a peaceful intervention for ecology, she had pissed off Gerry Duffy, and he had every intention of impressing upon her the difference.

Minor my ass, he thought. At fifteen he was peddling salt fish on the harbourfront. He was supporting his widowed mother at fifteen. They thought she was widowed; she may not have been Jesus widowed; his father had wandered off in a snowstorm and not come back. Gerry was up at five making bread every morning when he was fifteen, he delivered groceries in the dark, cold winter evenings. He cleaned the Newfoundland Hotel during the night, and had never had a mark below ninety at school, until he dropped out in Grade 10 to work on a construction site. At seventeen, the girl's age, he had a child on the way, the first of twelve.

Seventeen-year-old Colleen Clark would not be familiar with the nuanced understanding of limitation he had grown accustomed to by fifteen.

She's shameless, he thought.

Gerry had come to believe that hard work and missed opportunities had made him invulnerable.

Coming over Garrison Hill in a Ford pickup some years ago he had gripped the wheel tightly — it was a Sunday morning and mass was getting out at the Basilica, his youngest daughter had given birth the night before and he'd delivered a dozen roses and had seen the infant in her little plastic cot beside her mother's hospital bed. He had, earlier in the week, closed a deal for a subdivision that was three-quarters pre-sold and the church bells pealed and it occurred to him he was invulnerable.

Nothing would surprise him or overtake him. This is the thought he had going down Garrison Hill: he was equal to whatever came next.

Mrs. Duffy, Gerry's mother, had been a willowy Catholic who had accepted poverty, saw the honour in it, and allowed it to make her hard-tempered, vehemently selfless, and reclusive. She almost never left the house. She had once slapped Gerry's face for coming home from a card game with alcohol on his breath.

He used to cook for her each evening and hand over his paycheque. They had been sitting at the dining-room table over a meal of cod and mashed potato one evening when there was a knock at the front door.

Mr. and Mrs. Foley and their daughter, Mary, stood huddled on the sidewalk, rain falling like a string of rhinestones from Mr. Foley's peaked cap. Gerry's mother was standing in the doorway of the living room with her napkin clutched in her fist against her chest. Gerry saw that his mother was an old woman, much older than Mrs. Foley, who wore bright red lipstick and looked like she could be Mary's sister.

Mr. Foley said he was wondering if they might come in and have a talk with Mrs. Duffy and her son.

We've interrupted your meal, Mrs. Foley said. She could see the plates abandoned on the dining-room table.

That certainly wasn't our intention, Mr. Foley said. Once in the living room, he sat on the sofa but jumped up from it again. He tried to lean against the marble mantle, but it was the wrong height for him and he eventually stood in the shadows, in the corner of the room with his arms crossed over his chest. He worked at the post office on Water Street, and his face was grey and pocked like concrete.

We always eat at this hour, Gerry's mother had answered grimly. She meant they could be trusted to follow through in all things. No matter what the Foleys wanted to throw at them they would rise to the occasion. She waved her hand with the napkin vaguely in the direction of the table as proof of their consistency.

Mary, we'd like you to tell Mrs. Duffy what you've told us, her father said. The girl was staring at her hands, which were on the lap of her navy coat and looked very white. Her fine blond hair had come free of the braid that hung down her back and her face was bright red. They were going to have a baby.

The young couple married in the Basilica and shared the room across the hall from his mother until there were five small children and it was time to put his mother into an old-age home. The marriage was passionate and durable until Mary died of ovarian cancer after her last child, fifteen years later. The oldest by that time could take care of the youngest, and Duffy had already started on his fortune.

He was looking forward to this meeting with Colleen Clark. He'd driven over the highway at sunrise to get here on time. August was a busy time for him, but he was curious about the girl. He saw the sun come up over the barrens, all those grey, lichen-scabbed boulders tinged pink, one or two men on the side of the highway with fly rods. The ponds between the rocks like sheets of metal, the sun twinned in every one. He meant to make sure Colleen Clark remembered him every time she saw a sugar dispenser for the rest of her life.

COLLEEN

I WALK INTO the liquor store at the mall and they've got four people working there. This is the day before the youth diversion meeting and I'm revved up and anxious. I take a bottle of vodka off the shelf and a bottle of wine and I go to the counter and say, My friend bought me this, but I don't drink vodka so I'd like to exchange it for this bottle of wine which is almost the same price. It's a horseshoe counter and they have baskets done up with coloured Cellophane and bows, bottles of wine and corkscrews, fancy wineglasses.

If I have to, I can gently nudge one of these gift baskets off the counter. The woman at the cash says, Do you have a bill? and I say, It was a gift, which is why I want to exchange it, and the manager turns and says, Did she have that bottle in a bag when she came in? and the other woman who has just finished serving someone on the other register says, Do you have identification? The manager's arms hang away from his body, as if he were wearing an eiderdown coat, and he flexes his fingers. The girls behind the counter step closer to the manager. Either they step closer or they are already close. They form a phalanx, ready to pounce.

And I say, I'm not buying, I'm exchanging. And there's a customer behind me and I turn to him, a tall man, maybe six feet tall, with longish hair and gorgeous grey eyes though he's over forty for sure, old enough to be my dad, probably, and maybe he saw me take the vodka off the shelf, but the thing is, once I've imagined the absolutely worst thing I could do in any given moment I have to do it. I have to see how it will end.

I had come to the mall to buy striped socks but as I was strolling past the liquor store, I got the idea of stealing a bottle of something. I had to know how such a thing would turn out. I can feel my pulse, the thunk-thunk of blood, before what is about to happen and what has already happened. I say to the tall man behind me, I'm so sorry for holding you up. I try to sound relaxed and sincere. Even if he saw me take that bottle, he will doubt what he saw. He will doubt it for perhaps two or three minutes, by which time I'll be gone.

Now just a minute, the manager says.

I say, I can see you can't help me and I fully understand, I'll just have to regift.

I leave the store with the vodka and when I get around the corner I put on my jacket and sunglasses and put the bottle inside my jacket and I'm in the parking lot before they've even had a chance to shut their mouths.

MADELEINE

THERE'S A PROBLEM in the art department. The cinematographer, Guy Leblanc, wants to shoot the interiors with natural light so there will have to be skylights, holes cut in the sod roofs. Where in the budget does it say skylights? the art department wants to know. Of course, there were no skylights in the 1830s.

Guy had drawn a sharp breath when Madeleine mentioned this fact, as if she had slapped him. Film is an impressionistic medium, he'd said, as if she were an idiot.

You don't tell the truth, he'd said. But what you tell *becomes* the truth. He was pompous and irate. She loved his tirades. He could be so thoroughly French. She loved how he could dismiss whole libraries of historical scholarship by shutting his eyes and letting ripples of irritation run through him. He was bald on top with a ring of silver hair just over his ears, never combed. She had hired him because his raglan was ripped up the back, revealing a wine-coloured lining, because his hair stood off his head on one side, because he drank very good red wine and all he thought about was film. He got a far-off, concentrated look when he was on the set. She liked sincere, half-crazy men who took pleasure in their work. Her young, red-headed lead liked him too, Madeleine had heard.

I will not be a slave to the *facts* — Guy spat the word out as if it were poison. Who knows what the nineteenth century looked like? he'd said. I'll tell them what it looked like.

Madeleine lets him rant. He had come through for her on the winter shoot. Blizzards, sleet, ice; he had come through. He's the best in Canada, the best she's ever seen. What he could do with natural light made him worth his staggering fee. He might be shouting and spitting now, but on the set he was energetic and wise. He spoke to the actors with respect. He was unobtrusive and bold. They all wanted to do a good job for him, live up to his expectations. Not every cinematographer could deliver like Guy — what he had made of the Southern Shore in winter — it was a Gothic, vicious landscape, a curse, a new kind of beauty.

She knew he suspected she was thinking budget. The whole notion of a budget offended him deeply. He didn't care about cost, it wasn't his job. He cared about light. That was his job: to care immensely about light.

She's supposed to be working out the cost of skylights but for some reason she's thinking of the train station in Paris; why is the train station barrelling through her with such force? The glass rooftop of a train station: sheaves of light, clank of the rails beneath, chopping every memory up, twenty-four per second. Holding Marty's hand. She was gripping his hand and the straps of her knapsack dug into her shoulders. At some point they gave up holding hands; they became self-conscious about touching in public. A staid sense of coupledom settled over them. But in the cold station they watched pigeons flap against the skylights and he squeezed her hand so hard it hurt. Their shoes echoed and they promised each other they'd find the most expensive restaurant in France.

Let's blow our wad in Paris, Marty had said. But by evening they'd forgotten about eating. They had walked all day, every cobbled street they could find. They hadn't gone to see the Eiffel Tower and Madeleine found she was crying because she just was. She just was, okay?

She smiled at Marty and her eyes looked a rusty brown, through a glaze of tears, and he thought she looked insane.

There might be a strain of insanity in her family she had not mentioned.

If she had driven her Swiss Army knife into his forehead up to the hilt at that moment it would not have seemed incongruous to him. That's what he'd said at the time. But, he'd said, she was simultaneously dazzling and he thought whatever errant emotion had caused her to well up had also made her beautiful and he would let her plunge a knife through his skull if that was what she wanted. Whatever she wanted from now on, she could have.

Guy is whispering with full-blown fury: Don't speak to me about expense.

She's touching the tip of her pencil against this figure and that figure but what she wants is the afternoon alone. They all imagine she can carry the great weight of this film by herself. She feels her chest constrict and she pauses to draw a deep breath but she can't fill her lungs. Why does she always have to be fighting someone? Why is there always a battle? In Rothenburg they'd eaten putrid, green-veined cheese smeared on a baguette, then wandered through a torture museum. Marty had thrust handcuffs at her and wiggled his eyebrows suggestively and she hadn't found it very funny. She remembers exactly the smell of algae from whatever river it was that ran near the museum.

You're so demanding, he'd said. She was shocked by how stinging he could be. For some reason it stung. She was demanding, she knew.

Her arm is numb; she stretches her fingers but they're stiff. She can see through the frosted glass of her office window, the girls from the costume department, standing around the coffee-maker in the hallway, probably having a smoke. Did she pay people to stand around? Guy has drawn up a chair; suddenly bored with skylights, he's taken a crab sandwich from his satchel. He unfolds the wax paper and finds a packet of pepper. He tears it with his teeth. He opens the sandwich and taps the packet and slides half of the sandwich across the desk to her.

It's only a film, Madeleine, he says.

Guy, she says. He has almost won and they both know it.

The summer shoot will be magnifique, he says. He waves the sandwich in the air, to let her know he can foresee the entire shoot in all its glory.

Guy, she says. His mouth is full and he's trying to swallow so he can speak.

There will be colour, Madeleine, he says. She and Marty had met a German painter living in Marrakesh. Big abstract explosions of colour, orange embers falling through the night sky, smoke and it might have been the Big Bang or Dresden or a future apocalypse. They three stood before each painting and the German clapped his hands twice and a maid appeared with a bowl of tangerines and later they were told he was a former Nazi who liked little boys.

It was that afternoon they'd seen the snake. There was the snake in the medina; she remembers hearing the rattle inside a woven basket, an ancient shimmy-shimmer all about death. How many people get to hear that in a lifetime?

Guy has pulled the spreadsheet toward him from her side of the desk, he's running his finger down the columns of figures — intolerable — what does he know about budget, how dare he? But to let a man decide for a change, to give up the responsibility, just for a moment, to play dumb — she considers it.

A nearly naked man surrounded by a crowd in the medina had tipped the lid off a basket with his toe and played a reedy pipe. A weaving snake came up out of the basket, standing perhaps two feet high. Madeleine saw its lips were stitched together. A veil of perspiration sprang to her face, sweat dripped down the nape of her neck. The noise of the medina, the reedy, complaining music from the pipe had new, unearthly pitch.

A cart drawn by a donkey passed behind her and she suspected the squeaking of the wheels was an ingenious code, each wheel emitting a syncopation of dots and dashes of a frequency so high only dogs and ham-radio operators could decipher it.

Marty saw her eyes were glassy and she spent the next three days in a fever, puking, shitting, and shivering. It was an illness that never left her entirely, coming back over the years with renewed strength, making her feel as if she had been pummelled with a hammer, showing up in the darkest part of winter when she was in the throes of production. She was always in the throes of production.

Steady belt, her sister, Beverly, called it. I'll be down with soup, Beverly said, whenever Madeleine was ill. Don't get out of bed, I'll be down with soup.

But in Marrakesh, Marty had taken care of her. He'd pinched her skin to see how dehydrated she was and found himself running through the narrow corridors of the medina past the stinking vats of urine where they dyed leather, the light-pierced banners of fuchsia and violet cotton, and the stalls that sold spices all heaped in cones of soft mossy green and rust and brown, in search of a stall where he might purchase a thermometer.

When he took her temperature the red line crept beyond all the numbers and she was speaking in tongues and he wondered how he would get her body back to Canada when she died but on the third day she was fine and they decided to head back to Europe.

She drops the pencil, remembering Marty's relief when the fever broke. He had cried, his shoulders shaking. They were just kids on that trip and they'd hardly had any money.

If there must be skylights, it will have to come out of her own producer's fee, she thinks. Let there be light. She balls up the spreadsheet and prints another one.

FRANK

Frank hears someone say her name and she turns on the dance floor, her long hair flying off her shoulders. Her name is Colleen. She's dancing with her arms over her head, biting her bottom lip, her eyes are closed and her face tilted down and to the side. This is a look; men will bow down for this look, this slow undulation, this is a look of concentration and abandon. Her hips swing and he sees she has a rhinestone in her navel the size of a dime. The band plays "You Can't Always Get What You Want," nostalgic and embittered.

She's wearing low-slung jeans and a black halter top. She's doing a slowed-down hip swivel that's erotic and full of self-satire and her figure is skinny and her hips are pale in the blue spotlight. The rhinestone winks lewdly at him. What he wants is to put his hands on her while she dances.

He had been a St. Brendan's tap dancer, back when he was ten, in black pants and pink cummerbund, white shirt and bow tie. His mother slicked his hair down and he had a solo in a spot of light on the stage of the Holy Heart auditorium.

He could not see the audience but he could hear them in

the dark. He was told, from behind stage, to step into the spot of light that spanked the scuffed floor.

The spot was animate and neurotic.

He stood transfixed, terrified, gripping a fistful of velvet curtain, convinced that if he stepped onto the spot, it would fly up the curtains and the audience would bellow with laughter.

He'd peeked at the audience while herds of children, choirs from all over the island, moved on and off stage throughout the concert. Then he'd been given a hard push right between his shoulder blades and found he was on stage.

His taps made loud clicks and he moved over the floor to the edge of the spot of light. He stood on the periphery of the light and it blinded him, but it remained utterly still. The audience was — he felt a breathing mass — engulfed in a dark with so much depth and texture he felt in him the urge to hammer the spot of light down to the floor.

What he remembers: he willed himself to dance. He did not want to dance. He refused to dance. But his mother was in the audience and he would dance.

She had switched shifts as a greeter at Wal-Mart, had traded Christmas Eve so she could come to the concert. It wasn't her turn to work Christmas Eve but she wanted to see Frank on stage, so she traded Christmas Eve for the night of the concert with another mother. They were mostly single mothers or teenagers or older men who had suffered some version of emotional collapse that made them incompetent at their previous jobs. They were working at Wal-Mart because other options hadn't panned out. Nobody wanted to be there on Christmas Eve.

Frank's mother, besides cleaning people's houses, stood at the door of Wal-Mart and said hello to people and put lime green or orange stickers on the parcels they brought in with them.

She was on her feet all the time and she had varicose veins, zigzagging veins that were raised slightly above the tight, shaved skin of her calves. Her legs were as white as bread, and peppered-looking where she shaved, and the veins were lumpy and blue as ink.

In the evening she put her feet in a Tupperware bowl full of hot water and Epsom salts because her feet were swollen. When she took off her shoes, her feet held the indentations of the cotton ribbing of her socks, and the mark of the tongue of her shoe.

Frank watched her dip her feet into the steaming water. She put one foot in and lifted it up and crunched her toes and put it back in the bowl and did the same with the other foot, her face wincing each time, because the water was so hot. Frank watched her feet get red up to the waterline.

His mother was in the audience by herself on that evening when he was ten and he could not move and the music had already started and Frank had missed his cue.

The music started and it stopped.

He would have turned and run but his feet with the heavy taps were stuck and then the music came back for him.

It came back his way.

It was part reprimand and part consolation.

But there it was at the beginning again. He looked off stage where Dr. Callahan was sitting at the piano and smiling at him with an exaggerated clown smile, big, hopeful, and sinister. Dr. Callahan taught in the folklore department at the university and was a former Christian Brother and was all about preserving the old jigs and folk dances. Sweat was dripping down Dr. Callahan's ruddy face; his hands were raised over the keys for Frank to see.

His hands were about to come down and Frank must dance.

Dr. Callahan had one tooth in front that was grey, and the tooth frightened Frank because Dr. Callahan had said it was dead. Everything was in the tooth: all of Dr. Callahan's fight against despair and his private, mystical arguments with God and the complicated love he had for tap dancing.

Frank chose to concentrate on a part of himself that maybe didn't exist ever before, which he now thinks of as his will, and he made it burst into flame. He filled with something like rage or flame and decided to nail the goddamnjesus spot to the floor with his tapping so it never moved again.

He was, at ten, the best tap dancer in the province until Dr. Callahan gave him a beard rub.

Dr. Callahan said, Come and have a beard rub, Frankie. He took Frank's face between his hands and stretched out his unshaven chin and rubbed it against Frank's cheeks, first one, then the other, making his skin raw.

You danced well, Frank, Dr. Callahan said. The next day there was a rash where the stubble had roughed up Frank's skin and his mother saw it in the rear-view of the taxi and asked him about it and when he said how he got it the taxi driver opened the window and spat a big hawk. His mother lowered her sunglasses, which were sitting in her hair, so they covered her eyes and she turned to look out the passenger window and Frank never went to tap dancing again.

But he loved dancing. After his dance in the spotlight there was a pause and the clapping started. It came in overlapping waves and was multi-toned and fell away and was renewed and grew louder and louder. It lasted so long in the dark he started to wander off the stage but Dr. Callahan ran into the spotlight with Frank. The professor took his hand and lifted it and the clapping got even louder and it lasted longer still. Frank's mother had been surrounded by other parents who kept telling her how talented Frank was.

They couldn't even get out of the auditorium because of the adults pressed against his mother to congratulate her and to ruffle his hair and tell him he was a fine boy.

He'd like to dance with the girl, Colleen, that's what he'd like. He'd like to have his hand on the small of her bare back between the low-riding jeans and the knot in her black halter top, lay his hand just above the two dimples over her bum.

He'd like to move her around a nearly empty dance floor in Mount Pearl, or some other place where she wouldn't know anyone except him. A war veteran sitting at the bar probably with medals on his shoulder and five fat women sitting at the slot machines in the back and some red spotlights and blue spotlights and a dance floor with nobody else on it.

He wants that girl in his arms worse than he's wanted anything for a long time. It's an overwhelming inarticulate compelling want that makes him lose track of who he is.

He wants to tell her about his hot-dog stand and how hard he's worked to get it and how much money he makes. He wants to say I can make this much money in a night. He doesn't want to say it, but he wants her to know it.

He would like to say, I don't do drugs.

He would like to tell her about the Inuit guy who hanged himself in the apartment over his at Christmastime.

How would that be, if he told her that, him a total stranger? But he would like to get it off his chest. And about the Russians, the drug dealers who moved in above him when the room became available. He wants to talk to her about the waterbed he bought. He is swollen with pride because he had the foresight to buy a waterbed, just in case he gets a chance to mention it.

He would like to tell her, or have her intuit, how much respect he had for his mother and how empty the world is without her. He would like to explain how he feels like he has a hole in his chest. He would like her to put her hand on his chest and show him once and for all there is no hole and then he'd like her to undo his jeans and put her mouth all over him.

The door to the bar is open because it's so hot and the smell of pigeon shit and smoke and the harbour comes in very cool. And maybe the smell of those worm droppings that are covering the sidewalks in a wet muck and smell like cat's piss. Everybody's face is dew-struck and soft-featured because of the drinking and Frank's just stopped in on his way to the hot-dog cart.

He has to get to the hot-dog cart. But couldn't he just ask her maybe to dance?

He'll make money tonight hand over fist. There will be light breaking over the South Side Hills by the time he heads home. George Street will be covered in garbage, drunks lurching, the cops will be out.

Frank has a permit for the corner of George Street, which is the best spot in the city. This is a street with bars on both sides and is famous now for the festival, which is just drinking all night long.

He had to get down to City Hall before it opened and line up to get that spot. He paid good money.

A guy can move hot dogs on George Street.

He's seen a guy out by Sobey's Square have to depend on when the movies let out. The guy spends all his time looking at an empty parking lot. George Street in the summer and Frank can pull in close to a grand every week.

The taxi drivers keep him company. Gulliver's Taxis lined

up near the pizza place across the street, the drivers leaning on their cars, the ends of their cigarettes moving in the dark.

They're the kind of men who have a little timeshare trailer somewhere in the Florida Keys they drive down to because they are afraid to fly and their children are grown up and some of them have done a bit of time and they have faded tattoos on their hands to prove it, between the thumb and index finger, a sword and cross or a four-leaf clover, their wives want to go to Florida for their arthritis and you can't hang on to it one guy said because they put you in a home and the government just takes it and there's bastards sat off on their arses their whole lives collecting dole and doing fuck all and you know what they get? The same sort of bed in the same sort of old-age home as guys that worked all night long on George Street dragging vomiting drunks in and out of cars for the last thirty years. College kids losing their stomachs all over the upholstery, more money than you can bat an eye, they have to hose the van out the next morning, and so they spend two weeks of the winter in Florida because their youngsters won't get a cent after they're gone, the home will eat it all up, nest egg my fucking foot, and please, God, I'll be taken in my sleep before it comes to that.

The taxi drivers are something else, Frank knows, but they keep an eye on him because he works so hard and they kid him about being skinny and they say stuff about his wiener but mostly they watch out for him because when he leaves the corner of George Street after a night on the hot-dog stand he can have as much as five hundred bucks on him.

Just a kid, they tell each other.

At 4 a.m. everyone wants a hot dog, the taxi drivers tell him as they pull out their wallets and hand him a five and look off into the fog or rain and wait while the wieners barbecue.

Give me some of them what are they banana peppers my stomach will hate me, they say.

A crowd tonight, they tell him.

What have you got a cold drink back there, Frank?

Have you got a girl, Frank? I bet you got a girl, they say.

Look at Frank, look at the colour of him.

He must have a girl.

Some crowd tonight, Frank, they say. Give me a couple of them napkins. The taxi drivers come over and talk whether they want a hot dog or not.

Frank has never given a hot dog away.

The taxi drivers understand this perfectly.

There are people outside the door of the Ship Inn trying to cool down or having a smoke. She has a rhinestone in her belly button. She's slender, her arms are golden, her neck is golden, and there's an elastic riding over her hip, a part of her red thong and it makes him crazy to think about sliding a finger under that elastic. He'd like to take that elastic in his teeth. Her arms are raised over her head, and her face is turned down and to the side and she's biting her lower lip to keep from smiling to herself because she's so sexy.

If he could tell half the things about himself she would fall in love with him.

If he could have some of her time.

Just to tell her a few things.

He watched her dance with the guy who is the town simpleton, delayed person, and the delayed guy has on glasses that make his eyes googly and he is a type of thin that speaks medication and he breathes through clenched teeth, and spittle comes out but she doesn't seem to mind. She dances with her eyes closed and when she opens her eyes she smiles at the delayed guy. What is that smile, good-natured? It is without condescension and that's why he is starting to fall in love with her.

When the song ends the delayed guy goes to the bar and this is the moment Frank should ask her to dance with him.

He feels the moment getting bigger in his chest.

He is very close to just walking right up to her.

She lifts her arms and gathers her hair and twists it and piles it on the top of her head and he sees her bare neck and he should ask her right now and she drops her hair and gives it a shake and it falls in a curtain down her back.

The band is starting up — a retro band, joyfully ironic and smouldering with self-satisfied mirth. The girls love them — and she's just standing there almost all alone and he could go right up to her now. She turns slightly and the rhinestone catches one of the stage lights and winks and sends out a blue laser for half a second and the music begins and it's Meatloaf, "Paradise by the Dashboard Light."

She sort of rocks her hips.

She's looking like she might dance to Meatloaf and he should just put down his drink and go up there and if she said no that would be okay. If she said no he could just walk out but he knows she wouldn't say no. He knows she would say yes if his feet would just move but they are stuck and his chest is bursting now with the want to ask her.

She bites her lower lip when she dances as if the look on her face would be full of such profound sexual pleasure, it would be dangerous to let it show, so she bites her lip instead.

If he doesn't ask her to dance right now: but he doesn't.

And a guy touches her shoulder and she lays her hand on his arm and she is laughing and her hips are rocking and the guy touches her hip he lays his hand right over the red elastic thong on her bare hip above her low-slung jeans and her arms are over her head and her hair hangs down over her face and a red light from the stage falls all over her bare arms.

The floor is so crowded nobody can move.

Frank charges out of the bar, furious. Some people sharing a joint on the sidewalk open their eyes wide at him and he looks like he might kill them, except he also looks like he doesn't see them. He takes the stairs two at a time to Water Street.

He strides along Water Street and the couples go past, guys holding on to elbows or an arm draped over a girl's neck and their reflections in the big windows of empty storefronts stretch and lurch past.

There's music on George Street and the taxis try to drive through the crowds. The crowds take their time. Some girl lies over the hood of a car and the driver leans on the horn. Frank feels the drumming from the band through the soles of his sneakers. The girls have on miniskirts and little T-shirts with spaghetti straps. The straps slip off their shoulders and they have shiny bra straps and some of them are Americans from the cruise ship. Everybody tanned, mildly drunk, the high heels make the girls gawky and vulnerable and he could put a fist through a window he's so furious.

He passes a guy with a hot-dog stand. There's a lineup all around the stand and just the sight of it makes Frank want to take a bat to it.

He was in Sears buying the duvet cover that afternoon and the salesgirl said *wet bar.*

What you want is a wet bar, she said.

He didn't like to drink. He especially wasn't interested in stocking a bar. But he followed her down the aisle because she had a walk.

He followed her down the aisle because it was air-conditioned in the Village Mall. He'd bought a soft serve and sat in the food court where his mother used to take him for a treat.

He saw that there were a lot of handicapped people in the food court, and people who looked fucked up in one way or another, and then he saw the two Russians who'd moved into the bed-sit above his and they saw him and he finished his cone and walked through Sears because he didn't want to leave the mall right away in case they noticed and thought he was afraid of them.

They had come to his stand on George Street the night before and they stood on the curb just behind him and they watched him selling hot dogs. George Street was full of crowds, there was a band outdoors, people had plastic cups of beer, and the Russians just stood there watching him for more than an hour.

He had paid good money for the permit and it was his permit.

The guy named Valentin waited with his hands linked behind his back.

They just stood there and looked at the crowds.

Valentin had on a pair of sunglasses and the lenses were black and he wore a black leather jacket.

Some customers came and Frank put on some Polish sausages and he slit them with the knife and the fat leaked out and the flames sizzled. There were three customers and they took a long time dressing the hot dogs and when they left Valentin stepped up beside Frank and he said he wanted Frank's stand and he wanted the permit.

Frank put down the tongs he had for turning the wieners and he wiped his hands on his apron.

We will offer a good price, said Valentin.

The hot-dog stand isn't for sale, Frank said. Valentin lifted his lip then in a kind of slow snarl and a toothpick unfolded out of his mouth and he picked at his eyetooth with it and examined the pick and dropped it in the gutter. His black sunglasses were full of the coloured lanterns that were strung across the street. He turned and the lanterns ran across the black lenses, one after the other. The city had done up George Street to look like drinking was a Newfoundland tradition. But the old-fashioned street lights were brand new.

Valentin was taking all this in, this Old World look. There was a strip joint very near the hot-dog stand and the windows were covered with posters so you couldn't look in, but light leaked out the sides. Frank glanced over at the taxi drivers and he noticed Lloyd with his back against his car, his arms folded over his chest. Someone in the Sundance had started up the mechanical bull. They could hear the rodeo music and the metal wrenching kicks and bucks and the yowls of whoever was riding it.

The permit is my permit, said Frank.

I think you'll change your mind, Valentin said. At first Frank thought there might be something that wasn't translating properly.

I think you'll change your mind. He waited in case something else was coming. He waited for something else. He waited for things not to be the way they were.

But everything was the way it was.

He had understood perfectly.

Valentin had made himself understood.

Frank saw that things were exactly the way he had always understood things to be all his life. He had understood things to be this way when he was five and had to go into a foster home because his mother was hospitalized for breast cancer and had to have both her breasts removed.

He had understood things to be this way on several different occasions when he was, however briefly, a guest of the Whitbourne Correctional Institute for Juvenile Delinquents at the age of fourteen after a bout of shoplifting — he was caught, the last time, putting two T-bone steaks down the front of his jeans in the meat section of Dominion.

He understood things were this way when his mother was diagnosed with cancer a second time and when she explained to him that it was all through her, a phrase that has haunted him ever since, all through me, all through me, all through me, how thorough and definite such a phrase can prove to be, he well understood, and they wanted her to go to hospital at once because in the hospital they could manage the pain and there was a very good chance she wouldn't be coming out of the hospital and all of that proved to unfold exactly as his mother had said it would for the simple reason that that was the way things were.

And when the Russians moved into the bed-sit on the third floor, Frank had the uncomfortable feeling that things would once again prove to turn out the way things often turned out.

The guy named Valentin had been slapping a girl around the bed-sit the night before and Frank heard her screaming and he heard what he thought was her head smack the wall and then he heard her running down the stairs. They had one of her shoes and Frank went to his window and she was dishevelled and snot-nosed and the knee was torn out of her stocking and her knee was bleeding like she'd scraped it.

The shoe flew out the window and hit her in the head and she dropped to her knees on the pavement and the men were laughing and a Gulliver's Taxi came up and there was a long wait with her knock-kneed because of her tight skirt and she was dazed by the smack of the shoe on her head and the terrible predicament she'd got into because Valentin was yelling he would look for her wherever she went.

Try to leave, he shouted.

Just try.

Kneeling on the street and the back door of the cab opened and still she stayed and finally the driver got out, the guy named Lloyd. He picked up the shoe, took the girl by the elbow, and got her standing up. He put her in the back seat and a beer bottle flew out the window and smashed near Lloyd's heel. The glass glittering and rocking near the heel of Lloyd's boot and Lloyd didn't even acknowledge it; he just walked around to his side and closed his door. The taxi sat for a moment because Lloyd must have been asking the girl where she wanted to go and probably wasn't getting any sense out of her. Another beer bottle flew out the window and bounced off the roof of the taxi but it didn't break, it just rolled down the street. Then Lloyd drove away. He didn't burn rubber, he just drove off quietly.

Frank's mother believed there was no difficulty that couldn't be surmounted. This unending willingness not to be defeated kept his mother going, but she was also beaten down by it. Frank had learned from his mother not to give up on those things that are sacred. He could be yielding, but if something was sacred he would not bend.

What was sacred was he would not give up the hot-dog permit to those Russians because he had worked for it.

The girl at Sears had pink lipstick on, which made him focus on her mouth and the word *wet bar* sounded like an invitation to something altogether different; so he followed her to that part of the store.

It was black padded vinyl with vinyl-covered buttons that held the diamonds of padding in place. It had a shoulder of chrome and the part you'd rest your elbow on was a smoked mirror with gold veins running through it. It had a lazy Susan, which he had never seen before and thought ingenious. There was a lone bottle of Tabasco sauce in the lazy Susan. He had to admit it was an impressive piece of furniture.

The girl was chewing gum and she blew a bubble. She said she was getting married in a month to a guy who drove a bus and they had put this exact item on their registered wedding list and many of the guests had already put down as much as fifty dollars toward it. She said they had been buying furniture for three years always with the same plan in mind, when they had enough to furnish a small apartment they'd get married. They didn't have a single thing on credit. Her fiancé was going to the technical college at night. She wouldn't always be working at Sears, she said. What she wanted, and what she would eventually achieve, was accreditation as a dental hygienist.

Nothing is going to stand in my way, she said. Frank thought he could leave the mall now, the Russians had probably forgotten him.

I don't want a wet bar, Frank said.

You should go to school, she said. You look smart enough.

You don't know anything about me, Frank said. The girl blew another bubble and it got big and sagged and clung to her chin. She took the gum out of her mouth and peeled it off her face.

I can see when people got potential, she said. She slapped the bar twice and turned her back on him and sauntered down the aisle running her hand over the stacks of towels.

MADELEINE

WHAT SHE MISSES is convention. She misses security and not having to explain to people she's just meeting. She misses the way he sometimes held her at night when her heart was racing with anxiety. When she is afraid of having a heart attack, alone, dying alone, she misses him then.

Marty's mother and father had nine children, and his siblings were either domineering and wild-eyed or acutely shy. They were either Irish-looking with big blue eyes and black hair or they had a Spanish look, dark-eyed and vixenish. One of his sisters was a ballerina with a small company in Boston, another owned a consulting firm that assessed the environmental impact of new industry and was known to be impartial and thorough. There was a nurse who taught prenatal classes, having helped deliver hundreds of babies early in her career. She was cheerful and fresh-faced and had a deformed hip that gave her a strange gait and she told stories of women on their knees in elevators, and husbands fainting at the sight of blood.

Martin's sisters were good-looking, skinny, and energetic. The brothers were intellectual, three of them teaching at the university, two in politics. At family gatherings they were loud and drank as much wine as they could. Fights erupted easily. They were storytellers and fought each other for a chance to hold forth and slapped the table laughing.

The ballerina especially had a squawking laugh that turned her face red and made her gasp for breath. The table was always set formally and the men did not enter the kitchen. Madeleine loved being in the midst of them.

She loved the noise, the swish and grind of the labouring dishwasher, clatter of cutlery, laughter, and when the lids came off the steaming casserole dishes. But it wasn't a life she could imitate; it was too clean and big. Once she went in the kitchen and three of his sisters were whispering and she knew they had said something about her.

She demanded, What is it?

The ballerina said, You let him push you around. You'll never get what you want. Don't you have any ambition of your own?

Later he was furious and got on the phone. He made calls. She could hear him behind the closed door.

They had been best together when they were alone. Being in Rome with Marty: if she could do that again before she dies she would be satisfied. What would Rome be like now? They'd eaten at an expensive restaurant in Rome. There were chandeliers and evening gowns and the portions were small. Ostrich in truffle gravy, oysters and scallops, grapefruit champagne sorbet, a chocolate dessert that had seven layers, a bottle of red and they left without paying. They strolled out the lobby and the porter held the door for them. Madeleine bent to pat a miniature poodle in a tartan coat on the leash held by a woman draped in shawls. She patted the poodle, they walked around the corner, and they ran for all they were worth. They ran down laneways, took two twisting stone staircases, and caught their breath leaning on a stone wall that looked out over all of Rome. Then they heard the slapping shoes of two waiters in black tuxedo pants and white shirts and bow ties and they ducked and the waiters ran past.

She could not stand anyone who slept in. It was slothful, joyless behaviour, choosing, essentially, to let life pass you by, and it meant you were morally weak.

Mornings are the best time of the day, she'd said.

Marty hadn't looked up from his book.

Things smell better when you wake up early. He'd turned a page.

What are you reading? She put her cup down. What are you reading right now? Tell me the sentence.

It wouldn't interest you.

Tell me anyway.

The sentence I'm reading right now?

The very sentence, yes, I want to know exactly what you're thinking at this instant and every instant for the rest of your life, basically.

Okay, the sentence I'm reading now: We will see, for example, the wheel of a motor projecting from the armpit of a machinist, or the line of a table cutting through the head of a man reading.

She blinked at him. He shook off his shoe and put his stocking foot on her crotch under the table. He flexed his toes.

That's the Futurist Manifesto, he said.

Weren't they a bunch of fascists?

They wanted time and space to collapse. She put one hand over his toes, pressed the other hand flat on the table near her saucer.

Read me some more, she said.

They'd seen Fellini's *La Strada* and when they came out into the afternoon light she said, Anthony Quinn. That was all she said.

The thing was they were alone together for three months and everything they did amazed them. They were escorted out of a book launch by a woman with clotted mascara and a spot of blood in the middle of her left iris. They'd guzzled the free booze, picking up full glasses off one passing tray and putting down empty glasses on another, and Madeleine watched the tray she had reached for with an empty glass swivel out of reach the instant her fingers let go of the stem and it smashed and caused a stir.

When the woman let go of Marty's and Madeleine's arms on the front step of the library their legs turned to rubber and they collapsed in a heap on top of each other, squashing all the pastries they'd put in their pockets.

They were childless and willing to become something. Everything they did or said was stored up for the marriage that was coming. They felt nothing and saw nothing because they were in the present.

They were so much in the present there was no time for reflection, and if his sisters were right about him ordering her around, about her hanging on his every word as if he were a god, about the dangers of loving without reserve, there was no time to think about that either.

Anthony Quinn wrapped in chains, on his knees in the dirt, busting chains with his chest, the tendons in his neck, the impossible strength.

They kept moving until they were invited to sleep in a thatched cottage in the Black Forest. A musty-smelling sleeping bag in a slant-roofed attic.

Who owned that house? Who invited them? They took long walks in a tree farm. Acres and acres of trees whose trunks were all exactly the same size, each tree the same distance from the next, as in a nightmare. The forest must have been manufactured in the nightmare of a gargoyle or gnome, some Nordic creature only half-human or not human at all. The branches were bare and it was always raining, or finely swathed in mist or socked in with fog. Marty leaned her against a tree and ripped her jeans down to her ankles and he dropped to his knees and made her come and she was looking up into the woolly sky criss-crossed with black branches and when she pulled her jeans up the earth began to shake and thrum and a man in a fluorescent orange cap in a yellow bulldozer drove past, the first person they had come across in two weeks of walking through the Black Forest. He took off his cap and waved with his whole arm.

She had wandered in the uniform forest at dawn when the sky lightened evenly and the only sound was the crunch of her shoes on the leaves. She was falling prey to a mysticism that was smarting and potent. A crow in the trees felt like a former life or the life to come and when it flew into the air, cawing raucously, it frightened her out of her wits.

That was where she became who she was, Madeleine thinks, in that solitude. Everyone becomes who they are in a stark landscape of undiluted solitude and bad weather. It's possible to go through life without becoming who you are, but it is better, in the long run, to come upon yourself in an insanely ordered forest where nothing has been left to chance. She wishes every twenty-one-year-old girl a Black Forest of her own.

Is it true their first child was conceived under a thatched roof in the fairytale cottage lost in the enchanted forest? It is true.

COLLEEN

She had nearly been killed on the way back from sabotaging the bulldozers in the clear-cut. After almost an entire day of waiting on the side of the road a man had finally picked her up. It was already getting dark and she was soaking wet from the rain. As soon as she got into the van the man's cellphone rang.

He said, Russell here. He glanced over at Colleen wearily and he reached to turn up the heat and the phone fell down the neck of his coat. He scrabbled to catch it, making the van swerve. He listened and pressed his hand to his forehead and said, Sandra, Sandra. Then he put the cellphone on his leg. Colleen could hear a shrill voice rattling away into his thigh.

What do you think you're doing? he asked Colleen. Do you know how dangerous hitchhiking is?

Then he picked up the cellphone and said, Sandra, let me explain. He listened.

He said, Let me say something here. Let me speak. You were told. I already told you. Just let me. Talk, for Jesus' sake.

He glanced at Colleen. The woman continued, there was crying now. Then he quietly folded the cellphone and dropped it in his pocket.

Nice night, he said. The cellphone rang and rang in his pocket.

I'm getting your seat soaking wet, Colleen said.

Do you have any idea how dangerous hitchhiking is? I said to myself, Don't lecture.

The phone rang and they listened to it ring for a long time then it stopped ringing. When they were certain it wouldn't ring any more the man said, I didn't get your name.

Then the phone started again and he answered it.

I'm with someone, Sandra, he said. A hitchhiker. A young girl. She was hitchhiking. Yes, a hitchhiking girl. Yes, I told her. I said, it's not safe. I said, Girls your age. Sandra, I said all that. He looked at Colleen and rolled his eyes. The weeping on the cellphone started again. Colleen could hear it clearly, a breathy, snot-slickened crying, alternating with a high whine, a unique calibrated chuffing of breath.

Tell me this much, he said.

The woman began to outright bawl.

Sandra, Sandra, he said. And he hung up once more. Then, in the blooming quiet that followed the static and bawling on the phone, the windshield made a fist of itself. A fist of glass lined with silver wrinkles and cracks, and the fist punched Colleen in the face. The van had tipped over on its side, the passenger door scraping the pavement leaving a burst of orange sparks, her cheek against the window, and then it tipped again and they were upside down and the van slid over an embankment on its roof, a curtain of gravel and weeds racing over the smashed windshield.

They came to a stop, upside down, and nose first in a shallow pond, the roof of the van burbling with black water smelling of muck.

Colleen was hanging by her seat belt and the airbag was

jammed under her chin and there was a dust floating in the air, which she guessed was a flame retardant and it coated her tongue and tasted like metal filings and talcum.

The guy, Russell, it took her a full moment to realize, was speaking to her as if from a great distance.

Wake up, he said. They heard two vehicles zoom past on the highway above them, then three or four more.

I never got your name, he said. She felt her nose spread with homesickness.

Whatever was going on with her nose, it felt like acute grief.

But she couldn't remember what she was sad about. She had enough time to realize that whatever it was she was sad about was a tremendous weight she had been dragging around for a long time and whatever it was it was a relief not to remember.

She wanted not to remember for as long as she could because it was a tremendous relief.

Then she remembered: she missed her stepfather.

And because she had taken that brief break from thinking about his death, which she had been thinking about for four years, a break that had to do with having her face smashed in, a break that had to do with nearly dying herself, because of that very brief uplifting rest, the grief came back triplefold.

It was a sock in the gut and she lost her breath, which also may have had to do with the airbag and maybe a fractured rib.

She'd had a glimpse of something as they tumbled over on the pavement and then slid down the embankment on the roof of the van — every future moment would be without him.

Everything to come would not have David in it.

She hadn't really looked that far ahead yet.

Now she saw.

A door had slammed between the past and the present, with the same kind of force that had driven her into the windshield. Her stepfather was behind that door. There would be no reprieve from this, no let-up.

Colleen would become whoever and David would not see.

She couldn't ask, Are you proud? She remembered the dress she had worn to the funeral, but she could not think what shoes she had worn. This is what grieved her, hanging upside down in the van on the side of the highway with her nose most likely broken. She had wanted to preserve every detail of the funeral. But she could not for the life of her remember what shoes.

What happened? she said.

We hit a moose.

That was some phone conversation.

Or we hit something, he said.

You were asleep at the wheel.

I should have broken up with my girlfriend a long time ago.

Now it's too late.

I was suddenly struck is what happened, he said. She tried to think of the shoes. She could see herself getting dressed, brushing her hair, she'd put in tortoiseshell combs, she could see the tights — she never wore tights but she'd bought a pair for the funeral.

The next thing you're in the grave, Russell said. The water on the roof seemed to be rising. It occurred to Colleen the van might be resting on some kind of ridge and what if it gave and they sank to the bottom of what might be a deep lake and what if they were never heard from again. Brown suede high heels. She'd worn Jennifer Galway's prom shoes to David's funeral. Jennifer Galway had put her arm around Colleen in the parking lot of the funeral home and gave her a little pinch. She'd pinched her arm to keep Colleen from crying.

My stepfather died, she said.

And you're out hitchhiking in the dark.

I'm out in the dark, all by my lonesome.

What would your stepfather think of that?

I guess we'll never know.

Because we almost died ourselves here, he said.

Maybe we are dead. He turned and looked at her then and her chin, which he could see from the light in the dash, was covered in blood.

I don't want children, he said. Colleen thought suddenly of her mother.

Oh my God, she said. How angry her mother was going to be when she found out Colleen had nearly died. Her mother could not afford, emotionally speaking, to have anyone else she knew come anywhere near death, not remotely near, ever again.

I've got a couple of nieces, Russell said.

I'm Colleen, she said. The water had definitely stopped rising. She wanted to get out of the van. She should never have said her name.

A couple of nieces are plenty, Colleen.

But your girlfriend, she said. She could see Russell wasn't ready to leave the van. They might sit there forever as far as he was concerned.

My girlfriend can't take too much more.

Are my teeth broken?

You've got blood.

That's from my nose, but are my teeth?

Smile at me. Jesus, you're pretty.

I'm covered in blood.

But you're. What are you? You're up to no good. Let me get a tissue. The box of Kleenex that had been on the dash was turning in the water below them, a tissue stood up like the sail of a boat. Russell reached down and snatched the tissue and he handed it to Colleen.

This is for free, Colleen. There's only one life. There's not the life you are living and the life you might have lived. Do you know what I'm saying?

This has been informative, Colleen said. You're an informative guy.

I'm sorry about your stepfather.

Then they heard a strange warble, like a bird they might have crushed under the roof. Something crushed and submerged and it took them both a moment to recognize the faint green light under the water on the roof of the van as the cellphone. It made them giggle. It was still ringing.

Colleen wedged her feet against the dash and undid her seat belt and managed to work her way around the airbag so she was kneeling on the ceiling of the van in a foot of water.

She couldn't open her door but Russell had kicked out the broken glass from the windshield on his side and she crawled out through there and stood wobbly-legged, bleeding from her nose with a tissue to her face. She tilted her head to stop the bleeding and the stars were bright. There was a dark shape standing against the trees and it took her a long time to believe it was a moose. She did not believe until she saw it turn and disappear into the trees and heard the swooshing branches. She suddenly remembered her knapsack. She'd lost her knapsack and everything was in it. The remaining sugar and her diary. Some money, her name, her phone number.

Russell said she needed to get to a hospital. He was worried about whiplash and concussion and God knows what injury and insurance and who was her guardian?

She had already got a car to stop and several other cars had pulled over and he was talking to a man who had been in the woods hunting and she told him goodbye and he said, Hey wait a minute. But she got in and waved goodbye. Of course, back in St. John's, he'd made inquiries and she'd been caught.

MADELEINE

SHE'D TAKEN THE money from her producer's fee, which means she personally will make nothing at all, nothing to speak of. But now there are skylights for the set. Guy is happy. She would not be shouted at in front of the crew, she told him, just as if he were a child. She was harsh with him behind the closed door of her office.

I will not have it, she'd said. Then she gave in about the bloody skylights and his face got pink. He kissed both her cheeks. He left her office in a great hurry and no sooner had he closed her door than he'd opened it again and came striding in and leaned over her desk, knocking an empty cup to the floor, kissed her on the mouth and left, slamming the door, rattling the frosted glass. She was exhausted and she had broken a sweat and figured she wouldn't be around to spend the producer's fee anyway.

Never mind about the fee, she thought. She'd been having nightmares about the sequence with the white stallions in the snow. Every night she was dreaming the editing suite, the horses galloping in reverse, disappearing altogether. The whole film eating itself up until there was nothing left.

How much easier things might have been if she hadn't had a career. She thinks of it that way; the way women in eighteenth-century novels sit in drawing rooms and take up their embroidery. Some heroine slighted by a lover blushes fiercely, and takes up her sewing. She had taken up film and before film she was lost in the children.

She thinks of the suffocating, addictive sweetness of being a mother. How noble and foolhardy: to think she could care for two helpless beings. How enveloping it had all been, and over so quickly though it had felt interminable; the driving alone had taken a lifetime. She'd had to drive here and there in every weather, the birthday parties and Brownies and Cubs, swimming at Bowring Park, while Marty was at the office.

She thinks of the karate instructor. He is absolutely present to her; the cinematographer's stubble had stung her chin. Every move the karate instructor made was fluid and effortless; his foot was strong and frankly erotic and the loose pyjamas were erotic and even the fluorescent light was erotic, and the quiet squeak from his bare foot on the tile was deeply, deeply erotic. She was exhausted from all the driving with the children.

I could have driven with my eyes closed, she thinks.

Thirty years ago when the children were young, she'd get the script she was writing out of her purse for the red lights; she'd have a pencil tucked behind her ear, and she'd turn a page. People would blast their horns because the light was green. She didn't give a damn about other drivers. They would just have to wait.

She drove Melissa to ballet and Andrew to karate. Karate was new, a guy had come down from the mainland and he'd set up a school. She'd definitely had some kind of crush on the karate instructor, a tickertape parade drumming through her veins when his foot squeaked on the tiles.

This was before her career had taken off.

This was before she left Marty. The divorce had been nasty because he refused everything, would keep nothing for himself, and she burst into tears. Keep the leather couch at least, a battleship of a couch that had been in his family for years, but he said before the judge about the children needing good furniture, and all the courtroom saw she had failed to hold it together: the magnificent project that was true love. She had put her arms around it, locked her fingers tight, strained every muscle, and it had busted apart anyway. Marty had looked bewildered in the courtroom. It was not kindness — giving her the couch — he had no further interest in the couch. He'd watched her press forward with the details of divorce with numb, vivid bewilderment. He refused to sign things, left long pauses in the proceedings. Once, a brick came through her window at night but she could not be sure who'd thrown it. He held things up as best he could. And then, when the last *t* was crossed, he'd shown up at a party with a young cellist. He'd left an extra button on his shirt undone, showing chest hair. He had undone the button or had forgotten to do it up — such was the liberating nature of the relationship he'd fallen into with the cellist. In fact the shirt was buttoned all wrong — at a party thrown by their closest friends. The tail of his shirt hung out like a flag.

She'd left, in the end, because there were so many things she'd had to chase after — all the racing around. When she thinks of *chasing after* she sees herself in the laundry room on Lime Street listening intently for the origin of a leak. There was a pool of water seeping from beneath the washing machine. She ran her fingers over the pipes, feeling for a seeping crack. But it wasn't the chasing after. The truth was she had been unable to see her marriage from any kind of reasonable vantage point —

that was the problem — because she was so immersed. She had been swallowed up, forgot who she was.

Before she had any thought of making a feature film.

She drove Andrew to karate, she drove Melissa to ballet, that's who she was. You can drive and become a person who drives. Sometimes she and Marty would try to have an evening. They'd plan something special, a steak, good wine to shore up their relationship; they were deliberate about ordinary intimacy at this stage — but Melissa would cry out in her sleep.

The heater in their car was always broken in those days and the windshield frosted over. She had to drive with the windows down and it was below zero.

Andrew was just five and had his black karate suit that he wore with the white belt wrapped around twice and knotted, and was he ever smart-looking.

Twenty-five, thirty years ago, she guesses.

It wasn't the heater, it was the blower, Marty had said. The heater was fine.

Someone blasted a horn; she couldn't see a damn thing, frost all over the windshield and she wiped it with the cuff of her sweater.

A red light that said *check oil* had been on for weeks. Chicken thighs she'd slather in cream of mushroom soup and orange zest. She was an engine of love grinding away in the dark. She was a maker of suppers, a doer of homework. She was the person who drove.

She'd had a secret project in mind at that time, a documentary series about island culture. It would take months to write the scripts but she believed this idea would fly. Nationalism, ukuleles, grass skirts, and the darker things: sharks, voodoo, and gene pools the size of thimbles. She wanted to direct; it would require two years on the road.

She doesn't remember thinking, What about the children? Let Marty worry about the children, is what she thought. Men go off on oil rigs all the time, is what she thought; she didn't think. She didn't actually mention the series to Marty.

At the end of class Andrew was called forward and he did his courtesy bow and kicks and blocks and punches and he earned his yellow belt.

She was waiting at a red light and she tilted the rear-view and Andrew was asleep in the back seat. What an explosive blast of love she felt for the boy, especially when he was asleep. It was enough.

Snow slanted through the headlights and she hit slush and soaked a pedestrian. There was going to be an ice storm, the power lines knocked out, the streets would be glass and it came to her all at once: where was the bottle of champagne that had been in the hotel room on their wedding night?

Marty's sisters had given them a bottle of champagne. They had saved it for an occasion. But they should have it tonight, she thinks. Why wait for an occasion? How frivolous and redemptive to drink champagne for no reason. She remembers tucking it away under the kitchen sink but it's not under the kitchen sink, she's sure. She felt the car skid and she slammed the breaks and the car fishtailed and she thinks of the champagne in the dark corner of the cupboard, under the pipes, lying on its side. There's a car coming straight at them with her little son in the back and she shuts her eyes. She's driving with her eyes shut and they skid out of the path of the oncoming car.

Hands up to protect the nose, the karate teacher had said to Andrew. He had promised discipline and ancient wisdom, happiness, and self-esteem. She had her script on the passenger seat and a pencil behind her ear. A red light and soon the horns were blasting. Did they drink it already? They were saving it, she's sure.

They were on Brookfield Road, in the middle of nowhere, when the car died. She can't remember why the car died. She tried the key and tried the key. She smacked the steering wheel and hurt her hand. Cars came upon her and swerved and zoomed past.

She put on her hazards. The road was empty ahead. She and her sleeping son abandoned by the world, soon to freeze to death. Then a car came toward them, the headlights bouncing slightly, splintering the falling sleet and she had remembered.

The champagne had been recalled, that vintage had glass shards. Someone had found shards of glass. It wasn't under the kitchen sink. It had never been under the kitchen sink. It was a bottle of bleach she had been thinking of. She hadn't ever used the hazards before and didn't know where they were. But she found them, and she put the hazards on and the car engine would not turn over. She could hardly believe it; the car had died.

FRANK

FRANK LISTENED TO the Russians upstairs, there were violins. It was not like Newfoundland music. Their chairs scraped over his ceiling and they stomped their feet like they meant the music, they really, really meant it. The violins revved up and got turgid and squealed and poured like oil. They were drunk and their voices rose in argument. The violins got rougher, full of vengeance and craft and the music was sexual and melodic. It was the same as Newfoundland music or it had turned into Newfoundland music or all music is the same, always, and this was just another example of that.

It had been hot all day and it was still hot. Frank opened the window and put his feet up on a chair and had a coffee. He had a coffee every night before he went to the hot-dog stand.

The windowsill was covered in the elm spanworms and Frank got a rag and squished them and put the rag in a plastic bag and knotted it. He could see hundreds of worms on all the roofs and hoods of the cars parked along the street.

On the radio they said spray. Don't spray. The trees are finished, a scientist said. The worms have won. On the radio they said the worms would be gone by the end of August.

People called the talk shows about the smell. A pissy odour that got stronger when the sun warmed it. Picnic tables and the banana seats of children's bicycles, plastic swimming pools, everything that gets left outside was covered in worm shit. Don't track that muck into the house. Where had they come from? They had come on the wind or in someone's suitcase. They had come with a shipment of lumber, in a case of apples. Someone had dreamt them.

A crowd of perhaps two hundred people came up Long's Hill and gathered across the street from Frank's bed-sit. The man leading them wore a pirate hat and a cape. The man held a torch and he raised his arm and pointed roughly in the direction of Frank's window. All the people turned and were quiet and the guide began to lecture. He had tones, this guy, sonorous tones.

It was the Haunted Walk, all the sites of violent murder through the ages in old St. John's, tourists from the cruise ship, and the guy charged five bucks and Frank wished he had thought of it first. He could never make out what the guide was saying.

Someone had been buried in the basement of one of these houses, slowly poisoned and hacked to pieces, a hundred years ago.

A murmur went through the crowd at the same time each evening, all summer long. Awe and titillation, and the worms hung on their invisible threads making the leaves curl tighter.

MADELEINE

SHE WAS MEETING Marty for lunch because she was going to make him cough up the money she needed to finish the film. She would beg, she would cry. She would bring up all they had been to each other and force him to hand over whatever he had. She didn't care that he had a child on the way. That was his problem.

He had always been fastidious and this she enjoyed and despised. He had loved her for the thirty years that followed her leaving him, through a string of younger and younger girlfriends. He'd become more handsome with every passing year.

The women were all bursting with intellect, were earnest and buxom, the penultimate one had become a prominent architect in Toronto. They fell hard, but not hard enough to sabotage careers or to get knocked up. Until this last one, Gerry-Ann, whom Madeleine had never met.

She thought of her need to get out of the marriage by turns as a mild perversion and a bout of forgetfulness. Her need to get out was visited upon her and beyond her control and she tried to will it away. They had never been suited.

This is not true. She will not be untrue to how hard they worked and drove each other, and how they got up in the middle of the night to take care of the babies and had fast, fast sex in the laundry room when the children were watching cartoons, pasta boiling on the stove, he put his hand over her mouth.

Or sex in the living room, drinking wine, smoking dope, with the headlights of passing traffic sweeping the walls, they had tipped the great big leather couch over and broken a wooden strut in the back of it.

It was an enduring love; it had lasted all her adult life.

She never should have married him.

What was it that finally decided her? There was a leak in the flow of time and she found she could not account for all of it. Coming along Water Street, the sky over Signal Hill would be shaggy and darkness would come barrelling in off the ocean and she would realize it was November. This was November weather. She would look around her and see the pavement glassy, the world slithering askew, and put straight and ultra-clean with each sweep of the windshield wipers.

She'd had an appointment with the dentist and had forgotten it. She had left the children waiting for her in front of the school. They were soaking wet. She had left the oven on. She put her keys in the pocket with the hole in the lining and couldn't find her keys.

Projects started to come her way. She did industrial films about safety belts in cars and fish processing and prosthetic limbs.

They cut off the heat because she had forgotten to pay the bill. She shot a triple bypass and the doctor winked at her, clicking the tiny scissors, once, twice, like castanets, before digging into the splayed-open chest.

She shot a dummy crashing into a concrete wall in a blue sedan and the airbag puffed up and flame burst from under the hood.

You're not here, Marty had said. He was an implacable man who kept his own counsel, but she saw she had wounded him. She took the children to the park and felt a lump in her jacket and there were her keys. She'd found her keys! She dug them out and put them on the picnic table beside her.

They had said she would die of a heart condition when she was twelve and she remembers being on a stretcher, feeling the vibrations of the wheels hitting the edge of each yellowish floor tile with a subtle nick.

How thoroughly she had succumbed to the anaesthetic. The engulfing blackness that followed the needle prick had felt like absolution for a potent sense of failure.

She marvels now, that at such a young age, she could have felt so intensely the pressures of impending financial disaster. Her father's death had left them without any money, and her own operation meant she could not help at home.

They had almost lost her on the operating table and her mother went, during a snowstorm, down to Bowring's to buy her a confirmation dress that would be suitable to wake her in. The dress she would wear in the casket. The dress was pointed out to her later, hanging in the window at Bowring's; they returned it when it was clear she would recover. They couldn't afford dresses if there wasn't an occasion to wear them.

The sun was setting and she told the children: Down from the monkey bars, we'll go get an ice cream.

They wandered back home, taking their time and later the moon came up on the empty park, filtering through the trees, glinting on her car keys.

COLLEEN

Mr. Duffy of the destroyed bulldozers was a stubble-cheeked man in a blousy black and silver windbreaker and saggy jeans. His nose was shapeless and purplish at the nostrils. Colleen could see in his eyes a sort of intelligence she was unfamiliar with. An old-fashioned intelligence, more akin to cunning than what her mother had, which had to do with generosity.

He drained a can of cola, crunched it in his fist, and tossed it over Colleen's shoulder. She felt a breeze from its flight into a pail behind her where it dinged and jangled.

Colleen understood at once she was out of her depth.

She thought of her mother in the food court below, absent-mindedly tearing the paper lids off six creamers and tipping them into her coffee.

The social worker who was facilitating wore silvery panty-hose that looked like frost. They whispered every time she crossed her legs. She plunked a leather briefcase on the table and flicked through her files until she found the one she needed, which she pulled out and spread on the table.

Now then, I am Ms. Drake, she said.

Ms. Drake's sweater was pilled, tiny nubs of cotton clinging to the entire surface of her sweater. It meant she'd put it in the dryer. There was a whole history of resignation and maxed-out credit cards in her ugly sweater. Ms. Drake's skin was sallow and full of pores, she had a faint moustache and a polyester skirt and she would not likely care too much about pine martens.

Colleen shifted in her chair.

She was suddenly certain Ms. Drake would not know what a pine marten was if it leapt up and bit her ass.

Colleen decided to sit up straight. She thought of Julia Butterfly Hill, who had lived in a tree for two years in the middle of a clear-cut in northern California. They had chopped down almost everything around her. They had shaved the earth of forest but Julia, a sort of wood nymph Amazon hippie creature, had stood her ground.

Ms. Drake cracked her knuckles, first in one hand, and then the other, while she perused Colleen's file.

She jerked her head to the side, wincing, and there was another cracking sound. Then she shook her hands, making all the cartilage crackle wetly. Was it cartilage?

Julia Butterfly Hill had flowing hair to her bum and wore a woollen cap from South America. On the Net they showed her clinging to a branch as though it were a lover.

She might have been a model or a saint.

I made a promise to Luna, Julia Butterfly Hill had said. Luna was what she called the tree.

Wild-eyed, the *New York Times* had said. How strong and uncompromising she was. Imagine the shudder running through her tree when they put the chainsaw to the trunk.

Okay then, Ms. Drake said, seeming to have finished with her joints. She was shaking her head in disbelief at whatever it was Colleen's file had revealed and when she looked up there was not a whit of intelligence anywhere in her expression. Was she hungover or premenstrual? She seemed absorbed in some way that did not bode well for Colleen. There was a crackle of cartilage under the table and Colleen realized Ms. Drake had slipped off her sandals and must have been rotating her ankles.

Mr. Duffy, you may want to write a victim impact statement, Ms. Drake said. What that would be is a chance for you to put in writing how you feel about the damage Miss Clark did to your bulldozers.

I'll tell you how I feel, said Mr. Duffy. I feel put out. That's the best way to describe it. Do you know that feeling, Miss Clark? Write that down, Ms. Drake. Put out. I suspect Miss Clark hasn't ever felt put out. I would guess that, for the most part, things have pretty much gone your way, Miss Clark.

Here Mr. Duffy shifted in his chair to direct his comments to Ms. Drake, who had opened a pad to take notes but whose hand hovered over the paper, the pen wagging back and forth.

Colleen Clark will pay for putting me out, Ms. Drake. She will pay because I intend to invest heavily in her unhappiness. For example, I mean to make certain that if she ever expects to enter any professional trade, such as the law or medicine, she will find this act of vandalism following at her heels. There will be a panel of ageing academics reviewing her applications to those fields and grimly shaking their heads. Miss Clark is under the impression that the law is protecting her because she's a minor.

Now, Mr. Duffy, we are here to negotiate some conflict resolution, interrupted Ms. Drake. That's our goal.

Pardon me, Ms. Drake. My goal is to let Miss Clark know there are perfectly acceptable, legal ways around the law, which I intend to employ to make her life miserable. Should Miss Clark apply, for example, to be a teller at a supermarket or to work in some crappy little corner store she may find she does not get an interview.

Miss Clark should know that I have set traps for the fifty pine martens on my property and I intend to barbecue them and feed them to my dogs. If Miss Clark would like, I can send her the paws of each pine marten so she can keep up with my progress. I'm going to be personally responsible for the extinction of the Newfoundland pine marten. Consider it a pledge.

MR. DUFFY

DUFFY THOUGHT SUDDENLY of the girl's mother, the flaky mother with her hand on his arm.

Mr. Duffy, my daughter is a stranger to me, she'd said. Beverly Clark's eyes filled with tears. Her eyes were green and the watery film over them changed their colour; they became even more luminous, ultramarine. She was wearing mascara that made her lashes into sharp black spikes that seemed to hold her tears back. She caught her lower lip in her teeth and her eyes cleared and she laughed.

That's just what I didn't want to happen, she said. He knew he was being taken in.

She was not genuine; she was slippery and convincing.

Her hand on his arm, as though she'd mistaken him for the sort of man one might sway or indulge.

Yet it was pleasurable to have her smile at him while overcome with emotion. She was offering a weird intimacy, an unengaged, effortless form of flirting. He was astounded by it and miffed. He found, to his shame, he was flattered.

Mrs. Clark, you've raised a misguided little torment, he

said. He had meant to sound gruff. But it came out all wrong; it sounded courtly, like a compliment.

Duffy had a girlfriend, a young hairdresser who worked in Churchill Square. He'd had a plan for that evening: the Bulgarian restaurant. He liked to be lavish with the hairdresser. She was a good cook, and when he visited she'd have candles on every available surface, and incense burning, which he chided her about.

She had a little wooden jewellery box that had been carved in Kenya, inlaid with shell, where she kept her dope, and sometimes they got stoned together.

He was unable to say why it couldn't add up to much, except that they had become too comfortable too quickly. He'd never mentioned the relationship to his children. He wondered if Beverly Clark was still in the food court, waiting. Of course he had no intention of giving Colleen Clark's vandalism another thought. He'd had his fun. He put his hand on his arm where Beverly had touched him. Maybe he could catch up with Beverly Clark.

MADELEINE

MADELEINE WAS WEARING her shiny red kimono and she'd just made a cappuccino. She cracked a brown egg on a pot of boiling water and the yolk tipped over the jagged shell in one plop. The egg white stretched itself into opaque skeins and transparent veils and broke away from the yolk and frothed over the sides of the pot and settled back down. She splashed some balsamic vinegar into the pot. Madeleine had cleaners coming, two women from Placentia Bay who left the condo smelling of the artificial pine scent they put in the vacuum and every surface smelled of Pledge and she would smell Windex for days after they left. The smells made her hopeful and slightly congested. She liked getting the place cleaned.

She'd gone down in the elevator and out onto the sidewalk in her bare feet to get the paper. The concrete was cold and damp and she half hopped and picked up the paper. It was a warm morning, already warm. A dog was barking in someone's backyard. She heard a reverberating clank that rang out over all the empty streets; someone had dropped the lid on a Dumpster. A truck revving its engine. The cars parked along the street had blotches of rain over the roofs and hoods and someone had drawn a heart in the condensation on her windshield.

She picked up the newspaper and saw the photograph on the front page, first through a running blotch of rainwater that had collected in the folds of plastic. The water spilled over the picture and magnified the naked figure and warped him so his shoulder stretched and the black hood smeared and she tore off the plastic but she hardly knew that she had done so. She was only half awake and when she came inside, the hallway looked dim after the bright street. The hallway dimmed as if on a dimmer switch and she turned over the paper and stood still. The plastic fell out of her hand onto the floor of the elevator and she didn't notice.

The photograph was soft focus, a digital photograph that had an amateurish cast, a naked man in a hood standing on a platform. He stood with his cuffed hands over his genitals. One shoulder slouched, an almost girlishly coy slouch except for the hood that was large and black, and the brutal fact of his nakedness. The man's nakedness shocked her deeply. The photograph was low resolution, and looked like it had passed through a variety of media and the image had been degraded in the process. The hues in the print were off, an almost imperceptible wrongness of hue and focus, sinister in its casual ineptitude. Madeleine leaned against the wall of the elevator. She brought the picture close to her face to see if she could see pixels, how the colour had been reproduced; she tried to understand the image. A blooming horror made her skin prickle; what was this photograph? It was a homemade joke about torture, folksy and kitsch, full of abject glee and hatred. She had left the egg boiling. The egg was boiling over. She went back to the kitchen and put the paper on the table. The shock of the photograph receded; shock smacks and recedes. She would not let herself think the word *evil.* The egg was rubbery. The photograph was evil.

Her screenplay came to her in a dream the next night, she'd woken streaming sweat. There was something heavy underneath her on the mattress and she wanted to throw it on the floor. She tried to lift it, whatever it was, but it was too heavy. All the while, the dream unfolded, the plot and wrenching emotion and everything you needed for a film.

White horses galloping through a blizzard on the Southern Shore, and she managed to grip the thing that was in the bed and it was clammy to touch and cold and she couldn't throw it out of the bed because it was attached to her shoulder. It was her arm, paralyzed, and the paralysis was spreading into her chest and sweat ran down her temples or it was tears. She understood, though she was in the thick of sleep, that she was having a heart attack.

She had put the newspaper on the table next to a glass jug of orange juice. She poured a glass of juice and put the jug down. A parabola of light cast from the sun striking the jug jiggled over the photograph. A loop of wiggling, broken sunlight flickered over the humiliated Iraqi prisoner and it occurred to Madeleine his shoulder might be broken and she swept the egg off her plate into the garbage.

She'd written most of the script in six weeks and then she'd gone to Toronto to convince Isobel to come home: Isobel with her big, fraught, lonely, bursting life. Isobel had made a name in Toronto, finally, with her performance in *A Streetcar Named Desire.* Some newly arrived Eastern European director had the idea of blowing the dust off *Streetcar* — they were mad for

Tennessee Williams in Romania — and Isobel had triumphed. Madeleine was coming from the airport in a taxi, the cellphone shrill in her purse.

I know the best place for Italian, Isobel had said.

I want you to look at a script, Madeleine said.

Madeleine was driving near a concrete overpass and there was graffiti, bulbous and illegible; the sun struck the grimy windows of the taxi. Transport trucks tore past. She loved the way the outskirts reared up all around her, arched concrete spines and roaring traffic. She loved *Toyota* spelled in marigolds on banks of manicured lawns and the massive car plants with the grey stacks kicking out smoke and the chainlink fences and how the highways loop over and under each other in the distance.

Of course she has people to stay with, there's hardly a city in the world where she doesn't know somebody. She has friends in New Delhi, a young man in Iceland; Marty's sister in Jamaica is always begging her to come. But she's happiest in the hush of a mid-luxury hotel, with the paper sheaths for the drinking glasses, maids with hairnets, big views, and the ravaged food trays waiting outside bedroom doors in the morning, gnawed bones, greasy napkins, glasses with lipstick streaks.

Some women aren't meant for marriage, Madeleine had thought. They'd stopped at an intersection and a crowd surged in front of her taxi, a black man with three little girls, each with a strawberry ice-cream cone, passed in front of them — even if the conditions for love are exactly right these women can't help but want someone else — the taxi lurched forward and she saw a transvestite in a zebra-striped minidress, big red necklace — maybe truly independent women are never satisfied in love.

There's always someone else, Madeleine thought. One of her old boyfriends had become a neurologist; he worked on the spines of rats. She'd run into him at the airport.

You are exactly the same, he'd said. Do you remember the night I took you to the Starboard Quarter? It was every cent I had. She could not remember. You don't remember? You ordered the steak! She didn't remember.

And after all that, you married Martin, he'd said, giving his head a hard little shake as if to get rid of the idea. All what, she wondered. She doesn't think she's ever eaten in the Starboard Quarter.

Marty is having another child, she'd blurted. She reached out and gripped his arm — she cannot think of Marty being a father again without a mild wave of vertigo — but what a relief to suddenly speak of him. Here is someone who remembers Marty as he was back then, the elastic on his pant leg for riding the bike, when he was playing the sax downtown; Marty with long hair.

But he must be over sixty!

He's way over sixty, Madeleine said.

Every cent I had I spent on you, he said.

And now you work with rats, she said.

Just the spines.

A lucrative business, I guess? Madeleine said. She can't believe he has brought up paying for a dinner a thousand years ago.

I've done well by rats.

The driver lets Madeleine out and a doorman in gold braid and a black jacket, awful in this heat, takes her luggage while she struggles with her purse.

It meant she was alive, Madeleine thought, as she stepped into the air-conditioned lobby: to always want more; never settling. It was what drove her. She saw herself on a London street, clutching a map. Some street corner long forgotten, she'd had a date with an old friend and couldn't find the pub; the wind had taken her hat. Just look at how full her life had been; how many lovers, full to bursting. She drags her luggage down the hall to the elevator and talks on the phone.

Isobel, she says, I think you'll be impressed.

There was a crowd waiting to be seated but the waiter had a table for them in the back. He brought them past the deli counter with homemade pastas, sausages, and cured meats and the feeling Madeleine got was that the family was all in the kitchen and they were overweight and had made a religion of the preparation of food. There were white truffles in small jars under lock and key. The ceiling was stucco with bits of mirror and the tablecloths were checked and the balsamic vinegar and olive oil were poured into a saucer that must have a matching teacup in the back.

They talked the way they always talked, in unison, without listening to each other, their mouths full of pasta. They were campy and loud and full of themselves. They laughed while they were drinking and got wine up their noses and had to snort.

I want bleak, Madeleine said. What year are we talking? 1834. You want turnip soup and fish flakes and scurvy. I want pouting orphans with sunken eyes and scabby knees. And you see me? I see you, yes. I'm the lead? It's a big part. I don't know. You don't know? I've been offered something. What have you been offered? I'm this close, according to the grapevine. How close? A soap opera, I've been called back three times. You're kidding. It's a permanent job, Madeleine. You don't need a soap opera. I need something. Read the script, that's all I'm asking. I'll read the script. Read the goddamn script.

FRANK

He stood in the rain under the umbrella but the rain came in sideways. The rain shuddered and was enraged and held its breath and slapped itself down in ropes, but people were still buying hot dogs.

Frank wasn't going home if people were buying hot dogs.

A man drove up in the 97.5 K-Rock Hummer; it had an amber light on the roof that swivelled and the vehicle was pumping muffled music. It looked like people were squashed in, sitting on each other's laps, a shoulder against the roof.

The driver left it running and the exhaust lifted in ragged clouds that turned amber and there was a red shoulder smeared against the passenger window in the back seat. The guy had his raincoat up over his head and he ordered five hot dogs.

Frank could hardly see through the sheets of rain on the steamy windows, but the Hummer seemed full of girls.

He thought he saw a leg. One of the girls was pulling on a pair of pantyhose in the back seat; he watched this through the eye-stinging coils of blowing smoke and the rain spilling off the umbrella.

The rain glazed the pavement and shivers ran through the

water as it rushed down the street, wind-driven, and the hot dogs hissed and what he really wanted was to see how those girls fit in the back and smell their perfume and shampoo and why was she putting on pantyhose and what party were they going to and why did he have to be always standing in the rain.

He could not go home yet because he had not sold enough hot dogs to pack up and go home.

Frank got the five hot dogs ready and the man took them two at a time under his coat and passed them through the window to the women inside. Then he came back for his own and he only wanted ketchup.

The next day Frank heard Carol out on the fire escape pulling in her laundry. She had several pairs of underwear hung on the line, pastel colours, each pair flimsy and light-pierced. The panties were full of worms. They had gathered in the cotton-lined crotches of the underwear and made them look black. He was drinking his coffee on the fire escape above and she came up the stairs to talk to him.

They said about you on the radio, Frank, she said. They said about the hot dogs. A real entrepreneur, the guy said, standing out in the rain.

Then she whispered, Frank, don't talk to those men upstairs. I'm warning you, Frank. Those men, you can't reason. You're a nice boy, well-mannered. I can say to you Frank with conviction. I have a bad feeling.

Frank watched her absent-mindedly picking the worms out of her underwear as she spoke.

MADELEINE

THEY WERE GOING to an awards dinner, a gala, in honour of Isobel.

I should call Andrew, said Madeleine. She feels a panic about her son, who works for Médicins Sans Frontières in Ethiopia. What if Andrew is in trouble? There will be nothing she can do.

She thinks of him digging in the garden when he was a small boy; the day she found all the snails in the pockets of his tiny jeans, globs of moving slime and crushed shell.

Now he performs surgeries in canvas tents all over Africa with only a naked light bulb hanging from a pole and the sounds of gunfire in the background.

Her daughter, Melissa, is in Geneva and married to a heroin addict with old money. Melissa, in tailored suits and sensible shoes, striding down sidewalks lined with pristine fountains and gargoyles. She sends jewellery made from volcanic rock and woven wraps that snap under the arms and zipper across the breasts like straitjackets, the height of European fashion. She skis in the Alps and sends pictures of herself buoyed up by white wings of spraying snow.

Just tell me, though, said Isobel. Is this too ancient Greece? She had the hanger with the gold toga under her chin.

I'd have to see it on, Madeleine said.

Isobel pulls a black sequined dress down over her hips. The dress left one shoulder bare. She snapped the fishnet stocking, at her knee and at her ankle, and stood with her back to the mirror looking over her shoulder.

That's the dress as far as I'm concerned, said Madeleine. The director of *Streetcar* had bought Isobel the sequined dress. He had a raw-boned face and wild black eyes and Isobel might have liked him if he had not worked her so hard. He was tired of naturalistic theatre, he had shouted at them while they stood blinded in the stage lights.

Isobel Turner, he had screamed. Do I give a damn about Isobel Turner? They had been rehearsing for six hours in the heat. Isobel put her hand over her eyes in an effort to see him. There was a silence.

No, I don't give a damn about Isobel Turner, he screamed. She had slept with him the night before and this outburst was disorienting.

Audiences aren't paying to see Isobel Turner from Newfoundland put on a Southern accent. Haven't you ever lost anything? he screamed at her.

It was true there was something she didn't get about Stella.

Isobel would never have let them take Blanche away. Even if she did stand for the South and all that was corrupt and decaying. Isobel would have saved her sister.

She stood with her back to the mirror, looking over her shoulder at her bum.

I didn't get the soap, Isobel said.

Lately, Madeleine listens. Or rather, she doesn't speak as much. Part of it is that she's too tired to talk. She's got the phone pressed to her ear and the aluminum tree branches spread out on the floor. It's August, but she came across Christmas trees on sale in a bin at Canadian Tire. Fifty extras in the shoot with the stallions and there's the underwater shot. Five divers lined up and they know the tides and they have to get the horses out in the surf. But at night she stops thinking about the shoot. She is mesmerized by an aluminum tree.

She listens to Marty. They have conversations lately, in the evening, after his pregnant wife, Gerry-Ann, has gone to bed. They talk about his wife.

She's what? Madeleine said.

She's thirty-five and she's pregnant.

Are you having a good time, Marty?

She falls asleep in her soup, Marty said. The assembly instructions were in eight different languages.

Another child, Marty, Madeleine said. She fit the central pole into the stand; it was a sizable tree. They have talked about the baby a hundred times. Marty says bringing a baby into the world is a show of faith that she, Madeleine, is too cynical to understand.

Am I crazy or what? Marty said. She held a big silver branch before her face and shut one eye. It was still a big silver branch.

The crazy things we do, she said. She put the branch down on the carpet where the diagram told her to.

I've got four white stallions in the ocean later this month, Madeleine grunted. A whole crew in scuba gear. She inserted a final branch and gave the red bulb on its tip a little twist and the whole silver tree glowed hotly, infrared.

What are you doing? he said.

I'm trying out my new Christmas tree, she said.

In the middle of August?

It was on sale.

She picks up clothes while he talks, she sorts the mail. She smokes near an open window. She confesses to putting a fist through a wall, he confesses the same.

I miss you, he said. The tree is a blinking tree. The thing about a Christmas tree is to tart it up. Feathery red bursts of light tremble on the wall every twenty seconds.

She knew immediately how she felt about the tree; she hated the tree.

It was as though she had unleashed all of her loneliness. Her loneliness had been imprisoned in a tree, which happens all the time; and she had been forced by some evil spell to walk up and down the aisles of Canadian Tire, forgetting why she was there (clothespins), until she found the tree. When she got it home, the tree leapt out of the box, screaming absurd loneliness in eight different languages. A burning bush of shame, how old she is and weak-feeling lately and the film is lost and how profoundly alone with a ball and chain of a film around her neck.

Don't make me tell you what I paid for this tree, she said.

I miss you, he said.

You miss me, that's nice, she said. She calls him from the bath and is self-conscious about splashes, a bath seems too sexy for talking to your ex-husband, but then she doesn't care; what is too sexy? And she splashes all she wants.

She listens to Marty while she does the dishes; she loves having her wrists immersed in hot water; domesticity peeling away her daytime demeanour.

She likes being nobody in the late afternoon. She wipes the counter thinking about the cigarette she's been waiting for and listening to Marty who, it dawns on her, is angling to come over. Could he possibly want to have sex with her?

He does; he's angling for a languid tussle, something rich and familiar and longed-for with every fibre of his being.

There is no need to question the rightness of the tree. She wanted some stone stupid objects in her life that are irrevocably themselves. She stopped short of a tree that rotates and that was in the same sale bin for the same price and she has no regrets about this.

What she regrets, occasionally, is leaving Marty.

Occasionally, it's as though she's been struck in the forehead with a rubber mallet and she is overwhelmed with a feeling of regret. How much she loved Marty and what would have happened if she kept on loving him?

Just as quickly, she's glad. She could not have stood it; always having to answer for herself, always making allowances.

She remembers one bad-ass night of drinking during a festival in New Mexico, after the divorce, when a security guard shone a flashlight at her naked bum while she ran across the lawn to the hotel lobby in this little towel, a hand towel for God's sake, held over her crotch and went to bed with no one, absolutely no one, closed the door, full of giggles, on Bob Warren, who knocked with one knuckle and leaned heavily on the door, and waited. She heard the clunk of his forehead on the door: the one-knuckle knock again. She had her hand on the knob deciding, a light summery sweat, the chlorine and nighttime smell in her hair; they'd been skinny-dipping in the hotel pool.

Bob was handsome and single and if she moved now, turned the knob, he would topple onto her carpet like a gift, but she didn't move, was happy not to move, and she heard him wander off down the corridor.

And for this near miss alone she is glad she is not married. She had felt euphoria that night, falling onto the big hotel bed all by herself, and euphoria in the morning when the sun came up over the golf course and in through the window and she made a pot of coffee and she was writing and still naked from the midnight swim.

These irrefutable, stone-stupid near misses and the dalliances that came true and the men who found her fascinating because she stood on her own two feet — Trevor Barker upstairs, for instance, who had left three messages, who had turned out to be a more than passable cook — and the risks she took and fast friends she made and how she was the life of the party always. She wasn't married because she couldn't be married and she did not regret what she was.

If you fuck Bob Warren you'll be one of thousands, a producer friend had said the next morning, after the night skinny-dipping in the hotel pool.

And she had answered, So will Bob Warren.

When she first left Marty, she was desolate. Beverly had come over to the new apartment and found her bawling, the sort of scream-crying that has no sound. She had tried to sit in one of the children's plush cartoon armchairs, but it was too small and it was squashed beneath her and her knees were sticking out and she couldn't get up. She was wrenching up absolutely no tears, her face like mauled Plasticine.

Stop this nonsense at once, Beverly had said.

The tree is artificial and it has red lights like an alarm system, it's the middle of August and Marty wants to come over and it's more of an appliance really, a household appliance, it has more in common with a fridge than a fir tree. She decides she loves the artificial tree.

VALENTIN

When he came back for Isobel, she had three Tupperware containers full of green tomatoes. Each tomato was wrapped in a paper towel, nestled in rows, two layers deep, and she was wearing sunglasses.

He was pleased with how reconciled she had become to the idea of the fire. The sunglasses had white frames with tiny rhinestones. She was wearing a simple, dark red dress that hung loosely and rustled when she moved. Her shoulders were bare, except for the narrow straps, and she was tanned. He thought the sunglasses looked expectant.

Isobel had let the grass get too long on her front walk and the legs of Valentin's pants were wet with dew. He had seen, as he came down the path, that her front door was covered in worms. He had wiped most of them off the window with a flyer from her mailbox. Then he knocked on the door.

Standing in the sunlight he had the feeling the house was empty. What if she had called the police? He knew what her living room looked like at this hour, sunlight filtering through the trees, cool and full of leafy shadow. What if there were four or five police officers sitting around the living room quietly waiting? The gasoline was in the basement, all the gasoline.

He had put his hand on her throat and threatened to kill her and had promised, at the same time, about the money he would give her. Their faces were so close he could see her contact lenses lift with her rapid blinking and slide back down, slowly, over her irises. He was squeezing her neck and the pores in her skin on her cheeks looked large and there were tiny veins around her nostrils and these signs of age frightened him. She was old and he couldn't quite count on what she would do next. He had described how he would kill her and the alternative: the boutique with pedestals draped in velvet, each displaying a bottle of perfume worth so much money she would only have to sell one a week.

If the house wasn't empty, Isobel was probably sitting at her vanity putting in an earring. She had earrings that were peacock feathers weighted with tiny silver balls. She might just be sitting at the vanity with the wing mirrors on hinges, Isobel from several angles, letting him wait. He would wait. He didn't mind waiting.

The shadows of the trees and clouds and telephone wires were reflected in the front-door window. When he put his face to the glass he saw Isobel's sandals on the rope mat. The leather straps covered with clusters of colourful glass beads. He remembered how they sounded when she clipped down over the stairs.

He thought of Isobel coming through the front door and kicking the sandals off and walking barefoot into the kitchen. He thought of her crushing ice in her blender. She had tall glasses for summer drinks and he thought of how her skin looked flushed after a day of rehearsal.

There were bookshelves in every room, and there were open paperbacks, turned over on the coffee tables and the stairs and the bathroom counter. Isobel read in the bath and on the landing. She left scarves draped over the backs of chairs. He had walked into her bedroom one afternoon and she was naked, lying on her stomach; she was reading in the heat, her legs crossed at the ankle and swinging a little; the small of her back was shiny with perspiration.

Listen, she'd said. An ice-cream vendor. Then he heard the bells. But it was someone selling root vegetables. He had found her on another hot afternoon trudging fast on her treadmill, reading something else.

It was a shame about the treadmill. He knew he could get good money for it but he had decided not to take anything out of the house. It was a rule; he believed in rules. Anything that might weasel through the tight fist of his plan could be beaten back with a fast hard rule. Leave the treadmill. Leave the cat. Leave the piano and her scarves and books. Leave her jewellery and the pharmaceuticals. He wouldn't get caught for the price of a second-hand treadmill.

There was an open Chinese umbrella resting on the door to the living room. She had a collection of masks carved from coconut shells that were important to her. All of this would go up easily.

Over the summer she'd played her piano for him. She sat on the bench with her back straight and shoulders squared. It was music he could make no sense of, discordant and full of storm. Sometimes he leaned on the piano and watched her face while she played. Her nostrils flared and her eyes narrowed as if she were judging a grave matter. She had a habit of raising her chin slightly and looking down her nose at the sheets of music. Her hands were like claws, stiff and surprised. The water in the fish-bowl on top of the piano absorbed the vibrations of her playing and concentric rings trembled over the surface. The goldfish held still in the very centre of the bowl, electric and alert. Valentin could feel the music through his elbow and he watched intently as she closed her eyes altogether and her head began to sway or jerk, some quaking argument taking her over.

Once, she had invited him to sit in her backyard and she gave him a tall, wet glass of crushed ice and fruit, some pink, milky drink with black seeds suspended throughout.

Absolutely in*can*descent with vitamins, she'd said.

She had flopped into the chair beside him and they had been silent. She had tilted her face toward the sun and her lips were full and wet and she was smiling to herself. She was full of serenity and it agitated him. He thought about kissing her roughly, stirring her up. She had been wearing a navy dress with white polka dots, form-fitting and stiff, full of straps.

She took a deep breath and held it and he waited and then she breathed out and she told him to take off his shoes.

It's too hot for shoes, she'd said. When he ignored her, she got down on her knees in the grass and the slit in her polka-dot skirt rode all the way up her thigh and he could see the lacy trim of her underwear, which was magenta and satin.

She took off his boots and then his socks. She kneaded his feet until they hurt. She hurt him very sharply, digging with her knuckles. He knew his feet were clean and he'd used a powder for odour and he didn't mind her touching him in this way. She pressed her thumbs between his toes and pinched the skin as hard as she could.

You store your saddest memories in your feet, she'd said.

The dress was low-cut and her bra was the same colour as her panties and when he closed his eyes he could still see the colour on the inside of his eyelids. It was hot in the garden and he thought of the dentist's widow, how her baby had cried all night behind a rag of a curtain. He had tasted the widow's breast milk, sucking hard on her nipples, though she had tried to slap him away. In the morning when he got up he saw the house was surrounded in every direction by a field of lavender and the wind brought the scent to him and he thought the woman's breast milk had tasted like that, like the flowers.

Isobel pressed her thumbs into his arches and she talked, as if to herself, about how things were in St. John's and perhaps every town or city in the western world. She talked about an inside and an outside and she said she was on the outside, had always been on the outside, and the outside wasn't safe for a woman her age.

She said she could have done something else, but perhaps she couldn't have done anything else. There was a vast spectrum of emotion and she had, at one time or another, fallen prey to all of it. She had felt; it was her special gift.

Perhaps we are made a certain way, she had said. She kept talking and she was impassioned and soft-spoken and he could not follow her. There was no logic in what she said or else he couldn't translate it.

She said she was getting old and she had put nothing away. She'd had a faith in simply having faith. And it had turned out to be true, there were advantages to being outside, she'd said. But look at her now. She was lost. Financially, anyway, she said. She'd laughed and dug into his foot so hard it caused a cramp and he had to stand and shake the foot.

She'd put her hand over her eyes to block the sun and when she looked up at him her eyes looked too bright. He felt he had walked over a thousand miles of broken rock and that all the smallest bones in his feet had been crushed. She was talking about fate. He would never accept that any single thing was the way it was because it had to be that way. He would not accept it.

I have nothing to fall back on, she said. He saw tears come to her eyes. She had once cried for him on demand. She said she could do it in less than a minute and he had timed her.

They had been sitting at the kitchen table over breakfast. She put her elbows on the table and rested her chin on her hands and she became very still.

Go, he said. He watched her nose and cheeks and chin grow pink; he saw her chin crinkle a little and her lower lip tremble and then he saw tears drip from both eyes quick, quick down her cheeks. She had accomplished this in less than forty seconds.

She should have sprayed the worms, Valentin thought, as he waited by her front door. There was a suffocating laziness about her; she was too easily overwhelmed. If she had taken care of the worms he might have married her. He didn't care what she thought about, or who she was, she probably didn't know herself. Most people had no idea what they thought. He had a rigid, generous notion of love; it was without guile, full of sacrifice. It was fearful sex followed by overwrought, motherly tenderness. It was true he and Isobel had had sex like that; merciless, raw, religious sex they had passed through the way a plane passes through a bank of dark cloud to come out in the blinding red sun; but outside of the sexual act he knew she was keeping something in reserve. He might have married her, but at her core she was no more substantial than a soap bubble.

The night after Isobel had massaged his feet he'd woken in sweat, his heart tearing through his chest, and he couldn't get back to sleep. He had dreamt that someone in the mall had handed him a cellphone and his mother had spoken to him. It was her voice, just as if she were in the room.

Sometimes it wasn't a life at all, she'd said.

He stayed awake, thinking about his mother, until dawn. Her simple sentence had seemed cryptic to him, full of unmanageable heartbreak. The cellphone, with its shushing static, had sounded like a tomb.

They hadn't had sex since Isobel had accepted the idea of the fire. Seeing the sandals on the mat he felt glad he had decided to burn the house down. He wanted to teach her that things could change. It was a matter of taking charge.

He had imagined the fire and what he had seen for her was a small boutique of some sort. He didn't like her. There was nothing to like. She was not committed to anything. He had no idea why he saw her selling perfume, but that is what he saw.

She'd told him she never slept with married men because they had been formed by years of routine and she couldn't count on them to falter or be alert or to know what was at stake. She'd said she didn't have the stamina to stand in front of a camera any more. She had come back from a publicity shoot where she'd posed in front of a cliff that was encased in ice. Though it had been ten below, she was wearing a chiffon dress and a tiny white synthetic stole that had wide satin ribbons and that looked like a toilet seat cover. The photographer's knees were bent. He was crouched with the camera angled up at her, it was obscene. She watched the shutter flick and flick and flick. She had summoned what she thought of as her soul to the surface of her skin and stared into the lens with it.

Forehead, the photographer said. And chin.

She'd given her hair a toss, unfurrowed her brow.

And chin, the photographer said. She'd lowered her chin. She had been pouring herself into camera lenses since she was eighteen and she had done this for her entire career without questioning the effects of the transference. She knew, now, that she had been diminished. She had become unknowable. The thing is, we're all unknowable, but we usually mask it. Now her unknowableness had surfaced.

There's a point, she'd said, when there's more behind you than what's ahead. It's called regret. It can happen any time in a life — when what has happened is more vivid than what will happen. She had been twenty when she fell in love with Chris. She has been looking over her shoulder ever since.

Valentin leaned in again to look through the window and saw a flash in the band of sunlight that came through the window above the landing and then she was at the front door in her red dress, she held her white cat in her arms.

He had told her she would have to leave the cat, but there she was in the doorway of her house with the cat in her arms. He had told her to leave the garden as it was but when she peeled back the lid of one of the Tupperware containers and he smelled the greenness of the tomatoes, bitter and hard and full of promise, he let her take them.

It was plausible she would bring tomatoes, he decided.

The hallway was dark and cool and she passed him the cat and bent over the hall table to put on her lipstick in the mirror. He thought about wringing the cat's neck. He knew how to kill it with his hands so that it would die quickly and almost soundlessly. He was suddenly full of rage about the cat. He didn't want a cat in his truck and he had told her to forget the cat. He was angry that she had defied him.

He thought of wringing the cat's neck and throwing the limp body at her back. He was rubbing the animal's cheek with his thumb and it started to purr.

Isobel went into the kitchen and he followed her. She was barefoot just as he had imagined. He saw she had done the dishes, and this placated him. The dishes in the dish rack looked exactly as they should. They looked like an ongoing project. They looked like a middle-aged actress going off for a weekend to visit her family in Old Perlican.

She turned on the water and let it run and she took a glass from the cupboard and filled the glass and drank all of it and threw the glass at his head. She whipped it across the room, but her aim was off and it hit the wall above his head and smashed all over the floor. She wiped her mouth with the back of her hand.

He had her wait in the truck with the cat and her tomatoes and he poured the gasoline in all the rooms and on the staircase. The gas glug-glugged out of the plastic containers and sloshed over her books and clothes and he was careful not to get it on his shoes. He poured lots of it into her furniture and on her bed and doused all the curtains. He splashed the walls. He had an idea it needed to soak in. The fumes hurt his nose and he could feel a pain in his forehead, but he wanted everything soaked through and through. He wanted the house to go up all at once.

He drove Isobel and the cat to Old Perlican, stopping at the beach for a soft-serve ice cream. He had reached over during the ride and put his hand on Isobel's thigh and the cat hissed and pricked him with its claws and Isobel removed his hand. The idea of the fire had made her look less intense. He decided he liked her better this way, becalmed, pleasantly subdued. There had been too much pent up inside her to begin with. Whatever she was scared of, whatever she had wanted so much, all of that was over. She would just have to work the counter of a cosmetic boutique.

When they were driving past Northern Bay Sands she said she wanted to swim. She was tapping the window with her fingernail. He saw children with inflated air mattresses and towels and snorkels and he thought why not let her swim.

We can leave the cat, she said.

COLLEEN

WHEN I WAS a kid we went out in a glass-bottomed boat. This was a vacation in Barbados. My mother was wearing a white, semi-transparent blouse and orange bikini and a hat with a floppy brim. I was sitting with my feet on the warm glass and watching the fish flick past, orange and blue and red, transparent and silver. All these different kinds and coral and the sunlight refracted in the waves making lacy shadows on the white sandy bottom.

Mom was drinking from a coconut shell and she had already given me the little umbrella when something big and dark swam under us.

So dark and blurred it made me scream, but no one else had been looking down. I was the only one to have seen it. Back on the beach, in the brilliant sun, bartering for shell necklaces it was easy to believe I'd imagined it.

But the fish, I think it was a shark, has come back to me in dreams ever since. Not the glass-bottomed boat, or the way the sunlight pierced the weave of Mom's hat, making white freckles of light all over her cheeks, or later that night sleeping between Mom and David. What I dream is falling over. Some part of me wants to fall over. In every dream I am about to fall over the side and be devoured by something.

When I asked Madeleine about the alligator footage she said the man had suffered brain damage. The teeth had punctured his skull in several places and infection set in. But he had recovered. Or pretty much recovered.

He runs an ecological reserve in Louisiana, Madeleine said. He farms alligators and puts them back in the wild.

MADELEINE

FORGET YOGA, SHE's tried yoga. It feels like an iron clamp. Has she gone back to the doctor? She has not. Because (A) she has to finish this film and (B) she doesn't want to go to the doctor because she made him sign the physical and (C) it doubles her over and (D) it's indigestion.

You get an idea in your head. She wanted Newfoundland before Confederation because what kind of people were they? She remembers her mother's housekeeper tearing the skin off rabbits in the kitchen sink.

She wanted an actress who could melt the emulsion, someone hard done by and fast. She wanted the horses from Austria.

For two weeks last winter she waited for the phone to ring about the bloody horses. She would glance at the phone and will it to ring. These Lipizzaners can bow down on one knee.

She had them come on a freighter as big as a stadium last winter and the freighter got stuck in the ice.

Things get stuck in the ice, she was told.

Men go over the sides of vessels on ropes with chainsaws tied to their backs. The ice lifts on giant swells; jagged tiles, weirdly green, lift on the crest of a wave and slide down the other side. Tropically green. The ice makes a keening noise, and cymbal crashes.

And these men begin to hack at the ice. They chop a path that closes over as soon as it opens.

The freighter was stuck and she had a cast and crew numbering in the hundreds whom she had to pay to stand around, waiting on those bloody horses that she would not give up on because she had got an idea in her head.

She'd had a meeting with the premier at the Newfoundland Hotel. He was on his way to China, a trade mission. She wanted some leverage at the bank, that's what she wanted. They'd chatted about politics and she'd ordered bakeapple jam for her toast and insisted he have some of hers.

China, how marvellous, she'd said, pushing the dish of jam over the tablecloth. What an adventure.

She'd wanted him thinking of summer. She could not put into words about how she'd captured the history of Newfoundland in this film, new because she was inventing it, or how this film had spiritual implications, how it would transfigure human experience, how bloody gorgeous the landscape, the actress with red hair, and Archbishop Fleming and the church bells but she could distract him with the jam.

She watched his knife dip into the little pot. He tasted the jam and he was thinking and then he waved the knife at her about to say something. Something had occurred to him. He waved the knife like a magic wand.

She had a thought: I am having breakfast with the premier. She saw herself as if she were looking down from the rafters, her amber pendant and the rose-coloured blouse. She was stirring her coffee.

The premier put down his knife. He had closed his eyes and was nodding to himself about how right he was in whatever thought he was having. He had convinced himself of some small matter.

About your film, he'd said.

She'd been drinking martinis in a castle in Ireland — what was this? A year ago? A slate floor, cold underfoot, and there was a fire in the hearth kicking out a bank of heat. She was there with an international committee of filmmakers and the blotch-faced Irishman sitting beside her with the white, wax-tipped, handlebar moustache: he had a brother who ran a stable in Austria.

He was a person worth $27 million, a benefactor of the arts. That's how she justified the Irishman's hand on her knee: white stallions. What kind of man wears a handlebar moustache? She wanted to give it a good hard tug.

I think we can do something, the premier said. Let me jot this note. We can definitely get in touch with a shipping company. I can get those horses over here.

COLLEEN

There was a bouncer checking ID at the door but he let Colleen and her friends through because she stood in front of him with a tiny pot of lip gloss. She unscrewed the lid and dipped her pinky in the gloss and the crowd pushed behind her and she let them press her into the table. There was a lot of noise and smoke and the bouncer's muscles were gym muscles but he was unattractive and very slowly, drunkenly, she ran the tip of her pinky over her top lip and then her bottom lip and she pressed her lips together and made a big smack.

She made the smack deliberate and she was leaning near the bouncer, her breasts over the table, she couldn't believe how much fun it was coming on to an ugly bouncer in order to gain admittance to a wet T-shirt contest that she wanted to do because she was loaded and because she had big beautiful breasts and she might win $1,000. She was very drunk and desperate to get to the edge of an anger she couldn't describe because it was new. There was a neon sign in the window that said *Open* and the lime green light flushed through the tubing over and over and Colleen thought it was like the anger she felt, a surging, sobering anger full of neon. She wanted to commit an illicit act. It struck her as comedic — to undress before a crowd — both nightmarish and goofy. It was a banal act that had the potential to change her. It was none of those things. There was some part of herself she wanted to shed. She wanted to have fun. Colleen had waited through the whole month of July for the youth diversion meeting to be over and now she was going to be painting murals all of August to make up with Mr. Duffy and it pissed her off. She was with Sherry Ryan and a friend of Sherry's she'd just met, Leslie, and Jennifer Galway said she was coming later. Sherry Ryan has a new hambone mohawk and a tattoo of the local punk band Beaumont Hamel on her shoulder — she has a crush on the lead singer — but she didn't think Colleen should do the wet T-shirt thing.

It's kind of humiliating, Sherry had shouted over the noise, her hand cupped near her mouth.

What? Colleen shouted back.

Humiliating, Sherry shouted.

What? Sherry just rolled her eyes.

Colleen would take the wet T-shirt money and get on a plane in the morning, or the morning after that. She wanted to go to Louisiana and meet the alligator guy from Madeleine's video. She wanted to see the operation he ran. Saving alligators: that would be something to see. She could go for a long time with the prize money for beautiful breasts.

She smiled at the bouncer with her lovely teeth, recently liberated from years of braces and elastic bands and night guards and gathered everything she had ever seen on television sitcoms about looking sultry and she did it as a sort of joke, half serious. The bouncer jerked his head toward the bar and Colleen and her friends slid through the door.

A waitress worked the crowd with a tray of neon shooters; she had a tattoo near her collarbone that said *Kyle*.

A one-*thousand*-dollar prize goes to the winner, says the bartender, who stands in the centre of a small empty stage with a mike and he slithers the cord over the dirty floor.

Let's warm up with the wet boxers, he says. Colleen hears his spittle in the mike and it makes her feel like he's all over her with his wetness. He promises buckets of beer and a city-wide ride in a limousine. He gets the girls to clap, a slowly building beat that breaks into whoops and catcalls and laments about the absence of guys willing to have water squirted at their rods.

It's hotter in the bar than even a half an hour ago and Colleen's sweat smells like beer and she wants more beer. The girls have glitter in their hair, are wearing black eyeliner, push-up bras, fishnet stockings, and tongue studs that glint like a secret when they laugh. They look rumpled, unfocused, and full of lust.

Three guys lope around the stage, affecting a sort of good-humoured machismo. They look around the empty space as if they have to stake a claim. The one in the middle flexes his muscles, curling one arm and then curling the other.

Come on, Bell Island, says the bartender. Come on, Harbour Grace. Step right up. I want you to meet my lovely assistant.

The bartender's lovely assistant is chubby and acne-faced, but she works a gigantic, pump-action water gun and it's all over for the guys pretty quick. One of them strips off and his dick wags and swings as he does a triumphant trot around the stage. The bartender shakes his head and looks away.

Then the mood shifts. The floor is suddenly packed tight, maybe a hundred and fifty young men. Where did they all come from?

Get on with the nipple show, someone shouts.

The bartender calls on the bouncer and hands him the water gun. And there is Colleen standing on a plastic milk carton in an ultraviolet light with a white T-shirt that is phosphorescent blue and her teeth flash and the bouncer circles her and nods his head appreciatively, playing the crowd.

Boléro bursts from the overhead speakers and laughter goes up and the bouncer takes a camouflage hat from his back pocket and fits it on his head, and this makes everybody laugh too, he gets down on one knee in front of Colleen and pretends to squint through crosshairs on the plastic Uzi.

Then he sprays her face and the water is cool and she turns her head. Her mouth is open and the water sprays into her mouth and she looks like a kid with her face all scrunched up and blinking hard to get the water out of her eyes and then he drills her breasts with steely ropes of water.

The crowd presses closer and Colleen writhes under the water and the T-shirt is soaked. She grinds and feels naked and she's swaying to the music and the clapping, her arms over her head and she looks like she's having a pretty good time. She can't see Sherry Ryan in the crowd. Sherry Ryan has probably left.

Over at the other end of the stage, Peggy, from Grand Falls, topples off her milk carton onto the floor after the guy soaks her and she remains on the floor for a long time. Then Louise, on the milk carton in the middle, throws back her head and peels off her soaking shirt and holds a pose.

The crowd wants Colleen to take her shirt off too. They start to chant. The chanting gets more insistent, louder, faster, and then, out of nowhere, it has a slightly nasty edge.

There's a definite whiff of menace.

Colleen is oblivious. She's trying to high-five the half-naked girl beside her. Then a man separates from the crowd and it's the guy she's seen at the Ship who was watching her dance. He's not bad-looking, this guy.

She hears, exactly then, the menace in the crowd, the weird collective nastiness coming to a boil.

Someone throws a pop can and it hits Frank's shoulder and bounces off. The bartender takes Frank by the arm, but Frank shakes his arm free and puts up his fists and the bartender nods to the bouncer and the bouncer steps forward.

The bar has gone awkwardly silent.

It is part of the show, this stepping forward, this display of chest, clenched fist, and set jaw.

The cash register tings and the drawer flies open and the coins in the slots slap against each other. The ordinary noise of money changing hands and someone says about the hockey game and the moment passes. Everyone turns away from the stage and starts talking and handing around beer.

Colleen takes Frank by the hand and they work their way through the crowd and out onto the street and she says, Thanks a lot, whoever you are. It was a stupid thing for me to do, a wet T-shirt thing. Stupid.

Her hand is wet and her hair and her white T-shirt and her nipples are wet. A damp, fine gold chain, barely a thread, curves over the dip near her throat. She is holding his hand and he doesn't know where to look. He knows not to look at her breasts or her mouth or her throat or her eyes and he looks at all of it. She is shivering and when he looks at her eyes they are so full of excitement he is mildly shocked.

Maybe you'd like to loan me your sweater, she says. He works himself out of the sweater as fast as he can. He gives it to her and she disappears in it and then she says, Smells nice. Nice sweater.

I have a place, he says.

FRANK

AS SOON AS Frank realized all of his money was gone, he put on the kettle and got out the plastic coffee cone and put a paper filter in it. He got the sugar bowl he'd bought at the Sally Ann out of the cupboard. It still had the piece of masking tape with *25¢* written in ballpoint pen. The day he bought the sugar bowl, there was a woman trying on a wedding dress.

She was scrawny and bucktoothed and the bones in her face were so misaligned that she appeared deformed. The two women who work at the Sally Ann on Waldegrave were excited about the wedding and they seemed to know the groom-to-be, whom they called Johnny and who seemed to be mentally retarded.

Frank found the sugar bowl in a bin of kitchen junk, spoons with enamel thumbnail pictures of P.E.I. and rusty ladles and a plastic spaghetti strainer that someone had put too close to the heat and had melted the side out of it.

The sugar bowl was pinwheel crystal, which his mother had had four wineglasses of, the same pattern; some client she cleaned for had given them to her as a Christmas present.

He picked at the tape with his finger now, and peeled it off and there was left a little skim of gritty dirt in the shape of the piece of tape that he rubbed with his thumb and it balled up there and he flicked his hand. Something about this flicking made it real to him how absolutely alone in the world he was, because he looked absurd doing it but there was no one to see.

At the Salvation Army that day in January he had filtered through a cardboard box of junk for a lid to the sugar bowl, he knew it should have a lid, and was surprised by how much he wanted a lid. He did not want to be someone without the lids to things. He wanted whole sets of whatever he had, or nothing at all.

He wanted, when he went to the paint store, to get the trim they suggested went with the burnt sand colour he had chosen. He wanted, when he looked into the eyes of the idiot they had working there, who said he couldn't mix that colour but he could mix one pretty damn close, to grab him by the front of the shirt and shout in his face that he didn't want close.

He never wanted close again. He had been living with close his whole life.

He wanted to communicate how this acceptance of second-best infuriated him and the guy better find a way to mix the right colour.

One of the women at the Salvation Army was named Gert, and the other was Shirley, according to their nametags. Frank could tell by looking at them they were seriously religious women, and he saw they kept a stern eye out for shoplifters and they stood in the late-afternoon light with their arms crossed under their chests and watched the weather come in over the harbour.

Frank had been coming to the Salvation Army on Waldegrave with his mother ever since he was born, but he wasn't sure that they put him together with the baby and small kid he had been, or if they thought about his mother and wondered what had happened to her.

On the January day when Frank got the sugar bowl, Gert had pulled a chair across the floor and was leaning with a long pole to unhook a wedding dress from the ceiling. The dress was swathed in plastic and the plastic was covered in dust and Gert had to lean out too far and had lifted one foot in the air like a ballerina and Johnny, the groom-to-be, took her hand.

Frank saw how firmly he held her hand, saying, Hold on to me, Gert girl, before you break your neck. Everyone in the store was watching the hook sway slightly here and there around the wedding dress hanger, which was hooked over a waterpipe hanging just below the ceiling.

Gert lowered the wedding dress and shook off the plastic, clawing at it, and without the dusty plastic, the wedding dress, they all saw, was covered in sequins and it crackled with light and the girl with the misaligned face had covered her mouth with both her hands.

This dress was never worn, Gert whispered. She had fished a pricetag out of the froth and it said the dress was worth $1,500.

The girl gathered the dress up in her arms and went into the tiny dressing room and Gert and Shirley turned at once and started clucking and waving their arms at Johnny, telling him to turn around for the love of God and close his eyes.

After a few moments Shirley called out, Does it fit?

The door of the dressing room creaked open and the bride came out, and she was a scalded red with embarrassment and pride. She ducked her head into her shoulder and the beauty of the dress seemed more than she could bear. The red in her face made her eyes a dark, dark brown. Her misaligned face was lit up by her blushing and for a minute she looked weirdly beautiful.

Frank thought that maybe in the future this Johnny guy would beat the shit out of her, or they'd just live on welfare for the rest of their lives, or they wouldn't know about Canada's four food groups and the kids would be eating cake with blue icing blocked with sugar and chemicals and chips and cola and they'd be saucy and out of control all the time, and the parents would get something like cancer or they'd be alcoholics or have gambling addictions, but for now, in the middle of a snow-storm with the dress on, the girl, Frank saw, was ecstatic.

Frank saw her shoulders and neck were covered in deep brown freckles but below her neck the skin looked creamy and her body was pretty nice. Then he found the lid to the sugar bowl, his fingers had just brushed against it. It wasn't chipped and there was a small dip to fit a spoon in.

This sugar bowl, now in the cupboard in front of him, on the yellow mactac is shimmering, struck as it is by the light from the window and he takes it down and puts it on the counter and is humiliated as he remembers that he thought he would marry Colleen after a one-night stand.

He thought he would marry her.

From one night of making love he thought they were going to get married and everything he gathered together from that night on would be for her too. If he found a sugar bowl, it would be for her. If he bought an exercise bike or took cooking lessons or if they got into yoga or signed a mortgage, it would be for her.

He had allowed himself to be duped on such a grand scale that it made him light-headed.

He looked at the sugar bowl and this is what he thought: And I still love her. Because he thought of taking the strawberries from the fridge that were very cold and he had squashed one in his fist and tried to get the juice that ran over his knuckles to drip into her mouth but instead it ran down her chin and onto her neck and the smell of it on her skin when he licked it, and she liked what he was doing, which amazed him.

She licked his knuckles that were sticky with juice and she took his finger in her mouth and sucked it and he thought he was having the love tugged out of him. Tugging every single drop of love and loss and sexual-wanting-to-fuck and aloneness up out of his body through his finger with her gorgeous hot wet mouth, the way a magician tugs an unending line of knotted silk scarves from a gloved fist. Her mouth was a fist and he wanted it elsewhere. Her eyelashes were sooty and thick and her cheekbones and the strawberry smell was full of summer and when he lifted her up against the wall was she ever light.

And when she came, which he had never made a girl come before, he saw her eyes fly open and how startled she was, and that look was love he was pretty sure.

Even if she did take the goddamn money, which he knew she didn't need for anything, she just took it.

He took down the coffee jar and scooped out five spoonfuls. Then he tore back the bedsheets to check for a note.

For a minute he thought she might have left a note. He opened the door to the fire escape, half expecting to find the girl there.

When she wasn't there he felt the room behind him beat like a heart, thumpthump, thumpthump, and it was a very empty room and he realized that no matter how much it was clear she had duped him, he couldn't get it through his head.

COLLEEN

FRANK HAD FALLEN in love with her while they were having sex; she watched it happen. She fully expected to be caught and perhaps beaten up for taking his money. She had just met this guy in a bar and she went home with him and what happened was her eyes flew open and his eyes were already open and she'd had an orgasm, which was something that had never happened to her before.

And it had *happened to her*, unbidden and unexpected; her eyes flew open and his were already open.

He'd looked proud and shy. She'd been swallowing Jell-O shooters at the bar, layered globs of vodka and tequila and crème de menthe with a tiny wizened mushroom in the centre of each layer. She'd found herself convulsed with weeping after the orgasm: a wrung-out, lust-fuelled loss of self, an expulsion of her soul through her eyes and sweat glands and vagina and ears such as usually only happens in dreams.

Frank dealt with her crying the way one might treat a runover cat. He moved her gingerly and with lavish care until her forehead was resting on his collarbone; he kept very still. He smoothed her hair, which was full of static from his sweater;

he didn't actually touch her hair but patted down the brittle aura of electricity that circled her head.

Get it all out of you, he'd said. The bed rocked and gurgled with her sobs. He had hummed "My Bonnie Lies Over the Ocean" with such gravity and profound lack of tempo that it took her a long time to recognize it. She was almost asleep when she heard him say, I love you.

He told her he loved her and the words tumbled down the drunken, bottomless well of her with a sombre finality.

As a thirteen-year-old she'd started drinking and smoking dope in the parking lot behind her school among broken beer bottles and cigarette butts and the hopscotch games drawn on the pavement with coloured chalk. There were bushes at the edge of the lot and she'd gone in there and allowed boys to grope her and put hickeys on her neck and eventually to do whatever they liked, sometimes two at a time. It had all happened in a haze of camaraderie and coercion that everybody forgot, as best they could, the next day. Maybe she was crying for all of that.

Or she was crying because of a glimmer of self-doubt concerning the bulldozers. Maybe she'd been wrong about the bulldozers. Or she was crying because Frank had no idea how vulnerable he was. Frank's innocence was jolting and sensual and she felt the need to destroy it as quickly as possible.

In the morning, while Frank slept, she quietly put on her socks and reached under the bedside table for her shoes. She had the first mural painting meeting for juvenile delinquents in a couple of hours and she was still a little drunk. Her hand brushed against a cobweb and then a fat white envelope that she pulled out and opened. There were twenty-five hundred-dollar bills inside it. She counted them, careful not to let the paper rustle.

She tucked the envelope down the front of her jeans, one sharp corner digging into her hip. She bent to pick up her shoes and the room swayed. She stood up fast, holding the shoes near her chest. The room was mildly swaying in circles. It lurched and settled down and behaved itself.

The deadbolt made a screech. Frank's face was turned toward her and his eyelashes were very dark and he was engaged in a sleep full of trust. He was thoroughly spent and his cheeks were flushed and she thought of him as a solitary boy, more solitary than any young man she'd ever met.

He'd listened so intently while she talked during the night. She'd flopped onto his bed and it wobbled violently. She spanked the waterbed with both arms and felt the swells.

Once, I was nearly decapitated, she said brightly. She told Frank about being at the Confederation Building when she was seven or eight, one in a phalanx of overheated Brownies and Cubs, during an official occasion of some sort and an elderly gentleman, a former soldier in full regalia, had drawn a ceremonial sword, but it was too heavy for him and it came down over his shoulder and would have probably cut her head off cleanly — she was standing directly behind the old man in her little brown dress with all its splendid badges — except her mother, who had always been overprotective and doting, had pulled her out of its path.

I felt the swoosh, she told him. The breeze from the blade. She closed her eyes and imagined her seven-year-old head with its smart little Brownie tam still perched at an angle, rolling over the floor of the Confederation Building, Brownies everywhere stepping out of its path.

I think the mushrooms are kicking in, she'd whispered.

She opened the door very slowly, still clutching her shoes to her chest. The hinges yelped. She heard a slosh from the mattress behind her and froze, not even breathing, and then she was out in the hallway and down the stairs. She had put herself in peril, Colleen thought, and then retrieved herself from peril. She liked to see what she could get away with, how far she could go. *This time you've gone too far, young lady.* What she wanted was bacon and eggs. She didn't put her shoes on until she was around the street corner.

She headed for The Bagel Café and the cruise ship was still docked in the harbour and she saw a party hat lying in the gutter. It was a cone of silver cardboard with a print of birthday cakes all over it. It was rolling back and forth in the breeze and the sun sent a white flare running down its side. It looked like a dunce cap and she was seized instantly with remorse for taking Frank's money. A consuming self-hatred, a wish for instant annihilation, the sort of swoosh that would leave no trace. There seemed to be no getting beyond it. She had stopped in the middle of the sidewalk and the people in the cars driving past saw a bedraggled, washed-out girl staring at the ground in front of her, arrested, still as a statue, clutching her hair with two fists.

She withstood the remorse. She closed her eyes as she had seen her mother do when facing her own moral failings. If she had learned anything from her mother it was not to wallow in self-doubt. Doubt was a luxury, according to her mother, and it was always better to act, however unsure you might be. She would eat a big breakfast, she was starving, and find the mural painters at the Murphy Centre. She couldn't think of Frank or the pine martens or anything else until she was completely sober.

FRANK

IT WAS ALMOST midnight when Carol showed up at the hot-dog stand. She was wearing sweatpants and a cardigan and a black baseball cap; a pink curler hung behind each ear. Her fists were jammed into the pockets of her cardigan. He could see her knuckles pressing against the knit.

He'd never seen her on George Street before.

Frank, you've got to come home, she said. Frank handed the man in front of him his hot dog.

There's water everywhere, Carol said. Frank watched as the man tried to get some bacon bits. He was weaving slightly and wore a look of deep thought. Carol was pulling on Frank's sleeve.

Don't mix up the spoons, sir, Frank said. The man held the plastic spoon from the corn relish in the air; he was blinking in disbelief.

The different condiments each got their own spoon, Frank said.

Can't I have bacon? the man asked.

The plaster is after cracking off the ceiling, Carol said.

You can have bacon, just could you use the spoon for the bacon, Frank said.

There's an inch of water, Carol said. I'm afraid to turn on a lamp I'll be electrocuted. It's coming from your apartment, Frank. Could you have maybe put something down the toilet?

Go ahead, Frank said. The man was still holding the spoon in the air as if he were paralyzed by it.

Go ahead what?

Whatever spoon you want, Frank said.

A tampon or something, Carol said.

Is it real bacon? the man asked.

The girl you had up there the other night, I thought maybe a tampon is the first thing I thought.

It's bacon bits, said Frank. The man dug the spoon in deep and the bacon bits danced and hopped all over the spoon and mostly spilled on the sidewalk before he got the spoon to the hot dog. Then he put the hot dog down on the chrome ledge and staggered off without it.

Frank's apartment door was open when he got there and he stood in the hallway and listened. Carol stood beside him.

He turned on the light and saw everything was soaking wet. He pulled the covers off the waterbed and saw it had been slashed from the headboard to the footboard. One long gash.

His mother's urn was overturned on the wet carpet; the ashes had been dumped onto the floor and walked on. He saw the partial print of the boot treads. Carol stood just behind him and they both stared at the pile of ashes and she was still holding on to the sleeve of his shirt. Then she pushed past him.

Carol went down on her knees and stood the urn up and scooped up the ashes with both her hands. The ashes were clumping and smelled strongly like wet ashes. They smelled like what they were. Carol dragged her hands over the wet carpet until she had gathered most of the ashes and then she saw the lid of the urn that had rolled on its rim into the corner of the closet. She crossed the floor still on her knees and picked up the lid and crawled back over to the urn and put the lid on. Then she got up, which caused her to groan because of her back, and she washed her hands at the sink.

She used a squirt of the dishwashing liquid and then she dried her hands with a dishtowel. He had wanted to take the ashes to Signal Hill but he didn't want to give them up, so he had put it off.

Gradually the idea had occurred to him that he might keep the ashes. The idea made him afraid he was too much alone. It seemed to him the thinking of someone who was out of step.

He didn't imagine anything of his mother's spirit remained in the ashes, he recognized them for exactly what they were — what was left of his mother's body after it had been burned in the crematorium.

He understood, or thought he understood, the modern-day ritual of handing the ashes on to a grieving relative so that they may be scattered. He had imagined the sort of weather and the location along the trail where he could scatter the ashes.

The urn had cost $700. He doubted his mother had spent that much money on a luxury item ever in her life. The urn was solid brass and understated in design. For whatever reason he felt the urn was company.

Now the ashes were soaking wet and it was a travesty. He could imagine Valentin getting the door open and destroying the waterbed without compunction. The waterbed he saw, now that it had been slashed, was nothing more than a vanity.

But there was something so remote and alien about desecrating a grave that Frank felt weary beyond measure. He was also aware of the bald simplicity of the act.

If Valentin wanted money Frank would give him money. He would give him whatever it took because he understood, plainly, Valentin was stronger than he was. He sank to his knees and pressed the heels of his hands into his eyes until he saw flecks of light. First, he would see if money was enough. If not, then he would give him the hot-dog stand.

COLLEEN

COLLEEN HAD NOW attended the first meeting of juvenile delinquent mural painters who gathered at the Murphy Centre and the other delinquents were disgusting. They slouched, stank of body odour, and cigarettes, and they all wore velour pants from Zellers that hung down to reveal butt crack. They had chips and Pepsi for breakfast; their fathers were pimps and their mothers sniffed glue. They had the look, each of them, of low-intelligence, which was the nicest way she could think to put it.

Colleen felt very uncomfortable about spending August on a scaffold negotiating the class differences and flares of temper and social injustice that had created the divide between her and them, which was huge. They were assholes and she wasn't.

A huge divide, she figured.

She recognized a girl from Grade 8. Kelly Fitzgerald, known at that time as Fitzy, who had once attacked Colleen behind the school with her gang of stringy-haired, raw-looking girls from Chalker Place.

The girls taunted her and threw a few rocks and she had run but they were on top of her and had knocked the wind out of her. There were about ten of them and they held her arms and legs, though she writhed in the dirt below them and wheezed, desperate to get her breath back.

Fitzy had a stick with a used condom on the end of it. She held the stick over Colleen's head and told her to suck it or they'd beat the living shit out of her.

She lowered the condom an inch at a time, and the girls held tightly, grunting with the effort, murmuring consoling noises, as if they were administering medicine.

They asked her what she was going to do about it, and if she thought she was so hot now, and they said they'd heard she'd been doing the same thing Friday night with lots of guys and they'd heard she was good at it, and they promised it wasn't going to hurt a bit if she just did what she was told.

Fitzy had one of her knees pressed into Colleen's forehead and she had Colleen's jaw wrenched open with one hand and was leaning over her upside down and her face was red with exertion and her eyes sparkled. She was lowering the condom down toward Colleen's mouth with little jerks and Colleen saw there was a milky white glob of sperm in the nub at the bottom of it.

Colleen saw that Fitzy's mouth was open too, unconsciously mimicking Colleen's, the way a mother opens her mouth when spoon-feeding a baby.

The condom hung close enough to Colleen's mouth and nose that she could smell its humanness. It smelled of latex and rot and fish and some drunken girl in the back of a car because she had nowhere else to go and cologne and cigarettes and failure and shuddering release. Then a police car pulled lazily onto the Holy Heart parking lot and the gang took off.

And here was Fitzy again, at the Murphy Centre, the same girl, pinned beneath a pregnant belly on a couch with bad springs. She was splayed in the humidity, arms and legs dangling, and a look of sheer relief came over her face when she saw Colleen.

We were in school together, she said, patting the seat beside her on the couch.

You're Colleen, right? She wiggled her fingers at Colleen. What do you think of my engagement ring?

Colleen decided instantly she wouldn't be painting murals. Something had happened when she and Frank were having sex and she felt it and he felt it too because her eyes flew open and his eyes were open and he saw it. They both felt it, which, that's why she took the money and also because it was a lot of money. She got up from the couch.

Where are you going? Fitzy asked.

Way the hell out of here, Colleen said.

ISOBEL

WAVES TRAVEL A long distance without effort. They curl because they cannot not curl. Because when a wave is punched in the gut it caves. Because a wave is all show and no substance. The curdling spew rushes ahead. Foam scribbling over the sand, a note to say the wave is over. Because the glare on the water is in Sanskrit. Because the sea smells like the sea and she's got the dress wet already and it's clinging to her shins. Because she believes in submitting and has made a minor religion of it. Because there's a big fat red-haired man, pale as potato in a sunhat, charging through the water with an inflatable shark. Because the theatre is a cult and people give their whole lives to the cause, which is what exactly? Because perfume is looking good right now, making a living is looking good. Not having to worry about money is looking good. Because only women who have come and come and come and come or who wear thick silver bracelets or who have lost a lover or who have vision or who have lost everything or who know what limelight feels like could possibly understand her and there are none of those women left.

Because she gave up everything and came home to

Newfoundland. Because she had nothing to give up in the first place. Because early on she fell in love with Chris, who led her astray. Chris Morgan, who took her cross-country skiing, and they found their way out of the wilderness with a compass. He'd found the compass in a junk shop and had to hit it with his axe to get the needle to waver. Chris, who had drawn their supper out of a hole in the ice and built them an igloo with a fire in the centre so all night long they kicked off the blankets and slept naked and were soaked with sweat, and who made love to her in every single way it is possible to make love and the roof collapsed. Blocks of snow fell on their heads.

Chris, who was ridiculous, vital, super-horny, athletic, a liar and a cheat, who had a photographic memory, who always knew what regime had fallen where and what their major export was and how it related to the spoonful of cereal she was about to put in her mouth, who was untamable, who had introduced her to tahini and Tarkovsky, who was vigilantly agnostic; it had required a vigilance because his natural inclination was to believe.

And Isobel couldn't not think of him whenever she snapped the clunky silver bracelet onto her wrist, the bracelet from Mexico. They had taken an outdoor steam bath in the backyard of a minor politician they'd met while hitchhiking. The pool was cobblestones and fed by a natural hot spring and there were seven or eight of them. The steam rose and shredded when it met the night air and his naked thigh bumped against her with the hot bubbles and whir of water and she loved him. Or she loved something so huge it must have been him and later there was the bracelet on her pillow.

She had come home to Newfoundland because she had failed. She didn't get the soap and there was Chris, my God, directing a soap opera.

The anticipation of the hurling mass of the next wave, which is cold and mounting triumphantly and about crotch high, is huge, and if this wave hits her she's getting all the way in. Like the world exhaling. A hammering home of the truth. A refusal to be a wave any longer. The wave accepts the absurdity of being a wave, but also recognizes the beach for what it is: a reckoning. Who said it would go on forever?

Nobody said.

They said quite the opposite.

There is no cold on earth as unequivocal as this wave that is higher than her head and about to smash itself against her skull. It is as cold as cold can be. Because how can matter be so blasted with sunlight, so sparkle-riven, and curve with such blood lust and be so soul numbing? A wave is the bone around a marrow of light.

Isobel is standing up to her waist and wading out and she gets the wave full force, right in the face, up her nose, in her ears, in her mouth, down her throat, out her nostrils.

Valentin is behind her on the beach, overdressed. Even while she is deep under the water she can feel his eyes on her, the red dress billowing out and clinging, billowing out and clinging with every stroke she takes. She's a jellyfish making for the horizon. She knows she's safe for the moment; he won't risk getting his leather shoes wet.

MADELEINE

SHE HAD WOKEN in a sweat; Archbishop Fleming in the corner of the room, the ghost of Archbishop Fleming.

He was showing up in her dreams more frequently since she'd gone into production with the summer shoot. Fleming had wanted silver chalices for the Eucharist in every church on the Southern Shore. Archbishop Fleming cracking a whip over the backs of four white stallions, and they come tearing out of a snow squall like the wrath of God.

She'd invented the character, Fleming, on a blustery afternoon several years ago while reading letters he'd written to the Pope. She came out of the Roman Catholic Archives and the world had been transformed, a fresh blanket of snow. And now when she falls asleep in the afternoon, there is the archbishop standing in the corner with his white robes and scarlet cape and his staff.

The premier had said they could helicopter the horses to shore. Because of the ice, they had no way to get the horses. There was a sling they could use, and it was expensive and dangerous, but it had been done with racehorses in Kentucky.

The animals would be blindfolded of course, and they

would be lowered very carefully from the clouds. She had made a few phone calls. It was impossible, she had been told. It had never happened in Kentucky, or anywhere else. They would not helicopter the horses in, was she crazy? The animals would die of panic.

FRANK

He had told Valentin he would give him $1,000. They had met on the stairs and the Russian had said about cigarettes he wanted to buy cheap and sell at twice the price.

He wanted to borrow a grand that he would return the next day and even give Frank some extra for his trouble. Valentin said all of this casually, without reference to the ransacking of Frank's apartment or the desecration of Frank's mother's ashes. Valentin honestly seemed to be asking for the loan the way someone might borrow a cup of sugar.

We are neighbours, said Valentin. When Frank agreed to the loan the Russian took his hand and shook it vigorously and said he thought they would be great neighbours now.

We must be friends, the Russian said. I like you because you are a businessman. You are like me. This is what we have to understand: there is a system but it is like a suspension bridge, it has give. People like us must exploit the give, do you know what I mean? Frank said he understood.

With persistence and patience, Valentin said. He clapped Frank on the shoulder.

But now all Frank's money was gone and he could hear

the Russians waking up. He could hear the toilet and something boiling and the door to the fire escape banged against the wall and he could hear them speaking to each other in Russian. Valentin would be down soon looking for the money.

She was from a comfortable home where, Frank bet, she had never needed anything. She'd never been in a welfare office. She had never had to get a brown paper bag from the breakfast program at school. She'd never been evicted from an apartment because her mother was three months behind in the rent. She had never eaten Kraft Dinner for supper unless she wanted to. She had never worn a windbreaker, one of three hundred, donated by a sports store to a shelter for battered women and distributed throughout the city to needy families, a windbreaker that became an immediately identifiable mark of poverty, but had to be worn anyway because at all costs it was important to pretend to one's mother that one loved the windbreaker. She had never seen her mother live with a toothache rather than pay to get it fixed.

Yet, she had taken his money, and that's the way of it.

That is the way of money.

Frank put on a fresh T-shirt and picked up his keys and decided to walk down Duckworth Street to see if he could find Colleen. He'd get his money back.

On the street the boy from next door was playing with a bubble wand. He pressed a lever in the handle and the wand opened out into a large diamond shape and bubble liquid shot up from the clear handle and coated the plastic diamond when he tipped it into the breeze and a giant bubble wobbled into the air and lifted from the wand, and it caught the reflection of the landlord's Jaguar, which was parked outside the bed-sit and the black streaky gleaming car slithered on the curve of the oversized bubble.

The boy put out his hand to touch the bubble and it broke with a sun-sparkling mist and Frank started up the sidewalk and as he did he gouged his key into the side of the landlord's Jaguar and dragged it from the taillight all the way to the headlight feeling the paint crust against the tip of his key.

COLLEEN

I'M IN THE Toronto airport with a connecting flight to Louisiana in a few hours and I am so hungry I could pass out. I go into Swiss Chalet and the waitress has a tag that says Veronica. She's past middle age, perhaps forty, and she has her blond hair swept into a French twist and should I call Mom and tell her where I am? Not yet. Not yet. Veronica has a beauty mark on her cheek. I try to think who Veronica is in the Bible.

I know the boy in the kitchen, Veronica says, and I tell him you don't have much time, so he does me a favour. Veronica has an accent I don't recognize.

She winks at me and puts down the plate of chicken and a bowl of gravy and a finger bowl and I am so hungry. The chicken is moist and good.

Soon I'll be sitting in the plane while it turns circles on the runway waiting for clearance to take off. They'll turn off the cabin lights and the flight attendant will touch the overhead bins with her fingers all the way up the aisle. I can't leave Swiss Chalet without paying because this is an airport and how easy it would be to get caught. But once I'm through customs I'm through and it's so busy here, a table full of women in purdah, another table of five pilots, there's a toddler screaming her head off. I could slide out the door pretty quick. I should be able to keep going for a while on Frank's money, but it would be good not to have to pay for every meal. Swiss Chalet is a big chain, like probably part of some multinational. Veronica has her back turned. They're busy as hell, she's probably been on for hours already; she's probably exhausted. There are two entrances, and if I went out the one next to the bathrooms I wouldn't have to pass anybody. I could get out of here and it would take Veronica at least five minutes to see I'm gone.

MADELEINE

SHE REMEMBERS A luncheon in Sydney, Australia. Was she speaking about the art of documentary? Yes she was. She was speaking about how you could change the world with a good documentary. Earlier that week she had come close to drowning.

When she said *change the world* she thought of the sweat required to rev the engines of capital so you eventually got to say your piece. It took two years or more to browbeat the mucky-mucks and massage the concept and betray the concept, all the while remaining true. But if you displayed brazenness and fortitude, she had learned, you more or less got to say your piece. She was all for having your say.

She'd always start off a project by wanting to say a fairly simple thing, for instance: it was okay to kill baby seals, or wife battering was bad, or could we not help the people of Sudan before they all die in horrific, unimaginable ways? There were transvestites injecting gel into their chests so they would have tits and they were dying from it and this was bad. Cops carrying guns in St. John's was bad. Whatever she said, she would want the pictures to carry the message, and yes, there bloody well would be a message if she were going to raise all that money. You bet there'd be a message.

This must have been what she was saying at the podium in Sydney, Australia. But she was thinking, while she spoke, of how she had gone for a swim at Bondi Beach earlier in the week and the tide had dragged her out. From the beach she would have been nothing more than a speck. She could see several bodies in black wetsuits, needle thin in the distance and sun struck. They were walking with their surfboards, which looked like wafers and she watched them wade into the water and lie on their boards and paddle out and then rise up and skim the crests of waves with their arms aloft. She thought about her green canvas sneakers on the sand. Her gold watch and hotel key were in the toe of one of her sneakers. She had wanted to go for a swim and she'd thought, If someone takes the watch, so what. I'll get a new watch.

Yes there would be a strong message, she was telling them. But this is what she promised on the way. They'd get a story they weren't expecting. They would belly laugh at least once. They would not be exactly as they had been before. She was saying something of the sort at the podium. She was counting the promises off on her fingers. She was popping her *p*'s on the microphone.

The ocean wanted her, really, really wanted her. She discovered in herself a willingness to give up. Why not take the easy way out for once. When she thought of the sneakers on the beach she saw it as a shot, veils of sand blowing over them, half burying them, but it would have to be a quick shot or it would be cheesy. Why not cheesy, she thought. What's wrong with a little cheese? I'm dying here, after all.

She'd made a documentary about the cops carrying guns in St. John's, she was telling them by way of example, and the question had been would she be able to get the security guard who had gone into a public bathroom and sat down and laid his pistol on the back of the toilet and walked out again to talk on camera.

Who was she talking to anyway? Older women with hats. There were some grey-haired, frail-looking men. She didn't care who they were, she had almost drowned. Know your audience, she told them.

She was trying to keep it short because there was an elderly poet supposed to talk next and he had leaned over during the break and was trembling and had difficulty speaking, but his mouth was open and his eyes were earnestly trying to communicate his intent. He had to make fists with both his hands to wring out of his withered body what he needed to say and it was that he would die before the end of the luncheon if she dragged her talk on too long. He fought to go first but she was slotted to go first and she wouldn't give up her slot. Let the old geezer croak, she had thought.

A guy in one of those black rubber suits whipped past her on a yellow board. He nearly knocked her brains out and the board twisted in the air. He was flung into the sky with a blast of white surf and the board smacked down and he smacked down on top of the board. Then a wave curled over him, a fiery green wall of light and rainbow and mist. He was riding toward her through a narrow tunnel. The tunnel was clenching behind him, closing like a fist, and getting narrower in front and he had to crouch and she didn't have long left because there was no strength in her arms and anyway, it had been a good life. Then he was engulfed and oh well, that was that, but, the surfboard, which bobbed up quite close to her was tied to his ankle and he managed to get her on the board, never mind where his hands grabbed and pinched and how ungainly and squashed and unromantic and snot-covered and fat she was. Lady, he'd said.

He'd said, Lady, lady, lady. In that accent they have down there. He raised a fist in the air, flung the water from his hair, and made a whooping noise. She had nearly been swallowed by malevolent death to leave no remains, but instead — she could not believe. Here was a man, muscled, lean, young, everything she loved, and he was paddling them back to shore. She didn't get off the board until her dragging feet touched the sandy bottom and she was knee-deep in water. She saw he was winded but pleased with himself and they made arrangements for dinner because he had saved her life.

Later she sat in front of a big window looking onto Bondi Beach waiting for him. People were still surfing though it was dark but there was a moon and big lamps like those in ballparks. She drank her wine and waited and he didn't show up. How simply he had shown up before, and now, with comparatively few impediments, he did not make it at all.

She decided to call Trevor Barker upstairs and see if he felt like going to a play on the weekend. There was a new production at the Hall and she had tickets. And if the evening was still warm they could walk along the harbourfront afterwards. Maybe get invited on the cruise ship for a look.

BEVERLY

SUNLIGHT BOUNCED THROUGH the patio windows onto the high polish of Beverly's cherry-wood dining table. There was a white crocheted doily in the centre of the table. She placed the portable phone on her napkin. She was waiting for the phone to ring.

Helen French had made the doily — a high-school friend who specialized in christening gowns. Helen had sold christening gowns — it said on the tags that came with each purchase — to royalty in Germany and Malta. Colleen had worn one of Helen's gowns when Beverly had her christened at Corpus Christi, seventeen years before, by Father O'Brien. The backs of his pale, bony hands were covered in warts.

Beverly touched the cod with her fork and a flake fell away from the fillet. She'd put salsa on her plate in the kitchen, unable to stand jars on the table. She'd turned off the radio before sitting down, and the house became utterly silent. She braced against the silence the way a downhill skier might draw a breath before starting down a hill. She found silence both frightening and thrilling, and lately, more luxury than deprivation.

She'd picked up the phone once and checked the dial tone. The dial tone was loud. She hung up and put it down. Afraid she had not hung up properly she picked it up again and it was off and she turned it on. She turned it on to make sure the battery wasn't low. She turned it off and put it next to her plate. She was certain Colleen would phone. There had been a message three days before: Mom, I'm in some Louisiana backwater, heading for New Orleans, and I love you and I'm sorry for always letting you down.

She picked up her fork with the flake of cod but was transfixed by the garden. She had put out the sprinkler while the carrots were boiling. She watched as the water from the sprinkler lifted itself out of the shade of the maple tree, straight into the air, pattering the leaves for a moment before it began to topple over. The fan of spray stretched into the sunlight beyond the maple and became a semi-transparent, shimmering veil lowering itself gently over the grass and Beverly thought about how loving required a knack.

You had to have a knack for it, she thought. Without the knack it was exhausting. Love couldn't be forced. She had loved David. It was her greatest achievement, that effortless love, she thought, and the sprinkler raised its sun-flickered fan upward again, pattering loudly against the leaves of the maple like applause.

Colleen was an effort. She was an effort, but the love was definitive and instinctual and full of fear and need and the sprinkler tipped into the shade and stained the bark of the tree.

The grass had been mowed that afternoon while she was at work but it had not been raked. She could smell the wet, mowed grass from the open patio window. Closer to the glass she could see a swarm of gnats or mosquitoes or flies rising in a tornado of fuzzy chaos. The sun was setting, a red ball between the two bungalows that were behind her garden.

She'd had the thought falling asleep last night: a knack. She spoke the word out loud because it occurred to her that it might not be a word.

Knack, she said. But she was entirely unaware that she had spoken.

Colleen's christening had taken place on a Monday afternoon in late March. The snow had been creeping back off the sidewalks; crocuses pushing up through the wet earth like an army of bayonets on the banks of the Waterford River, ragged ice tumbling in the current. The streams spilling over the cliffs of the South Side Hills were still frozen, covering the rock like candle wax on the sides of a wine bottle.

The cod was poached. It was supposed to be poached in champagne but Beverly had used water. There was fresh parsley on her plate, and three wedges of lemon.

Beverly had worn a raw silk, bubblegum-pink miniskirt and matching jacket to the christening. She bought it at Bowring's and had paid a lot and was proud of her legs, but Father O'Brien made an unpleasant comment about the length.

That skirt is not an appropriate garment for a new mother, especially in the house of the Lord, he'd said.

He took off his heavy, black-rimmed glasses and screwed his eyes shut, and moved the smudged glasses in concentric circles outward, outward elucidating the pedantic, inevitable feelings of the church, the positions they held, how they must be firm, now more than ever, the churches in Latin America breaking away, the evils of birth control. Then he put his glasses back on, opened his eyes and blinked, as though he had been an unwilling vessel for the nasty message and he was just coming back to himself. He put a warty hand on Beverly's shoulder and pushed her into the dark coolness of the church.

The snug cap that went with the christening gown — Beverly's favourite part of the outfit — was covered in mother-of-pearl beads, the beads so tightly bunched that the cap was as hard as a helmet, and the gown's train was spread over the hardwood floor around Beverly's high heels. Madeleine and Marty were Colleen's godparents even though they were atheists. David stood beside Beverly, holding a bottle full of expressed breast milk. She had wanted Colleen christened because she believed in ceremony and in God. She believed welcoming a child into the world required enlisting the sacred — incense and prayers.

Beverly had packed a picnic of Kentucky Fried Chicken and potato salad and wine they were going to enjoy at Bowring Park with plastic utensils and paper cups, but the weather had changed while they were inside the church — lightning had cracked and there was a roll of thunder in the distance — and they ended up eating in the car while rain drilled the roof. They passed the bucket of chicken back and forth over the front seat, wiping the grease off their faces with paper napkins while the baby slept.

The rain rushed down the windshield and the duck pond was stirred up and brown. A swan lifted its impossibly large white wings against a sudden wind and was blown across the pond with such dramatic force that Beverly felt her milk spurt through her nipples in a great gush. The raw silk jacket was stained forever.

Three years ago, Beverly had run into Helen French in the bakery section of Dominion on Ropewalk Lane. Colleen had turned fourteen and Beverly was picking up a birthday cake.

She had been standing with her arms folded tightly over her chest, tapping her foot on the tiles while the girl behind the counter worked a squeeze bag of pink icing through a plastic nozzle. That morning someone had defaced Beverly's home with shaving cream.

Helen gave Beverly a light smack on the arm and Beverly had been startled by the touch. She had been frightened by the graffiti on her windows — but when she saw Helen she was overjoyed.

Helen, who had given birth to six children, and her husband had taken up with a woman from the mainland, and there had followed a commission from Saudi Arabia for a tablecloth. An Arabian prince of some sort wanted Helen's work throughout his palace. Helen had gone to the desert; there had been a picture of her in the *Telegram* waving from the back of a camel, wearing a safari hat. And here she was in Dominion, clutching a zucchini.

Hadn't Helen remarried? The young girl behind the cake counter was biting her bottom lip in concentration. Beverly saw her lift the plastic nozzle with a flourish when she had made the letter *n* in *Colleen*.

Helen said, My God, Beverly, I heard. I'm so sorry.

It had been unexpected, to have David's death mentioned like this, early on a Saturday morning in the supermarket. Beverly had picked up two lobsters for a special birthday dinner and she saw one of the lobsters in her cart tentatively raise a claw with its green elastic band, and lower it, as if exhausted. She had always left David the job of dropping the live, moving lobsters into boiling water. She'd felt a tingling through her scalp that might have been the start of tears.

The girl had placed the cake in a box and was taping the sides.

It doesn't get any easier, Beverly had said. She had admitted this to absolutely no one before and she covered her mouth with her hand. Grief was on the outer rim of human experience. She had been on that rim for too long and now they had sprayed her house with shaving cream. Someone was threatening her daughter, she was sure that's what the graffiti was about. They were threatening a fourteen-year-old girl who had lost her father. A threat or an insult devised to make Colleen unsure of herself. The girl behind the counter was writing the price of the cake on the box with a Magic Marker — she held the cap in her teeth — Beverly had felt such an overwhelming feeling of gratitude, that Helen had understood, had made her say in the middle of the supermarket that yes it was hard, it was hard — she was so brimming with gratitude that she had ended up ordering seven custom-made doilies for every available surface in her new home.

Helen, I must have them, she'd said.

There was steam rising from the cod. Colleen will phone from an outdoor booth. Beverly knows this suddenly and unequivocally. Some gas station — she's probably hitchhiking — on the side of an eight-lane highway. Rural Louisiana, her last message said.

The flake of the cod was quivering on the tines of her fork. There was a wine-coloured vein, thin as a strand of hair, visible in the translucent fish. Beverly had been dieting for six months. She had given up alcohol and sugar. She had given up butter on her toast. The diet meant she was hungry all the time.

The fish wasn't cooked. It should have been whiter. The phone will ring as soon as she puts the fish in her mouth.

Colleen is walking across the parking lot toward a bank of phone booths, Beverly can see her plainly. The phone booth will be hot from the sun and smell of cigarette smoke and a faint tinge of urine or spilled beer. Colleen's skirt will bell with the warm Louisiana breeze.

Beverly had left the house early on Colleen's fourteenth birthday to pick up the cake. The cake would be a surprise. She'd started the car before she saw. Then she saw. The front of the house was still in the shade. She turned off the car and got out and shut the car door as quietly as she could. Each of the four panes of glass in the bay window had a letter sprayed on it spelling *slut*. S-L-U-T. White globs had dropped into her rhododendron bush and had scattered across the lawn.

She trotted through the gap in the hedge. She felt a great urgency. She had to get the word off the window before Colleen woke up. She didn't want Colleen to know. She would protect her from this; it was important that she never have to face this kind of wickedness. Beverly thought of it as a wicked act. The dew on the grass made her stockings wet. One of her spiked heels wiggled beneath her. Beverly pressed against the rhododendron bush, stepping into the cedar chips at the base of the old tree, and reached in to scrape at the letter *S*. Half the letter came away in her hand. The shaving cream had developed an outer crust in the cool night air, but was spongy beneath the crust and when she squished it between her fingers the smell was sharply chemical and flowery. She leaned in toward the window, which was black in the shade of the eave, and saw the shaving cream had left a hard transparent line like the trail left on a sidewalk by a snail. She scratched at the trail with her fingernail and it broke up like peeling skin in a glittery brittle crust. She leaned in to wipe away what remained of the *S* and nearly screamed with fright. There on the other side of the glass was Colleen. She had got out of bed and come to the window. Their faces were so close they might have kissed.

She picked up the portable phone and gave it a little shake. She put it back down on the napkin and ate the fillet of fish in three fast mouthfuls, hardly chewing.

LOYOLA

You live here by yourself? Colleen asked. He was cooking crawdads for her because she'd never had them before. A giant pot boiling on the stove and big piles of steam floating into the light over the fridge. He had put out candles.

She'd come up the walk at the end of the day and paused to read the *Closed* sign that hung on a string. She cupped her hands around her eyes and put her forehead to the screen and she saw him sitting behind the counter.

The sunlight was behind her and it shot through the screen door, under her arms and in her hair. She had on a skirt and the sun came through it and he saw the outline of her legs, which were long and shapely. She paused and read the sign and she came in anyway. The door slammed behind her and there was something familiar.

He knew this kind of girl, he'd grown up in the swamps, spent his life around alligators and tourists. He was prepared for a vast range of behaviour.

I keep my own company, he said. He shook the crawdads out into a bowl and put them down on the table.

His wife had left eight months after the accident. She had

nursed him through the roughest part. He'd got an infection and it made him delirious and he became violent and babyish by turns for a week and his wife was told to prepare for the worst.

But on the seventh day the fever broke and he began to get better, although he never fully recovered.

His wife had said he wasn't the man she'd married.

You're not the same man, Loyola, she said.

She had heaved her suitcase into the back of her Chevy Impala, a car that had once been baby blue but had become so sun-faded it was almost colourless except for the rust, like scabs on the fenders.

The girl had her hands in the back pockets of her skirt and she was looking at the framed pictures on the wall. She was looking at the picture of him with his arm around President Bush, standing near the airboat. He had taken the president on a tour of the reserve and he liked the man and he found himself agreeing with his decisions in Iraq. Since the accident he sometimes had fits and they left him anxious and he had developed a second sight.

He had seen the girl coming down the path moments before she appeared. He had been totting up figures and he felt her presence and could even intuit the colour of her hair and that she wore a blouse of Indian cotton with two glass beads hanging on red threads near the neck.

Do you get lonely? the girl asked.

You're full of questions, he said.

His wife's car had been blotched with swampy shadow, the sun already warm. The slam of her door was a damp slam. The engine sounded phlegmy when she started it up, the back tires sent up a splash of mud and the car was stuck. Then she turned off the car and sat unmoving, looking out the side window, thinking hard.

She sat like that and the blue heron that lives in the swamp flew over her and it was bluer than usual, a feral blue, and even at a moment like that the beauty of the bird confused him, knocked him off-course.

His wife got out of the car and her heels sank in the mud, which was funny but also part of the reason she was leaving or the whole reason. Her heels sank in the mud and she just turned around and got back in the car and this time black smoke came from the spinning tires and you could smell the rubber but something caught and the car flew backwards and she drove off backwards the whole length of the driveway and then she jerked the car around and was gone.

Kindness is the last thing to leave, he said. He put the bowls of melted butter on the table and a pot of boiled potatoes. He had some asparagus that he almost forgot.

Just dip them there crawdads in that there butter, he said. I don't touch them myself.

Kindness shakes hands with disappointment at the door and they squeeze past each other, he thought. But kindness goes out like a match. Once it's gone, it's gone.

There was something about Colleen reminded him of his ex-wife. She reminded him of the Impala and his wife's guitar and the oily black coffee beans she preferred. The girl looked lit-up the way his wife had looked lit-up.

You got an appetite, girl, he said. He had given up eating and was just watching her. She dipped the crawdads in the butter and sucked the meat out and tossed the shells. She had butter on her chin and a thumbprint of butter on her cheek that showed up in the candlelight when she bent forward for her beer. He didn't know if she was old enough to drink and he didn't care.

This is the way it was with his wife: she was always funny

and sexual. She was always in those jeans and she could cook and he liked to watch her shop. She haggled: bruised bananas, a dented toaster, she could work shopkeepers down and they ended up feeling flattered by the attention.

Sometimes when he was in the swamp collecting eggs she would spend the afternoon practising the guitar. She had taught herself classical, though what she sang in the bars was the raunchy twang of her childhood. By the time the stars were out he would come upon the trailer and the music would be dark and rolling and when he got inside she was distracted and hardly herself and he liked her that way.

I saw your wedding picture, Colleen said. He had forgotten about the wedding picture. He hadn't looked at it in months, years, maybe. They'd been married by a cross-dressing Queen Elizabeth impersonator in Las Vegas and he felt that might have cursed them. They'd been brash and inattentive to the mystical in the occasion, he felt.

He wished he could be that way again.

His wife had told Queen Elizabeth she revered her new husband, and the word struck him as biblical.

He had begun putting his head between the jaws of alligators when he was eighteen. He knew the animals. He knew exactly how slow and fast they were. He knew how cold they were, and what their breath smelled like.

Queen Elizabeth had touched them both on their shoulders with her sceptre and tossed confetti. They weren't thinking permanence because they were too young to imagine it.

They were thinking it but they had no idea what it meant.

What it meant was the trailer he had on the edge of the swamp and the house he'd built by hand and 112 alligators and the guy he kept on for the tours, the skins they sold and the freezer full of meat.

It had eventually meant he had nearly been mangled to death by one of the animals. He shot it afterwards, when he got out of the hospital, and had it skinned and hung the skin over the fireplace and his wife continued to sing in bars.

The girl got up from the table and he asked her to come closer and he wiped the butter off her cheek with his napkin.

He had touched her without a thought and their eyes met and he pushed back his chair with embarrassment, which he tried to cover up by taking his plate to the sink but the incident shook him a little and he smashed a glass and she got the broom, all of a sudden full of industry and questions about the housekeeping.

We were just kids, he said, because he saw the girl was standing in front of the wedding picture again. She was rubbing it gently with the cuff of her shirt.

She had the Impala and she began to get a following in the bars. She was writing her own material and people took notice.

He should have known that marriage vows were sacred and should have stayed away from the Queen Elizabeth impersonator.

He should have known the event required decorum. If he had respected the inherent power of the ritual it might have stuck.

They were just nineteen and eighteen, not even pregnant.

But maybe even the guy with the Queen Elizabeth dress and the crown and the giant corseted gut could not sully the event of their marriage.

Maybe it hadn't been sullied at all. Perhaps they had been at their purest then. They were too young for sacred.

He saw in this girl, Colleen, a similar kind of sadness; the same dark thing his wife had.

Do you always wear your cowboy hat at the table? she said.

She had taken a swig of her beer and wiped her mouth with the back of her hand. He removed the hat and laid it on the table between them.

It was as though all the ugliness in the world affected these women, he thought. They had no way to turn it off. They felt everything. They wanted to save everything. That was it; they wanted to save everything.

The alligator farm was dense with green light and the smell was virile, like sex itself, but he was alone. He had made a miscalculation with that alligator. Or maybe that one animal was a rogue, or it was as simple as the drop of sweat that had done him in.

Eight months in hospital and he was not the same afterwards.

There had been infection in the brain and he had trouble with simple things for a long while afterwards. He couldn't tell the time. His vision was blurred. The fits started.

The sacred had busted out of them; it had a kind of deafness, it spilled in his inner ear and made the room tilt.

The sight of the Impala bouncing backwards over the rutted road: it could not be repeated, or contained, or understood. It was an altar and a wordless story because he'd never really spoken of it. He lost his purchase when his wife left.

He became sensitive about his appearance. And he forgot he had an appearance. The leather cowboy hat was an example. How he had come to a place in his life where he would wear such a thing was a mystery. The events that had led him into a souvenir shop in Mobile and drew him to the rack of hats were absolutely lost to him. But the crown had darkened with oil from his scalp and he was never without the hat. He remembered standing in a shopping mall confronted by a bin of white underwear and coming to understand the absurdity of the bin and the underwear and of being unattached.

He lifted weights in the evening listening to Bjork or Lucinda Williams or Thelonious Monk. He attended to the reservation and the alligators and the tourists.

What he did: he attached himself to an idea. The idea was to make money. He had no need for money other than the action of making it. There is in the making of money a propelling forward. Energy is exerted and boardrooms come into being. They form themselves seconds before you open the door and there they are when you open the door and if they are in Houston the walls are glass and there are seven or eight men in suits and a blast of sun that eradicates history.

Money moves by instinct, he'd found. It will lie still and then it will move. He found he could keep in his head the trajectories of futures as easily as he could make his breakfast in the morning.

His sister called from the hospital in Houston when she was delivering her second child, moaning through the call, telling him again and again how much it hurt and how much she loved him and would he come for a visit and he sat in the house by himself with the phone to his ear and tears streaming down his face and nodding his head silently. But he found he did not like to leave the reserve. He had the tourists to deal with and the alligators and premonitions about investments and that was enough.

His sister called one day to say she'd heard Meg, his ex-wife, was singing in Nashville. For several weeks he slept with a waitress who worked in a bar sixty miles away. But after a while he couldn't bring himself to drive that far every weekend.

The girl who showed up was from Canada and she had hitchhiked from the airport, or maybe stolen some money and he let her have the trailer. He had met her aunt, the girl said. A woman from Newfoundland, she'd said, but he couldn't remember ever meeting anyone from Newfoundland before and the girl had left it at that.

Might as well let her sleep in the trailer, he thought. She was young and she reminded him of when he and Meg got married and he thought he might tell her about the Queen Elizabeth impersonator.

She wanted to see the reserve.

After supper, he kicked open the door of the trailer and light came through the lime green curtains that were sun-faded and she looked green in the light. He had an airboat and he said he would take her out in the morning when he had to collect eggs, before the regular tours started. Then, if she wouldn't mind, he'd like to give her some money and get her on a plane and send her home.

It didn't seem right to him, a girl her age, wandering around when her mother didn't know where she was. He showed her the phone and he told her he would be much obliged if she'd call her mother that night and never mind about the charges.

He explained about the ecological reserve and how he was putting the babies back in the swamp.

She asked if they were dangerous and she immediately burned bright red because of his face.

He said he'd seen them swallow a few dogs, and an old woman in Florida with a lawn mower had been attacked. But people felt it was the lawn mower that agitated the gator and if she hadn't gone near it with the noise the attack wouldn't have happened.

He said, If you keep your head out of their jaws you do pretty well.

They like marshmallows, he said.

MADELEINE

When she thinks of her childhood home she thinks of Beverly playing piano for all she's worth. Madeleine watching the snow through the window on the landing; she was almost a teenager. The window was beaded with water droplets, and beyond, lazy, fat snowflakes fell and lifted in the wind. A Sunday-evening dimness crept from all the corners of the house, mingling with the smell of boiling cabbage and the pies. Partridge berries. In the Sunday late afternoons of her childhood she liked to sit on the landing of the stairs and hear everyone moving through the house. She just sat on the worn Persian runner and listened to Beverly play.

Mrs. McCarthy, the housekeeper, had skinned the rabbits on the kitchen counter. Her knuckles whitening as she ripped the fur from flesh. The purplish flesh wrapped over tiny bones lined with skeins of yellow fat. Five rabbits in the sink, cold water splashing over them.

The cleaver came down and a paw fell off the cutting board. Madeleine put it in the pocket of her dress.

Mrs. McCarthy smoothed her chapped, red hands over her apron and lifted the kettle off the stove. A comb hung by a strand of wrinkled hair from her loose braid, her face was mottled.

That Sunday they'd gone to the Basilica for five o'clock mass, Father Dunphy raised the Eucharist. Something flew from one perch to another in the rafters. Christ's red glass robes lit up with sunlight, the white of his downcast eye, his hand, the blood. The choir sang, Mrs. Hill's high-pitched trill above everyone else. Mrs. Hill had arranged the turkey tea, two hundred paper plates with tiny pieces of fruit cocktail in green jelly and the beet-coloured scoops of potato, dry turkey, and a pearly grey slice of processed ham rolled around a raw carrot stick.

In the dark living room, Beverly digs notes out of the piano, playing it as hard as she can. The low notes send a vibration through the wooden spindles of the stair rail. A flood of light hits the glass, a passing car, and each drop gets full of burning white. The shimmer leaps from drop to drop. Beverly hits a discordant note but she recovers; she's a skater racing across the pond and the tip of her skate hooks, her heart, her red mitts — what was it? Mozart? — but she regains her balance and she sails on, the last few notes like the sweep of the headlights illuminating all, catching, lastly, the cut-crystal decanter on the side table, busting it open so bits of light zoom over the walls, the piano, Beverly's back, the portrait of their grandfather in the convex frame, his eyes, and the coat of dust. A pot cover drops in the kitchen.

Beverly stops playing. The piano bench creaks. There are forbidden chocolates in an enamel bowl and Madeleine can see Beverly reach for a chocolate. Madeleine is startled by the audacity. The chocolate melts in Beverly's mouth. Then tires crunch on the gravel. Beverly tentatively touches the keys, the music is more viscous, the cherry centre and the sour liqueur, dark chocolate.

A man has come to the door, snow whirls in around his pant legs and there is Madeleine's mother, her hand on the door and the smell of fresh snow, the frigid air, the wind crashing through the branches outside. This is the end of Madeleine's childhood. She holds the spindle of the stair rail, from here she will lose faith, she will go hungry, she will be fuelled by anger and sex and a desire to make every moment tangible; she isn't thinking about making films, of course, she has never heard of making films, she's not quite a teenager, this is St. John's — the light passing through each raindrop on the window in the stairwell — but she decides she will make films.

It is decided, whoever decides.

Madeleine watches the man speak to her mother, the brim of his hat, and her mother's shoulders crumple. She hugs herself and her shoulders quake with little shudders. Their father has finally died.

Madeleine has been making films ever since. She has made industrial films to support documentaries with radical political slants. She has made television cooking shows and political campaign ads. She has made films in India and Africa and Australia. She has made films about the Yanomami and the Inuit and the Andaman Islanders and the more obscure members of the royal family.

The film she is making now will be better than any film ever made by anyone. Better than Bergman. This film will contain everything. It will contain everything. It will contain everything.

COLLEEN

I CHECKED THE sheets and they were clean, but there was a musty smell. The door was rickety but there was a lock. There was a single toothbrush in the holder over the sink and it was stiff and crusted with toothpaste. I smelled it and it smelled like toothpaste. I ran my thumb over the bristles and the toothpaste came off in a little cloud of powder. I opened the medicine cabinet and there was a tube of toothpaste and dental floss and a bottle of Aspirin.

I heard him go back along the path and I heard the screen door.

I brushed my teeth and I put the cap back on the toothpaste and put it back on the shelf and closed the door to the medicine cabinet. I stood there looking at myself in the mirror.

If you look at yourself for a long time without blinking your face starts to change shape. I looked at myself that way and I felt afraid of the ride through the swamp tomorrow and I blinked hard. Then I just looked at myself and something black and fast ran from my nose to my lips and it was blood.

I tried tilting my head back but then I could taste it.

After a while the nosebleed stopped and I lay awake for a long time and the sounds of the swamp didn't frighten me as much but I was wide awake.

His face was shredded and flaps of skin overlapped other flaps and there was a loose web of lines all over his face and head. He was almost bald and I saw where the teeth had punctured his skull. His hands had a constant shake, he nearly spilled his beer. At supper there was a moment, maybe thirty seconds, when he stared into space and didn't seem to hear me.

He has a compound for the alligators, and there are bridges all through it where the tourists can walk for five bucks and the whole compound is surrounded by a chain link fence and there are more than a hundred animals.

At first you don't see them and then you see them. You see them on the bank and just a strip of their backs breaking the water and they look like floating logs in the green algae. The algae are luminous and there's a dank smell and they don't move at all but when they move they're fast. They flick their tails and they are like monsters.

I knelt down near the fence and looked into the eye of a giant alligator that was very near the fence. The alligator did not move and did not move. I saw myself kneeling in its eye and I was tiny and fragile-looking in a long velvet tunnel and I wasn't ever coming back from there. Then the animal turned and waddled over the hard-packed, cracked mud and algae. Its tail swung with lazy muscular swishes. Then it sank into the water and glided out of sight. He told me to get my fingers off the fence.

FRANK

FOUR BOYS ON skateboards appeared to float momentarily on the crest of a hill on Gower Street and then gathered speed.

Their arms hung by their sides, they wore baggy jeans and bright polyester hockey shirts. They came down the hill accompanied by a growing rumble and just before they smacked into an oncoming refrigerated truck advertising meat, all four jumped and the skateboards leapt from beneath their feet into their hands and it was exactly as though they had never been on them.

They waited on the curb for a break in the traffic, then strolled across the street and one called after Frank. There were quick pulses of lightning followed by a distant crack.

On the other side of the street the boys dropped the skateboards with a clatter and stepped onto them again. Their bodies dipped and rose three times as they kicked themselves up to speed, then they followed each other in lazy, swerving paths around the corner of Prescott Street and out of sight.

Kevin Nolan was leaning on a door frame sucking hard on a cigarette. Frank realized with a peculiar clarity, heightened, it seemed, by the smell of ozone, that he would ask

Kevin for the money he needed and that Kevin would give it to him.

It meant he would have to endure Kevin's company for perhaps an hour, then outright ask for the money, and it meant the end of the fragile, important friendship the two young men had nursed since they were five.

Come in and have a cup of tea, Frank, Kevin said.

There was a narrow hallway that led to a cramped kitchen smelling faintly of mould. Kevin took out a frying pan, looked at it closely, and then tapped it twice against the counter dislodging a shower of mouse shit onto a waiting piece of newspaper. He put the pan under a running faucet and wiped it carefully with the bottom of his T-shirt. He tipped it into the light until he was satisfied the pan was clean.

He waved the pan toward a kitchen chair and Frank sat down. There were several marijuana plants hanging from the ceiling in macramé holders, and more on a table by a window that looked out onto a small backyard. Kevin's T-shirt had a picture of a skeleton holding a beer can in the bones of his hand.

I'm doing small machine repair up to the technical college, Kevin said. There's nothing I don't know about photocopiers.

It was Kevin who had got Frank the part-time job at the photocopy place.

He dumped a half-bag of frozen fries into a saucepan on the back burner. The saucepan roared up, spitting boiling fat.

Kevin took a step back and then reached over the stove holding his shirt close to his stomach to hit a button on the fan. He had the waxy complexion of an insomniac, an open cold sore on his upper lip, and the dark eye sockets of a heavy pot smoker.

A rapacious vitality kept some part of his body always tapping, he made weird noises, softly whispered expulsions of air that mimicked machine-gun bursts or the feedback of amplifiers, kapow kapow kapow kapow, yeah, uh huh, yeah, va-voom, all the while slapping his thigh with both hands and Frank felt sorry he had come inside.

Kevin was thoroughly unlovable with his Adam's apple raw from a recent shave, the home-done tattoo of a skull peeking out from behind a torn heart, and, most painful to witness, his baldly searching look. He sold hash but was discreet with his money and might have become an IT specialist — he had a vicious intelligence and was intuitive with computers — except for bouts of depression that kept him on a couch for months at a time.

Frank thought of the first day they had both gone to daycare together with Mrs. Hallett, the foster mother they had shared for six months when they were five. Frank's mother was in hospital having her breasts removed and Kevin's mother had left him standing under a tree during the St. John's regatta. She said she would be right back but it took a month.

When Frank got inside the daycare he could smell chicken noodle soup. The lukewarm, piss-coloured, salty broth in bright plastic bowls dimpled with globules of oil and sinking noodles engulfed him in despair.

Three weeks before meeting Kevin, he'd glimpsed the gauze taped to his mother's weirdly boyish chest. He'd watched the doctor lift the gauze, look beneath, and touch whatever was under the bandage with his gloved index finger. He gingerly taped the gauze back down and it was the extreme gentleness his mother required that spread the same fear through Frank that had caused him to wet his bed for months after that first operation.

Mrs. Hallett, Frank's foster mother, was a heavy woman with thick curly black and grey hair that tumbled around her wide red face and onto her shoulders. Her cheeks, close up, were covered with a minute network of capillaries, broken from laughter and exertion in her extensive garden. Her eyes were a light brown, fringed with black lashes, and she had a space between her front teeth.

She was always grinning, glowing with excitement, unless she was lost in thought, bent on her knees in the bathroom checking the temperature of the water for the boys' baths. She would grunt, absorbed by some inner argument, and push herself up with the knuckles of one hand down on the floor. He can see her pressing down the pastry cutter, too, a tan-coloured bowl tucked into her hip.

She was a nurse and kept her house perfectly clean and made them eat a piece of fruit each night. Frank's mother had only ever bought McIntosh apples, with the white flesh, barely tinted green.

Mrs. Hallett bought kiwis and mangoes and pomegranates. Frank felt sorry for his mother, that she didn't know about the diversity of fruit, that her five-year-old son knew more than she did.

The aroma of chicken noodle soup was more than Frank could bear that first visit to daycare, he dug his face into Mrs. Hallett's thigh and whispered he wanted to go home and she peeled his hands off her and he slapped them back on, clinging to her skirt. She told him she had to go to work, that he was a big boy and she would buy him an ice cream and they would visit his mother.

She left and he threw up. He could remember Kevin looking on solemnly as Frank covered both their shoes with half-digested Cheerios and watery milk. Kevin patting his shoulder as he trembled and shook with dry heaves and eventually Kevin was hugging him, and promising him full ownership of a remote-control airplane, the only toy Kevin had brought with him to the foster home.

Kevin himself had spent the evening of the regatta at the police station and when nobody could be found to come and get him he was sent to the Janeway Children's Hospital and didn't see his mother again for a month, by which time Social Services had decided she was unfit to raise him.

After that, she and Kevin met every second weekend, usually at McDonald's, and in the presence of a social worker. Kevin played in a glass room full of climbing tunnels and coloured balls while his mother and the social worker read the newspaper on the stools outside the window. Sometimes his mother came into the room and yelled up through the tubing for Kevin to behave himself, or to leave the little girls alone, though he was always scrupulously polite and fair with other children, or to come down and finish his milk.

Mrs. Hallett kept Kevin until he was sixteen, visited him every weekend when he moved out. She still took Kevin's laundry and brought him homemade suppers in Tupperware containers, and slipped twenty-dollar bills in greeting cards on every possible occasion.

Blue smoke bulged out from the lip of the saucepan with the boiling fat and curled up and then rose obediently in a straight column to the fan.

Frank took off his baseball cap, put it on his knee, and tried to calculate when he could leave without being rude. He wanted to leave. He didn't want Kevin's money. He would leave without the money.

Kevin slapped margarine into the frying pan and put the burner on high. He opened the fridge and Frank saw it was empty and brilliant white except for a bottle of mustard pickles and a package wrapped in butcher's paper. Kevin tossed the package onto the counter. Frank could smell the margarine turn brown.

Photocopiers I'm specialized in, Kevin said. Mostly it's the carbon tray empty when there's a problem. Utensils hit the back of the drawers noisily as he slammed them with his hip.

My ex-girlfriend laughed at me buying this pan. This is Teflon and you can't use metal or nothing like that on it. And where is the Jesus spatula, Frank, I wish I knew. My girlfriend said when she saw the pan you'll have that all scratched up before the week is out. You'll never own anything worth anything is what she said. I don't know how many times she said that. I'd like to see someone try to point out a scratch on this pan though, Frank.

It looks to be working pretty good there now, Kevin, Frank said.

Kevin turned from the stove and looked out the window. He had a garden, Frank saw, with a little patio and two chairs and a rusted wrought-iron table with a glass top. The garden darkened and a wind showed the grey side of the whispering aspen's leaves and let them flop back washed green and lifted them again.

The rain came down hard, drilling the metal garbage tin, rising up like white fur from the slabs of concrete that made up the patio, spiking off the arm of the plastic lawn chair. Kevin unwrapped the bologna and, peeling off the wax rind, dropped each slice in the sizzling margarine.

Frank saw there was no way he could leave while the rain was heavy and before the fries and bologna were done and decided to take the money.

He needed the money; he would take it.

He felt angry with Kevin for making the money mean so much; for having enough of it to lend in the first place.

I hear your mother died, Frank, Kevin said.

I still have her ashes, Frank said. He couldn't think what had made him admit such a thing.

The fries are done perfect, Kevin said, ladling them out of the fat with a slotted spoon. He put a salt shaker and the ketchup on the table. Then he got the pickles out of the fridge. He put a plate in front of Frank, piled with french fries and a piece of bologna, and Frank began to eat.

My girlfriend left there the spring, Kevin said. He cut the slabs of bologna with the side of his fork, slapping both sides of it in the ketchup and folding it into his mouth. He stabbed the fries until the fork tines were jammed and he ate the plateful in less than three minutes. Tipping his chair onto its back legs he dropped his plate into the sink behind him.

I need a thousand dollars, Frank said.

KEVIN

Kevin lowered his chair to the floor and he ran both his hands up and down his thighs. He stood and pulled a thick wallet from his back pocket. The wallet was attached to his jeans with a retractable cord that he tugged on and then drew out several bills and put them on the table beside Frank. He put the wallet back in his pocket and Frank heard the cord slither into place.

Kevin sat down again and tore a piece of paper towel off the roll in the middle of the table and wiped his mouth. He folded the paper towel and rubbed each corner of his mouth carefully and folded it again, and just patted his lips gently with it and stared forward, out the window.

When they told my mother she wasn't fit, my mother smirked. It was a smirk, Frank, Kevin said.

He put the folded paper towel under the bottom of the ketchup bottle. He was thinking of an afternoon when he and his mother were walking up from downtown and a parade passed by them. Cadets coming down Long's Hill. First the older men, looking straight ahead, their lower lips firm with the grim promise never to look anywhere but straight ahead, because everything depended on that. They had agreed to look straight ahead and they could be true to their word.

They wore black pants with a red stripe down the leg and jackets with brass buttons and the man in front wore a high black fur hat. He gripped a sceptre near his chest and the silver knob at its tip caught the sun and glowed like an incandescent light bulb. Above, on the hill by the Kirk, a bagpipe player in a kilt stepped onto the ridge from amid a patch of alders and began to play.

The music swelled out and carried down the hill toward the harbour and vibrated in Kevin's chest. There were some women who wore their hair in tight buns below their folded caps and they looked ahead too, just like the men. Then came younger cadets, their blue nylon uniforms whispering loudly as they marched past and he watched them go all the way down Long's Hill, their hands swinging together, sunlight on the polished shoes and his mother swept him up in her arms and kissed his face all over. She kissed him so much he lost his breath.

She wrestled him onto the sidewalk and put a knee on his chest. She was laughing and saying, Who's my boy, who's my boy, who's my boy, tickling him until he was overheated and shaking with laughter.

The sun dropped spears of light through the maple trees that leaned out over Long's Hill, as the wind ruffled the leaves. He needed her to stop, he could not breathe, and when she did stop she was flushed. Her smile was big and her eyes were pale blue and the blue patches of sky through the leaves above her head were painfully bright.

Then she gripped his head, her hands over his ears, and she looked into his eyes with an intensity that had nothing to do with laughter.

It was a kind of intensity that had to do with the horror of her addiction and her struggle against it. He could see a vein in her temple pulsing, her breath smelled of cinnamon gum, her sweater was a pale pink angora and her jeans were acid wash and she wore lip gloss that smelled like watermelon. No one will ever convince him that she did not love him, that she had not always loved him. He was pressed under her knee on the sidewalk, the wind nearly knocked out of him, because she was afraid of losing him.

From this experience he learned that authentic love is capable of disappointing you. This disappointment can be paralyzing, but it does not diminish the quality of authentic love. Watch out, if you stand in the path of that kind of love, he thinks. It can leave you blazing and numb. It may not be worth it. But it is worth it.

As soon as the money was produced Frank had burned a dark red. He sat inert before his plate. It seemed to Kevin as if Frank saw no way to avoid putting the money in his pocket but neither could he bring himself to do it.

They had each felt a binding loneliness as children that they had no words for, nor would they have wanted to articulate it, if they could, because it was shameful and something they would struggle to avoid acknowledging for the rest of their lives. But each boy had felt the presence of this absence in the other and felt a reciprocal and grim admiration because they had both more or less withstood its gravitational pull.

Kevin stood up, got himself a spoon, and took a tub of ice cream from the freezer. He ate directly from the tub and then saw a smear of blood on the spoonful of vanilla ice cream he was about to put in his mouth. It was blood from his cold sore and it turned him and he swore softly and gave the ice-cream tub a toss into the garbage.

He cleaned the spoon off, opened the back door, and the sound of the rain and a fresh briny ocean smell filled the kitchen. Kevin began to sing a scat with hisses and machine-gun putt-putts and the grindings of a photocopier. Then he threw the spoon he had been tapping against the door frame into the sink and said, Fuck it, Frank, it's only money. It doesn't have to ruin our friendship, such as it is.

Kevin thought of the backyard at Mrs. Hallett's, the heavy plastic jungle gym with wooden beams, knotted ropes, and a rubber tire that filled with rain. The grass, early Saturday mornings, was covered in dew that was greyish silver, almost frost, and full of sparkle where the sun struck.

When he and Frank wandered the rolling lawns they left two green trails of footprints in the fogged-over grass. From the garden they could see the patio window behind which Mrs. Hallett was ironing blouses, or one of her pale uniforms.

Because they knew she was just beyond the dark glass, they could forget her and be absorbed by a trail of ants sometimes carrying a dead ant out of the path of the others. They watched the sun light up beads of dew on a spider's web that jiggled violently with a breeze. They watched wasps crawl from their papery nests and hover and pitch and crawl back in. These miniature garden dramas absorbed the boys so thoroughly they became, for that brief time in their childhood, almost as one.

It was a wordless union based entirely on mutual wonder in a big garden. Frank took the money off the table and put it in his breast pocket and buttoned the flap.

Good luck with the small machine repair, Kevin, he said. He was ready to leave and Kevin wanted him to go now, but he stood still.

FRANK

DID FRANK THINK? Yes, he did. He was exceptionally lucid. He was in the centre of a ball of fire. The air was jellied. He couldn't get air into his lungs. He had been locked in a house and the house had exploded into flame and his clothes were on fire and his hair and his face. He had woken up in a blazing room with no memory of passing out.

His windpipe was scorched and his lungs were scorched and the blood that rushed through his veins and capillaries toward his lungs, desperate for oxygen, was hot. His arms were bubbling; he saw rather than felt the blisters coming up. But all he knew was he could not breathe.

He thought of the door and where it was in relation to the centre of the room. Glass crashed; the mirror over the fireplace splintered and then fell from the wall in jagged pieces. The flames were swaying around his knees like a field of long grass and the heat climbed each piece of furniture and gave the piano a liquid glaze. The piano top was a rippling lake and the heat twisted around Frank like bedsheets, and he kicked out of the sheets of flame and got to the door and when he touched the doorknob it was already too hot to touch. He lifted his shirt over his mouth and nose. Time was not behaving, he knew. He was in the room for no more than a minute. Five minutes? But the minutes had melted and warped. Time, without oxygen, collapsed. It couldn't have been more than a minute.

He threw his shoulder against the door but the door didn't budge. There was one way out and it was this door and the door was not opening. A massive blast of tumbling heat tore through the living room to funnel up the staircase and on the way it smacked against Frank nearly knocking him down and it transformed upon touch into more flame and it licked him all over his back and ran up his spine and shoulders, and it had grabbed his scalp, tugging viciously at his hair. He could feel a blister form on one eyelid. His eye was closing over. He couldn't keep it open. He wiped at the blister with his fingernails and it broke and the water ran into his eye. He was gasping, there was nothing in his lungs.

He stumbled back into the centre of the room and he saw the goldfish in the bowl flicking madly back and forth. He understood perfectly that Valentin had jammed something against the door.

He'd had a shot of vodka in Valentin's apartment but what followed was out of all proportion to a shot of vodka. What followed was a weak-limbed euphoria, an easing up of gravity and everything grave. Frank hadn't had a good rest since his mother died. Whatever had been in the vodka, it was odourless and colourless and extremely potent. It made him feel rested.

He knew Valentin had dropped a match; that much he knew. Everything that had come before, his mother's death, the evenings at the hot-dog stand, the way Colleen had clamped her body against his, all the rain that had fallen over the summer, the money, the hunger for it, the need, the compelling need to accumulate money, the stark ugliness of his bed-sit, and the infestation of worms, all of this had been forgotten, briefly, gently, thoroughly forgotten when he drank from the shot glass Valentin had given him.

Valentin had put the glass down in front of Frank and he had a shot glass for himself and the glasses were small and printed with Christmas trees. The glasses matched, Frank had noticed. Valentin had pulled out the chair opposite Frank's and he sat with his elbows on the table, hunched over, and watched Frank drink. He was intent and patient. Valentin's brown eyes had a beer-bottle colour, amber flecks.

How are you, my friend? Valentin said.

They had gone down the stairs and got into Valentin's truck and then they wandered into the house on Morris Avenue where the furniture needed to be moved.

He was supposed to be helping Valentin move furniture.

But here he was, standing in the centre of the fire and he reflected on the nature and texture of his exhaustion, which he knew to be physical and having as much to do with the vacuum created by the fire, the loss of oxygen, as with his spiritual fatigue. Spiritual fatigue was a term his dance teacher, Dr. Callahan, used to use and it was a term Frank had forgotten completely but it came back to him in the fire on Morris Avenue and the phrase was so apt he nearly wept while the flames ran up the arms of his nylon jacket and made the material shrivel and burned runnels into his arms. He felt his forehead tighten because his eyebrows had sizzled off his face. He felt all his facial hair, even the bristles under his skin, burn away. Here's what happened: he woke, he threw himself out a window. But later the goldfish came back to him.

Being in the very centre of a fire is a religious experience, Frank thought. He had been told the house was empty, someone had moved, and there were household items for sale.

There was a stereo he could have, Valentin had said, for next to nothing.

The Russian had passed him on the stairs and said, Just come and have a look, my friend. I need help moving some furniture.

Frank had given him Kevin's money, right there on the stairs, without a word, and Valentin clapped him on the arm and told him it was very good. He held the money in his fist and shook his fist for emphasis and he said the money would be doubled in a few short days. But he still insisted Frank go with him to move furniture.

You could use some furniture, the Russian said. It was a reference, Frank knew, to his mother's ashes and the ruined waterbed.

They'd gone up the stairs to Valentin's bed-sit for a drink.

First we will drink together, Valentin had said. The Russian's bed-sit was tidy. There was a stuffed flamingo on the floor in the corner with long lime green legs; it must have been a prize from the regatta.

I have a young son, Valentin said, nodding toward the toy.

I'm sure he'll appreciate it, Frank said.

It was that or a teddy bear.

You went with the flamingo, Frank said. He downed the shot and it hit him like a pillow fight. He felt gently bashed and full of wonder.

An Inuit guy hanged himself in this room, Frank said.

There's a strong smell, Frank had said, when he walked into the house on Morris Avenue. He knew it was gasoline. He was putting it together as he spoke. If his body was found after the fire, the police would think he had started it. Just as he put it together he had passed out.

VALENTIN

He had the accelerator jammed to the floor and Frank had slumped against him. The boy's head had fallen onto Valentin's thigh and it was as heavy as a bowling ball. Valentin had dragged him over the grass to the cab of the truck with the boy's arm flung over his shoulder. When he gripped the boy's wrist he felt a blister burst under his hand. The water made his grip slippery. The boy was heavier than Valentin had expected and when he became semi-conscious his feet tripped all over themselves on the driveway.

Valentin had given the boy a larger dose of the drug than he thought was strictly necessary because he didn't want him to suffer. He had seen this drug work on women, had seen them sleep for almost a full day after they'd been given it. He couldn't understand what had roused the boy once his head had dropped onto his chest.

In the cab of the truck the boy's eyes were rolled back in his head and his eyeballs were bluish. The eyelids quivered but didn't close. The whites of the eyes stared up at the roof of the cab and Valentin was taking the corner on two wheels. Froth bubbled up from the corners of the boy's mouth; his breathing was ragged; his lips were moving as in prayer. The boy was reciting something to himself, something ancient and ordinary, full of rote spirituality. The wordless praying was interrupted by rough, weak coughs full of phlegm and it sounded like the boy's lungs were irrevocably damaged. Blisters had come up all over his face and neck. The truck stank of melted plastic and smoke and the boy's burns. His windbreaker had shrivelled in rough glittery scales, like the skin a snake leaves behind.

They had entered the house in the dark. The boy was stumbling and incoherent but he had noticed the piano as soon as they entered the living room. He had bent over to read the sheet music that lay open on the wooden ridge above the keys. It was too dark to read the sheet music but the boy continued to lean, his face close to the paper.

Valentin had said, We don't need the lights.

Frank stood that way, apparently reading in the dark, until he began to weave slightly, forward and back, and had to put his hand out to steady himself. He avoided falling face first into the piano by pressing three fingers against the lid, which was closed over the keys. A passing car sent headlights zooming over the walls and they hit the fishbowl on the lid of the piano and the goldfish flared a fierce, pulsing orange and quivered all over and the aqua-coloured stones on the bottom and the plastic palm tree were all full of surging brightness and then, just as quickly, fell into shadows. The fish lost its colour and sank slowly to the bottom of the bowl. The boy turned his back on the piano abruptly and swayed sideways like a punching clown and righted himself.

I need to sit down, he had said. He had spoken in a formal tone, and he had closed his eyes in the effort to enunciate the thought. Valentin took him by the shoulders and helped him to the chair in the centre of the room.

I need a rest, Frank said.

You are a good boy, Valentin had said.

I'm pretty tired.

Sit down in this nice chair.

He waited until the boy's head dropped. Frank was very still and then his head rolled back and his mouth hung open and he snorted deeply.

He would feel absolutely nothing. He would suffocate before he burned. He would never wake. Valentin waited before dropping the matches. He waited for an eternity, but the boy didn't move. The boy was out cold. He struck a match and lowered it carefully toward the carpet but the flame leapt up from the floor to greet the match.

The fire ran in ribbons from the match he dropped. It traced the invisible ropes of gasoline, it ran down the hallway and into the living room and kitchen and the flames looked like something that had always been there, but had been lying in wait. Valentin had splashed the walls as well and the flames traced the splashes that had sunk into the paint. Through the living-room window Valentin saw flames leap from one curtain to another curtain. They leapt up the stairs like weasels. He saw one of the upstairs windows go bright, then the next window, and finally the third window on the second floor.

Valentin was outside in the fresh air and shoved the stick he had chosen beneath the handle and he tried the door but it wouldn't open. He pulled hard on the doorknob and the stick dug itself deeper into the ground and the door didn't open.

Then he ran down the path and got in the truck. He was pulling out of the driveway when he saw the chair come through the window and the boy hurl himself onto the lawn. He saw this in the rear-view mirror and he leapt out of the truck and grabbed his shovel from the back.

The boy rose up from the lawn on his hands and knees and the flames stood up on his back like the fur of a hissing cat. The boy stood up with his arms held out from his body as though he were a conductor about to address a choir. The house held its breath. Then Frank flapped his arms wildly. He whipped his arms through the air and the house bellowed behind him with one long, sustained, sonorous boom.

The windows in the front of the house blew shards of glass all over the lawn and knocked the boy down. The fire reached as far as it could out the windows and then it flowed upward. It poured into the sky like a river falling in the wrong direction. Flames tumbled up and raced over the backs of other flames and flicked at the leaves of the trees that grew near the house.

And then the trees went up. The flames moved from tree to tree and the trees shrivelled up and crackled and spat sparks. All the worms hanging in the trees were lit up for the second it took them to turn to carbon.

The boy stood up again and turned around to see what had knocked him down. Valentin ran from the driveway into the wall of heat. The hairs on the backs of his hands curled and disappeared and it made the backs of his hands itch. He saw, through the front window, a yellow film of heat engulf the piano. He saw the sheet music curl and disappear. He thought of the possessed look Isobel wore while she played and the way she nodded at him to turn the page, how imperious and frantic her face had looked, how important it was to turn the page at exactly the right moment, how concentrated he had been in order to do her bidding, but the sheet music had disappeared the instant the flame touched it just like any other kind of paper. The armchair was a sunflower.

The boy was slapping the flames on his back, he was turning in fast circles and arching his spine and ducking and slapping at himself. There were tattered flames on both of his swinging arms and flames at his ankles and he was trying to twist out of them. He appeared to be wrestling himself to the lawn, finally knocking himself down and rolling. The fire covered him in a flimsy straitjacket the boy couldn't get out of.

Then he was out cold again. Valentin was dragging the boy to the truck before he knew what he was doing. Everything took time and was mired in the time it took.

He had taken the shovel out of the back of the truck. He would bring it down on the boy's head and throw him back in the fire where he belonged and put an end to this at once. He knew the shovel would never work but it would have to work.

Then he saw the woman across the street, under the street light. She stood with a dog on a leash. Valentin dropped the shovel and dragged the boy across the lawn by the back of his jacket but the jacket came apart in Valentin's hand. He knew the woman was watching and now it was necessary to think before he killed the boy. He managed to drag the boy's body over the lawn and he got him into the cab of the truck. He slammed the passenger door but the door bounced back and he slammed it again and it bounced back, and he slammed it with all the force he had, spit flying out of his mouth and the door bounced back. The woman across the street watched him and it occurred to Valentin that it was over. He would not implicate Isobel. He decided that in an instant. He did not love her, he hated her, but he would not implicate her. He would say he had acted without her knowledge. He would say he was a jealous lover. He would go to jail forever but he would leave her alone. She could have the insurance money; that's what he decided. He would stand by her. It might be the honourable thing.

The door of the truck had made him limp with rage. The boy was supposed to burn in the fire. First he would pass out or he might even crawl along the floor and breathe the smoke and perhaps find his way to the door but the door would be jammed, if the boy made it that far, and the boy would slump against the door and the firemen would find whatever was left of him there.

Valentin gave up. He accepted that he could not close the door to the truck and that the boy was alive and he could already hear the fire trucks and the police and it was over and then he saw the boy's sneaker was in the way.

He pushed the boy's foot in and slammed the door. There was another low deep boom from inside the house and black smoke was dragged across the lawn and shifted direction and lifted itself up over the burning trees. Two people were running toward Valentin's truck and he got in behind the wheel and one of the men was waving him down with a baseball cap.

Valentin tore out of the driveway and took off down Morris Avenue. He drove through a red light and nearly side-swiped the fire truck and a fireman in his yellow gear looked into Valentin's face as he went past. They saw each other.

He pulled into the Bannerman Park parking lot to stop from trembling. He was trembling all over, especially his hands. He sat there with the truck idling and saw teenagers hanging off the monkey bars. He would take Frank to the ship in Harbour Grace and keep him there until he was certain he had got away with it. No one had followed him. He could put Frank in his old bunk on the ship until he knew for certain what would happen next. If he got caught, it would be better for the boy to be alive. They would have the make and colour of his truck, but he had removed the licence plates. He would put the plates back on when he got to the highway. He needed to stop trembling in order to drive. He needed to drive slowly.

He reversed the truck and slowly pulled out of the lot. He

drove down Monkstown Road and when he was near the Riverdale tennis courts he saw there were women playing tennis under big lights. They wore white shorts and tiny white T-shirts and one woman jogged over to the chainlink fence and she was waving her racket, trying to tell him something.

He rolled down the window and the breeze revived the boy; the boy started coughing and muttering again.

Watch out for the dogs, the woman shouted to him. She dipped the racket downward, pointing to the road in front of his truck.

The dogs are fucking, the woman called. She covered her mouth with her hand; she was giggling. Then she trotted back over the courts and her ponytail swung and she bent, lifting one foot in the air, and picked up a luminous yellow ball and she whacked it to the other woman and he heard her racket cut through the warm night air.

There were two dogs mating in the centre of the road, right in front of his truck. A small white poodle so closely shaven Valentin could see the pink of her skin under the silky, silver sheen of fine hair, what was left of her coat. The dog on top of her was twice her size and black and white and it hung on to her and jerked with a deliberate and awkward ferocity. The poodle tried to withstand the weight of the male, but her front legs, which were straight against the asphalt, threatened to buckle and she stepped daintily forward to maintain her balance. She turned toward Valentin's headlights and her eyes went a weird luminous green and the tuft of white on top of her head was incandescent.

Valentin realized the radio was on and had been on the whole time and there was talk about an all-expense-paid trip for two to Orlando, Florida, for the first caller who could name all the songs on the countdown.

The boy began to mutter and Valentin heard the word *harmonica.* Frank was pawing his chest as if he had something in his shirt. He was calling for his mother. His eyes were still rolled back in his head, but the pupils became visible for a moment and the boy looked at Valentin. He looked at him and said he needed a harmonica. Then he was convulsing with a fit of coughing.

Valentin had dropped Isobel before a curve in the road near her aunt's house in Old Perlican. She had come out of the water at the beach with the red dress clinging to her and her hair gleaming and in the truck she smelled of seawater. The cat was pressed against his leg because Isobel was wet. She was trying to wipe the wet sand off her feet. He could see the lace of her bra under the wet silk dress. She was breathing heavily. Perhaps what he felt was love.

He had watched her walk down a dirt path with a ridge of shiny grass down the centre and the branches of the alder trees met over her head and the light through the trees was green and full of clouds of golden mosquitoes. Her dress was wet he could see the straps of her bra and underwear. He had seen the red dress waver and flush beneath the water. She had been swimming near the sandy bottom and she came up for breath and went down again.

FRANK

THERE IS A monstrous chasm between being alive and being dead, two very distinct states; and the trick is always to be alive.

He would remain alive until he saw Colleen again because he wanted his money back. He thought about having sex with her and he wanted that to happen again even though she had stolen his money and he made a ball of himself and he flung that ball at the window.

There are blisters all over his body and his face is raw and the blanket hurts him because the wool has rough fibres that rub against his burns, but he doesn't stay conscious long. He is being rocked gently, and sometimes he knows it's a ship but mostly he has no idea where he is. A naked light bulb swings gently above him. He loses consciousness and regains it and sometimes he sees the two Russians and he wants the girl back, whoever she was, he wants the girl.

COLLEEN

I AM WRAPPED in a blanket and the guy is shouting at me and I'm shivering all over and my teeth are chattering. The way it started was he cut the engine and let me listen to the sound of the males. There were several males and they were making a vibration in their throats like engines, like lust, a calling out to the females; it makes the hairs on your arms stand up, and the surface of the water vibrates. The water was like glass and then beads of water rose up, bounced up off the surface, just as if rain were falling down but the water was falling up. Little beads of water dancing all over the surface and a strange warbling noise like a metal filling when you touch it against tinfoil, like fingernails on a chalkboard, like the pulley of a clothesline. This is how the males attract the females.

We saw a few slide off the banks and Loyola said about the scars some of the old ones have because they can scrap at this time of year fighting for the females. He cut the engine and the sun was coming up and we just floated a little after flying over the surface of the water in his airboat, hitting bumps of air and lifting and knocking spray all over the place and getting flicked with mud and water. We saw the blue heron he said has been in the swamp for years and it was standing on a stump that was sticking right out of the water, all the twisty branches of the trees and the hanging green moss were reflected in the muck green water and he said, Did you call your mother? and I didn't answer him.

The heron flapped its big giant awkward wings and it flew up and became graceful. Then Loyola putt-putted over to a little island, a hill, big enough for one tree, in the middle of the swamp and he showed me the alligator nest, which was a pile of twigs and grass and a hole dug into the earth and he said about insulating the eggs and how many he might find there. He got down on his knees and he was knocking the twigs back, just to check.

He was out of the boat and he had a stick and the mother was gone off and I stepped out of the boat to get on the bit of ground where he was. I had one foot on the boat and one on shore and the boat eased away from me and I thought there was land under me but there wasn't.

The water was deep and I screamed and I could feel weeds clinging to my jeans and he hauled the boat in and I tried to get onto the little island of mud he was on but the land kept giving way under me and he jumped into the boat and I saw an alligator slide off the shore.

I had not seen it before and then I saw it. I thought I saw it. A shape that sank almost below the surface, just the ridge of its back visible, gliding quickly toward me. It moved with the same slow-fastness that things in dreams move with, it dipped under the surface but the wake, a soft V in the water, plaiting itself behind some invisible thing coming my way.

And then he had me in the boat. He reached over the side and hauled me up, which, how he lifted me I don't know. I lost a shoe and he was screaming how stupid I was how crazy and stupid and he stopped shouting and he got me a blanket and he was crying with his face all screwed up with rage, tears rolling down his cheeks, and then he just stood over me patting the blanket and he stared for thirty seconds or so and I said his name and he didn't hear me and then he started shouting at me again. How stupid I was.

I said but there weren't any alligators around. There weren't any around, I screamed back at him and I was crying too, and when I said that there weren't any alligators, there was a whack against the side of the boat.

The aluminum rang out like a gong and the suffocating humidity of the swamp held the reverberations of the aluminum and made the echo last and last.

Get off my farm, Loyola shouted. I said I would. He said, Get off my farm. I promised I would. You get, he said. I said, I promise. I want you out of here so fast, he said. He had flung an arm out, rigid, his sleeve was soaking, and a finger pointing back over the swamp in the direction of the farm, but I couldn't see anything except trees and moss green water and algae. I want it to be I never laid eyes on you, he said. I said I was going. Don't worry I was going. And I said I was sorry, I was sorry, I was sorry. But he sat down and he turned his back on me and he wouldn't start up the boat for a long time.

FRANK

THE DOOR OF the room he was in crashed open and there was Valentin.

Where am I? he said. Valentin hauled him out of the bunk and punched Frank in the face and Frank felt his jaw break. He heard the bones break and it was a sound inside his head. He tried to move his teeth so the bottom ones were under the top ones and they would not go that way. It felt like a pedantic thing to insist upon, that the teeth align, under the circumstances. He was aware that he was having a small, private moment with his teeth in the middle of a larger argument, which was he'd probably end up dead.

That's so you don't open your mouth, Valentin said. Something was catching in Frank's throat and he coughed it up and it was a tooth. Then Valentin punched him in the gut and Frank fell against the wall and Valentin kicked his head and Frank lost consciousness.

Frank came to hours later and focused on the cot he had been hauled out of. He thought he could drag himself up to the cot and he managed to grab the blankets and he pulled with all his might but the blankets and the pillow came down on top of him. He decided that would have to do because he could not move.

He lay there and listened and wished he could fall asleep or die and then he heard something and it sounded like a rat moving over the wooden shelf above his head. He heard the clatter of tiny claws and then stillness, then the clatter of tiny claws again and it sounded as if a rat was pondering which direction to take, where it might find food next, which was not possible, Frank decided. He decided it was not possible that there was a rat in the room and he fell asleep.

CAROL

SHE TIDIED UP her room for the police officers and made a pot of tea but they came with Tim Hortons coffees. One of the officers had been to the house before, when the Inuit boy committed suicide, and Carol mentioned that she remembered him and that they'd done a fine job that time and that the incident was a tragedy and she hadn't felt right about the bed-sit ever since it happened.

She patted the couch, which had a crocheted throw of orange and lime green Phentex yarn that she'd made herself, and one of the officers sat down and she said about Frank's hot-dog stand.

That boy was like clockwork, she said. Something awful has happened to him, I just know it.

If the officers wanted, they could check with the taxi drivers on George Street, that's how regular Frank's hot-dog stand was. She had gone down there herself last night and the night before last and there was no hot-dog stand on the corner and no sign of Frank. She told about Frank's room being vandalized and how he had forbidden her to contact the police. He said it would be very dangerous for both of them if the police got involved. And Valentin was gone from the third floor and the other Russian he sometimes had sleeping in the room with him, the whole building was as silent as a tomb.

The police went upstairs and they knocked on both doors and there was no answer. They went away for a couple of hours and when they came back they forced the door of Valentin's apartment the same way they had done when the Inuit boy had hanged himself, and they came out with two beef buckets full of tiny bottles with rubber stoppers that were some sort of prescription drug.

Carol stood in the door of her bed-sit wringing her hands as the officers went up and down the stairs, and then they came out with several armloads of cigarette cartons. It took them a lot of trips over the stairs to confiscate all the stolen goods.

He was off that ship in Harbour Grace, she said.

She reached out and took one of the officers by the sleeve of his uniform and she said she was afraid Frank was dead.

When the police left she stood in the centre of her bed-sit trying to think what she could do. She got down on her knees and she gripped her hands under her chest and she prayed to St. Anthony, the patron saint of lost souls, and she prayed for Frank's safety, she begged for it. She whispered. Please, please.

Later in the evening Carol heard someone walking around on the floor above her head. She had been watching television and she turned it off and listened. She heard footsteps and she got her housecoat and went up the stairs very quietly. She didn't turn on the hall light.

Frank's door was ajar and she pushed it open and the hinges squeaked. There was a girl standing at the window looking out onto the street, her dark, curly hair hanging past her shoulder blades.

Beyond the girl, Carol could see out the window to the street, and the crowd from the haunted hike had gathered under the trees.

Are you Frank's girlfriend? Carol asked.

I owe him some money, the girl said. Carol walked up to the window to look out at the crowd.

I stole some money from him and I want to pay it back, the girl said.

The trees across the street were white, as if there'd been a snowfall. The window screen was covered in moths. Carol saw, on the roofs of the cars below, and on the hoods, a blanket of white moths, the wings opening and closing. A transport truck roared up the hill and moths lifted all at once and it looked like a Christmas card.

The worms, the girl said. They've transformed. The deflated waterbed was still in the centre of the room, the bedclothes lay on the floor from when Frank had hauled them off the bed.

Frank is gone, Carol said.

FRANK

HE WOKE IN the hospital and his jaw was wired shut. Everything he ate had to be liquefied. He could eat Jell-O, applesauce, and eggnog. He became an expert on what liquids had the most protein. He had an IV and most of his nourishment was coming through a tube going into his hand.

The nurses had poured sterile saline over the fabric that had melted into his skin during the fire, mostly patches of the nylon windbreaker, and they removed the nylon with tweezers and he gripped the metal bar of his bed and broke a sweat while they tugged at each piece. They let him rest between strips of fabric, for a moment or two, and water ran from the blisters. They told him he was brave, and it was going well, and it wouldn't take much longer and it would all be fine soon. They said when they were done he could have a nice rest. They said these things while they let him rest but when they were tearing the fabric from his skin with the tweezers they worked in silence. He couldn't feel the fabric they took off his upper arms and torso because the burns were deeper and the nerves there had become insensitive. The nurses were in agreement that his chest was pretty bad; there would be substantial scarring on his chest.

But there were blisters all over his face and the nurses said not to burst them and they said they were pretty sure there wouldn't be any scarring where there were blisters.

You were lucky, the nurses said. A doctor asked permission to show some interns Frank's burns and when they came into the room one of the interns fainted.

Anything you could suck from a straw. Kevin had been keeping vigil. Kevin had gone to Ches's and got an order of fish and chips with gravy and dressing and he put everything in a blender and brought it in a jar and Frank tried it. He tried it and it tasted just like fish and chips and he asked for more salt, but it was too much work getting it through the straw.

Kevin came four days out of ten and he sat there while Frank slept and he wiggled his eyebrows behind the nurses' backs and made lewd gestures. He leaned forward one evening and stared into Frank's face and said there was something funny he couldn't put his finger on. Then he realized Frank didn't have eyelashes any more.

One evening Frank woke and he could hear Kevin asking one of the nurses to a movie, just outside his bedroom door. When he came in and sat down, Kevin was blushing and Frank said, I'm sorry I asked you for that money. Kevin took a newspaper from under his coat and the story was still front-page news. Valentin ducking the camera, his hands in cuffs; he looked wary and unrepentant.

ISOBEL

MADELEINE IS DEAD. Madeleine died and Isobel got a phone call from the production assistant. Isobel was asleep and could not believe someone was waking her.

She sat up on one elbow and listened and then she was wide awake and she put her glasses on and she kept saying it can't be true and she saw she was holding her fist up to her mouth. She was staying in a bed and breakfast on Gower Street until the insurance from the fire was settled. She saw herself in the mirror on the wardrobe door and no matter how much she whispered it couldn't be true she knew it was true because there was nothing dreamlike about the phone call or the square of sunlight on the hardwood floor or the weight of the cat on top of the blankets. She could smell toast burning.

She and Madeleine had gone for a hamburger in Donovan's Industrial Park because that's where they ended up. Madeleine drove and she talked about the film and Isobel said nothing because she had decided she would tell Madeleine about Valentin and the fire he had planned for the following weekend. She felt certain Madeleine would intervene. Whatever it took to intervene, Madeleine had it. She would reroute the inevitable, take charge. Isobel sat in the passenger seat with her hand against the dash and her foot pressed into the floor as if she had a brake of her own and she listened while Madeleine talked budget.

Anyone who has to confess is better off closing her eyes. Isobel had planned to order a hamburger and while waiting for it to arrive she would grip her fork and knife and close her eyes and tell Madeleine everything. Some part of her believed the fire would never happen.

It was hard to get a word in with Madeleine. She was obsessed with the bloody horses and believed she was being haunted by an archbishop and she had never been able to shut up for five minutes in the whole time Isobel had known her. Isobel had decided to close her eyes and say about the fire.

Madeleine told the waitress she only had a forty-five minute lunch. She said about the burger: she wanted medium-rare, she didn't want rare, she didn't want well-done. Did the girl know what she meant by medium-rare, Madeleine wanted to know. Do they do that here? she'd asked.

Isobel had worn her silver bracelet. She fiddled with the fork. She opened her hamburger when it came and scraped off the mayonnaise.

You don't meet men at weddings, Madeleine had said. Everybody at a wedding has a date. I'll tell you the place.

Isobel put salt on the tomatoes. A wide man in a flannel shirt hefted a cheek from his chair to swivel all the way around. They were two beautiful women being too loud in Donovan's Industrial Park.

Funerals, said Madeleine. Nobody brings a date to a funeral. The men come out in droves.

The emergency ward is good, Isobel said.

Funerals, Madeleine insisted. Her mouth was full of lettuce. She put the hamburger down.

What is so bloody hard about medium-rare, can you tell me?

The production has shut down, the production assistant says. The director will be waked at Caul's Funeral Home and in lieu of flowers people are asked to send donations to Médicins Sans Frontières.

Madeleine had said, Look, I'm dying. She was waving her fork, making a point about the burger. The point was if she was dying, really dying, couldn't the universe conspire to give her a proper hamburger. She had given up meat and now she was treating herself and look what they had served her.

She was dying and she said Isobel was free to bring a date to the funeral. She waved the waitress down and explained again about how, exactly, she wanted her burger. When it came back it was burnt.

Isobel wanted to tell her about the fire because Madeleine would deal with it. Isobel knew she couldn't trust herself. Something was wrong with her. She was in the grip of a powerful man at a bad time in her life. She was being crushed. She would shut her eyes and grip the fork and knife and say *arson*. She would say about his hand on her throat, how tight, she would say about all her belongings going up in smoke. How off-kilter and afraid she had become. She would say about the pills she'd been taking.

I have to tell you something, Isobel had said.

I don't have long, Madeleine said.

FRANK

IT HAD RAINED for most of December, icy rain and the afternoons were dark but there hadn't been any snow. The rain lashed against the houses and the sidewalks were slippery and sometimes it turned to sleet. Frank had been cutting business cards at the photocopy shop for most of the afternoon and it was almost closing time. Lana had finished the floors. She turned off the buzzing lights and her yellow rubber gloves looked luminous in the gloom.

She stood for a moment leaning against the doorway, holding the mop handle with both hands and resting her chin on the tip.

He could smell the ammonia floor cleaner. It was a smell that reminded him of his mother. He could see his mother in a short-sleeved shirt, her elbows eczema-crackled.

Ammonia reminded him of cancer, the eradicating, indifferent swath it had cut in his life, and the July evening when he was five and Mrs. Hallett brought him back home, after his mother's double mastectomy.

Your mother is getting out of the hospital, Frank, she'd said. And he was afraid to trust it.

Mrs. Hallett had taken him to Middle Cove Beach for caplin when he was five. He and Kevin scrabbling over the rocks, picking up the wiggling fish with their bare hands. Someone had a flashlight trained on the curling waves and he saw the caplin twisting on the breaking surf like a silver scarf. Mrs. Hallett had got down on one knee and had taken hold of his elbows and said that his mother would be home when they got back to town. She was bringing him directly to his mother's apartment. You can show her all your fish, she'd said.

Afterwards, he'd stood on the sidewalk on Water Street and a window opened on the third floor and there was his mother in her flannel nightdress, elbows on the sill, leaning out, waiting for him. He'd opened the Dominion bag for her to look, caplin glinting under the street light.

There was a funny phone call, Lana said. Water was still gurgling through the pipes somewhere on the fifth floor. But the building was empty. Why, when you turn off the lights in an old building like this, does everything alter? He could hear the wind outside. Everything was about his mother tonight; it had something to do with the weather. The giant cola-tinted window of the photocopy shop overlooked the harbour. It was covered in beads of rain. She was so proud when he brought home a good mark. She'd take both his cheeks in her hands and look into his eyes.

Look at me, she'd say, holding his cheeks. It means the world to me when you do well in school, she'd say. Once he'd brought a math test home with a gold star and she'd moved her thumb over it and when she looked up she was exultant.

The wind made the raindrops on the windowpane shiver and then drove them sideways cross the glass. He brought the paper cutter down over the last stack of card.

Some girl looking for you, Lana said. Frank lifted the blade.

Lana pulled the bucket behind her so the wheels rattled over the tiles. He listened to her moving around in the other room, emptying the bucket, flushing the toilet.

Lana was washing the coffee mugs and called to him over the running water.

You know I'm taking Monday, she said. Then she jumped because he was standing behind her. He had a way of creeping up.

I don't want to talk to anyone who's phoning me, he said. Lana looked at him for a long moment, then picked up a rag and started on the counters.

A call comes for you, I mention it, she said.

He knew it was Colleen. He wanted his money back. Lana was some sort of Gypsy. Her husband was a fisherman during the crab season and worked at Stoker's Auto in the winter. Lana had talked once about roasting goat on a spit over an open fire. You could see the snow coming through the mountain pass, she'd said. They'd eaten eggs and bacon fried on the engine of a car when she was growing up.

We moved in caravans, she'd said. I saw all of Europe as a child. It made Frank wish he had known Lana back then. If he and his mother could have travelled in caravans and eaten goat.

It got dark, Lana said, while we chewed the bones and afterwards the violins came out.

ISOBEL

Give the lines the time they need to materialize. This is essential. Actors forget this and it's the only thing they're required to remember, let the lines materialize.

There was a girl of twenty standing in the middle of the classroom, her hair drawn back in a ponytail, wearing sweats, holding a script.

Get up and take a book off a bookshelf if you must, Isobel said. Be deliberate and vague at the same time.

She told them she had once played Napoleon. Even Napoleon had to look uncertain. She'd worn one of those hats.

Here was her advice: Watch a person get on the bus or peel the paper lining away from a muffin. See how lost and present they are. Emulate this. That is acting: the alchemy of absence and presence. Embody the character, agree there is no character; there's only a series of linked gestures, fudged acts, reprieves. She was teaching an evening course at the university. They had a growing drama department and she was finding she could pick up at least one course a semester. She was thinking about dinner theatre. There was a growing market with the cruise ships. It was something she could do easily.

What people don't understand about regret is that it incubates; this was her strong hand. She knew regret and it was a hue in her palette the younger actresses didn't have. They could not muster that tone. Regret could cast shadows in a performance: to have fucked up grandly, that could make you an actress of note, especially if you hadn't got caught. There was talk of a big shoot the following summer. She'd received an e-mail. There was talk of a Hollywood actor, someone halfway big, and they wanted local colour.

First, you think the lines out, and then you say them. Say the lines as if everything has already been settled.

He had called once, after the fire. He said he was going to cover for her. She hadn't spoken because she was sick about the boy. She hadn't known — no part of her had guessed — he was capable of it. His capacity for hatred was stunning, shattering.

You'll get the money, he'd said. He waited for her to answer. He had left the boy to burn alive. Isobel had slept with him, he had touched her.

Don't hang up, he said. Please.

She couldn't speak and the receiver was slippery in her hand, but she didn't hang up. She couldn't. She could feel through the silence in the phone that he would not call her again. Wherever he was going he would never come back; he would never get out. He knew it. She would not hang up on him.

I don't have anyone else, he said.

She waited.

The wind nearly took the door out of Frank's hand. Isobel ducked under his arm.

I was driving past and I thought my card might be ready, she said. She took off a clear plastic rain hat and pulled it taut by the ribbons and droplets bounced out.

He was taken aback by how beautiful she was. He almost said it out loud, without thinking, but they were alone in the room. It was just a few minutes before closing time. He turned the lights back on.

Let me get the mockup, he said. She watched him disappear into the back. She had once acted with a Polish troop. They'd rehearsed naked in a forest in northern Ontario. Chris was directing. It was after they had first met, working on an Artaud play in Montreal. What was the play in the forest? One of Chris's actors was almost seven feet and had a canary yellow mohawk. Chris made them roll in the mud, naked. She had been twenty, the youngest in the troupe.

What had he said when he got her alone in that stand of birch, white and pink and blue with the sun slashing every which way? She was standing naked, the rain running through the mud down her shins, mud on her face — someone had smacked her in the face with a mud cake. Most of them were on acid. She was on acid. Chris had been videotaping them. They would do *Macbeth* on acid, had been Chris's idea. He wanted them to say the lines as if they had already been said.

She was hardly able to see for the rain.

What she would have given to believe wholeheartedly in his project, this relentless living he had proposed. He said security would nullify them. He'd raised his naked arms to the skies and yelled with his head thrown back, Nullify.

Be convincing, he said. That was Chris's advice. The ultimate lesson for the actor, the content doesn't matter.

Deliver, he said. He wanted her emptied out. He wanted her to give up herself. Chris said to remember they were not the thing they were pretending to be. He wouldn't have that sort of moral turpitude, that Stanislavsky slop. They had to be who they were and who they weren't at the same time. He would accept nothing less. We convince, he yelled.

And when she did run into him later it was at the soap audition. She'd come into the room and could not see because of the footlights. They turned off the lights and there he was. His eyes were the same crazy eyes. But it was a soap opera; he was directing a soap.

And walking along Yonge Street afterwards, she had cried. Because she'd wanted the naked afternoon in the woods to be true — the mud and rain and acid and all the emoting. She wasn't willing to live like that herself, but she wanted it to endure.

She was standing with her hands behind her back looking at the giant corkboard of sample business cards. Frank slid her card across the counter and she picked it up. She held the card out at arm's length. She was shaken slightly, being in the boy's presence, though he didn't know who she was. She had wanted to see him with her own eyes. She needed to know his face wasn't scarred.

She snapped the arms of her glasses open and put them on the tip of her nose. She wore one of those cords to keep the glasses around her neck and she seemed too young for it. She was frowning at the card, her chin crimped.

You want, she said. Then she took a deep breath, raised a hand in the air, fingers spread. A giant ring covered most of her index finger. It was a dragon.

Spaciousness, she said. She snapped the card down on the counter.

This is too busy, she said. She pushed it across the counter to him with one finger. Frank picked up the business card. They had gone over every detail together on the phone. It was a card advertising dinner theatre.

We could adjust the font, he said. I don't know what you think of italics.

A business card, she said. You want it to feel as roomy as a golf course.

Frank scissored over the low counter and he was standing beside her, holding out the card for her to see. He was all ready to print. He'd spent hours. He'd done it exactly as she had asked.

Some people are fond of italics, he said.

Isobel turned around and looked up at him. He lifted weights, she could see. The shirt was ironed and she could smell fresh air. There was no scarring on his face. That was why she had come. They'd said in the papers the more serious burns were on his torso and limbs. She wanted to know for certain about his face.

The business card has to work, she said.

What it does, Frank said. It gives people an idea.

I almost wish the card could be empty, she said. Imagine if it didn't say anything at all.

Frank felt the building pulse. Pa-boom. It was the furnace, or the water pipes. This woman was undeniably beautiful — shiny hair in loose curls, her eyes were big and blue and her mouth was wide.

The insurance money had come through and it was just enough to keep her going for a year or two if she lived in an apartment. The dinner theatre might fail, everyone said it would fail, but she would try. She wanted to try. She'd got a government grant for publicity — posters, business cards, a few radio spots.

A business card has to have the name of the business on it, Frank said. She suddenly looked very fierce.

I guess, she said.

I have something, Frank said. He left her for a moment and came back into the foyer with a sheaf of paper.

This has weight, Frank said. He opened the package and worked a piece out and handed it to her. She held it to the light.

I'd like to leave it blank, she said.

The point of a card, he said.

They have to know what it says at a glance, Isobel said.

So you're going to have to say something, Frank said.

MADELEINE

SHE'D HAD COFFEE with Beverly. They'd stood for a few moments on Water Street while the wind lifted a paper cup up off the pavement and dashed it against the concrete. Mike Dower passed by. Mike Dower ran the Roman Catholic Archives and had shown her Archbishop Fleming's letters.

Not a man at all, an instrument of God, Mike Dower said.

That is what she'd wanted: to bring the instrument of God down onto the snow-swept barrens, Archbishop Fleming's brute desire to colonize the shore with Catholics, to have bells clanging in the grey sodden skies all over the island. Madeleine saw wan-faced children in rags watching wide-eyed as the archbishop ranted from the pulpit, his frosty breath hanging in the air.

Colleen is back, Beverly said.

It's too hot to run away, Madeleine said. The girl had rebelled — of course she had. Look at the world — there was a blast of flame on the front page of the paper, flame in every news box along Water Street. Was it Iraq or the Sudan? Why wouldn't the girl rebel. Who could walk past these boxes and do nothing?

The pain in her chest is monstrous in the late-August afternoon and she sits in her armchair and reads. She cannot work. She imagines Fleming standing in the room, by the wardrobe. First, it was *as if* he were in the room. Then a presence in the corner of the room made itself indisputably felt. The archbishop's presence accumulated like a snowdrift in the corner, except the heat in her room is unbearable. She should get up and draw the curtain but she's too tired. They all thought the film was her swan song. There were the letters about Fleming's decrepit mother, and the soup he'd made her, onion soup. Fleming had the Vatican's ear. He had put up a number of churches. What is the word: *raised* churches. He would have obeyed the summons from the Vatican, coming as it did from the Holy Father himself, but he was on his knees in the dirt pulling up onions for his ailing mother. I'm certain His Holiness will understand.

She sees Fleming with the ocean behind him, robes billowing with wind and he raises his arms and so begins the hammering, the sawing; the hoisting of a bell. He wanted silver chalices in every church along the coast.

We all want something.

Some mention of horses in a letter, says Fleming, standing in the corner. He was ingratiating and acerbic in his letters, each sentence bloated with hate and desire. He would have visited the Pope but his elderly mother had required nursing. Someone had wrapped the Eucharist in paper and brought it down the shore that way and Fleming bellowed there would be silver chalices from St. John's to Renews within the year.

In paper, like you might wrap a piece of meat, the body of Christ. For days there'd been a tingling in her arm, the side of her face. And a mild paralysis she mentioned to no one. Not now. Fleming, florid with passion, his yellow teeth, he is shouting at her in Latin. Why shouting?

She's in the grip of a pain that won't let her catch her breath and she dials Marty's number. Maybe she has to go to the hospital this time. She wants to talk to Marty.

She wants regret on the screen, and Isobel could do regret. If the film doesn't get finished, Isobel will turn her hand to something else. The phone rings but there's no answer. Perhaps Marty is out walking the new baby. The baby has made him ten years younger.

Madeleine, he'd said. You should see her.

This giving in to the darkness of a nap, but she can't afford it right now. She has to stay alert for the phone. If the phone rings she will hear it. She is waiting to hear about the horses; no, the horses have arrived. She is waiting for Marty. She has completed the winter shoot and Isobel was perfect. The horses galloped out of a squall. They disappeared; they ate their own tails. Marty will ring and she'll tell him she needs an ambulance. The young girl sat up in bed. She has to get those horses off the freighter, someone said a helicopter. The film will be a monument.

The trouble is to stay alive until the shoot is over. Then she'll go to Cuba and rest. She'll drink her face off and turn black on the beach. Just let her get through the shoot. She will rest, act her age.

I want to love Colleen again, Beverly had said.

And you can't? Can't you love Colleen?

Beverly crossed her arms under her chest and dug her fists into her sides.

I want to, she said. Of course I do. I love her.

She is telling the archbishop. She is giving him this much, since he won't leave. They can both wait for the phone. No, the animals have arrived already. They've completed the winter shoot.

The great monuments, she tells him. You go out of your way to see them but they never stick in your memory.

She'd visited the Taj Mahal, arriving at sunset as she was advised. But she rarely thinks of the Taj Mahal. A particular alley is what comes back to her as vividly as if she were standing there now. The dusty alley persists, returns briefly, sweeping through her, like a current tossing some old shell at the bottom of the ocean where it's pitch black; a lost afternoon from forty years ago. And yes, she admits to Fleming, this might very well be a heart attack. She's dying in a chair she bought at the Salvation Army and refinished herself.

The archbishop raised his arms. The horses come by helicopter, pawing the clouds with their great hooves, a snowfall of moths. The city is covered in fluttering white snow. Moths on their hands, on their arms, on their upturned faces.

ACKNOWLEDGEMENTS

FIRST, I WOULD like to thank my husband, Stephen Crocker, basically for everything, everything.

My big, extended family makes writing possible for me and I want to thank them all. I would especially like to thank Eva Crocker, Theo Crocker, and Emily Pickard.

I would like to thank everyone at Anansi for the tremendous effort that went into the creation of *Alligator*. Sarah MacLachlan has been extremely supportive throughout the process of writing this novel. She goes at every aspect of publishing with uplifting gusto and I am very fortunate to have her energy and experience behind this book.

Martha Sharpe is a very gifted editor and working with her was a privilege. Heather Sangster and Kevin Linder were also exacting, eagle-eyed, and generous with their editing skills, for which I am thankful.

Laura Repas is an excellent publicist, and I am grateful for her work on *Alligator*. Thank you also to Matt Williams. It has been my great fortune to have the aforementioned team at Anansi behind *Alligator* because of their expertise and passion for writing and because I have also become friends with them and I am thankful for that. I am grateful to Bill Douglas for *Alligator*'s beautiful jacket design.

Thank you to my agent, Anne McDermid, for, among many other things, her friendship.

These are the people who offered their valuable reading time, friendship, considerable knowledge, and love of writing while simultaneously holding off the men in white lab coats, at least until the novel was finished: Mary-Lynn Bernard, Libby Creelman, Eva Crocker, Rosemary Crocker, Stephen Crocker, Susan Crocker, Michael Crummey, Ramona Dearing, Barbara Doran, Gail Faurschau, Holly Hogan, Bob Howard, Dr. John Lewis, Mary Lewis, Lawrence Mathews, Sourayan Mookerjea, Elizabeth Moore, Lynn Moore, Susan O'Brien, Beth Ryan, Rose Smart, Medina Stacey, and everyone in the Burning Rock.

Michael Winter, Nan Love, and Claire Wilkshire went way beyond the call of duty and I am forever indebted to them.

I would also like to thank the Canada Council for the Arts and Memorial University of Newfoundland for having me as writer-in-residence, thereby providing the necessary financial assistance for the writing life.